UNFORGOTTEN

THE GREAT WAR 1914-1918

UNFORGOTTEN

THE GREAT WAR 1914-1918

Short stories and poems by Swansea and
District Writers' Circle

Published by Accent Press Ltd 2014

ISBN 9781786150769

Contents Page

Introduction

I've wanted to write since I first realised books contained stories. In infant school I was punished for writing a tale about pigs falling down a well and landing on the moon when I should have been practising 'joined up' writing. I wrote 'novels' all through primary and grammar school and refused to stop even when my teachers warned, 'People like you don't write books.' My favourite college tutorials were with the charismatic fishing correspondent of the *Daily Express*, Clive Gammon, who occasionally said, 'enough of literature, let's talk writing for publication.'

Naïve, to the point of stupidity, I stockpiled the output from my portable typewriter (computers weren't invented) add waited to be 'discovered'.

I wasn't.

In 1976 I read a life-changing article in Swansea's *Evening Post*. It mentioned Swansea Writers' Circle. I had no idea what a Writers' Circle was but I rang the secretary, Peggy Carter, who was warm, welcoming, and soon to become a lifelong friend. I entered the first meeting with trepidation. Peggy had warned me that as well as beginners, many members were well published.

I was greeted enthusiastically and given the advice I craved. The most valuable lesson, along with how to lay out and submit a manuscript for publication was so obvious it had eluded me. If you want to appear in print, 'write for a market'.

Decades have come and gone. I've met many of my closest friends within the Circle. We show one another our work, (when we wouldn't allow our nearest and dearest to glimpse a line) encourage one another through the rejections, (we've held a competition for the most humorous), and the entire circle celebrates when a member has work accepted for publication simply because the next success could be theirs.

This anthology not only contains the work of the winners of our international short story and poetry competition but that of our members. It showcases the quality and diversity of their writing. My own contribution was penned in one of our monthly Writers' Circle workshops.

The encouragement, counsel, and guidance I've received over the years has been priceless. My long-suffering husband calls writing 'a disease'. If he's right, I'm grateful to have found a haven with fellow suffers. Swansea Writers' Circle has many illustrious names among its past members. Here's to the future publications of present and new members, who will carry on the tradition of encouragement and friendship into the next half century since the Circle was founded by Edith Courtney in 1952.

This anthology has only come to fruition through the sterling efforts, and hard work of our members, especially Fiona Riley, Steve Jones, and Dawn Smith. The entire circle owes a debt of gratitude to them and the staff of Accent Press for their achievement in bringing it to publication.

I'm a proud member of the Circle and extremely proud of each and every one of my fellow scribes. I hope you enjoy this anthology and look forward to seeing you at a meeting should you care to join us; I promise you a sincere and warm welcome.

Karen Watkins/Katherine John/Catrin Collier

https://www.facebook.com/pages/Swansea-and-District-Writers-Circle/183386015060585?fref=ts

http://www.swanseawriters.co.uk

Hello, Sweetheart
Cheryl Leend (SDWC)

Dear Journal,

I hate it! I hate it ... this bloody so-called 'Great' war that we were all excited about! And I'm *so* scared ... *all* the time. The noise, stench, and filth is unbelievable – and constant. My gun still feels alien and heavy in my hands despite using it so often and I hate the smell it makes when it's fired ... but I don't feel safe without it. My life consists of staring at sky, or mud walls. No chance of popping up for a quick look-see with snipers ready to take your head off. I've seen it happen too often. Men become so claustrophobic they need to have just a quick peek – bam, half their face blown away. I hate this war. I hate it with all my heart and wonder at the utter futility of it all. It's not a *Great* War, it's a massacre. So much for being over by Christmas!

I can't believe our stupidity. We thought it would be fun, me and the lads; but war is not a game. It seemed a good idea at the time, joining up with a group from the Brigade; a few months' adventure, we thought. I get angry when I think of the *responsible* men and women who encouraged us to join the 'Call to Arms'. Naïve, enthusiastic patriotism does nothing but get you killed; so many friends gone for ever. Sometimes I want to go home and scream at the men who have placed all our young lives in such precarious and deadly conditions. Promises of 'Those who volunteer together should serve together' should be changed to 'Those who volunteer together, die together'. I dread going home to face the families of those who have lost their sons.

Ned sighed as he put down his journal, and picked up a postcard.

Hello, Sweetheart,

When I write to you, it helps take my mind off the war a little, thinking of you and your lovely smiling eyes. It's a bit boring here at times, but it's nice to have friends around to share a cuppa and chat or game of cards.

It's a good job we did all that drilling in the Boys' Brigade, because it's helped us follow orders quickly and the gymnastics certainly gives us a bit of extra strength and agility.

I'll write again when I can.
With all my love, my beautiful girl,
Ned xxx

My Darling Ned,

I'm so proud of you out there, doing your bit to save us all. I'm glad you've got the boys with you for a bit of company. I think of you every day and imagine you being as brave as you are at home. I was a bit worried you might find it difficult to adjust when you left because you are so quiet, but obviously they have come to know what a lovely, gentle man you are.

We've been told that we can send you parcels. Is there anything you need over there?

All my love,
Your Violet xxx

Dear Journal,

Oh yes, my love, there is something I need … desperately. I'll take some sanity in a mad world; the comfort of your arms around me; and to be clean again. I'll never take the feel of being clean again for granted. The sensation of warm water trickling over my body, getting rid of the stink of my armpits and grime from hair and folds of skin would be heaven. I can't remember the last time I felt fresh. *Everything* itches. My head aches from the constant noise of guns, my groin has a nasty, smelly rash from sweat and dirt, and I've got boils on my backside.

Rats foraging around us have grown obese from gorging themselves on putrefying bodies in no man's land; they eat out corpses' eyes then burrow into the crevices. Not content with this glut of food, they run over us whilst we sleep, infesting us with fleas as they snack on our rations or exposed ears.

And lice! Good God, the little bastards are everywhere! I'm constantly pinching and burning them from seams of clothing – but of course they are back straight away because we are living on top of each other. The itching was so bad one night that I went to the MO, but after smearing the ointment all over, I swear the little buggers thought I'd laid on a feast for them as it made it a hundred times worse!

We try to keep our spirits up by sharing fags, cups of tea – even dirty pictures. I wonder what a naked woman feels like. Will I die before I get to have a woman?

Hello, Sweetheart,

Thank you so much for the parcel from home. The lice powder has helped a bit. I use your fancy lavender soap sparingly to make it last because it reminds me of you.

We share lots of things that families send us from home,

but I won't share the socks you made for me. They are special. You wouldn't believe how often we are made to check our feet and change our socks, but they say it stops our feet getting sore.

I'll finish off now, because it's my turn to make the tea.
All my love, my wonderful woman,
Ned xxx

Darling, darling Ned,

I was so happy that you liked my little parcel – especially the socks. I used my best wool for them. I had a little smile when I thought of you making tea – that's usually my job, isn't it? You'll have to show me how good you are at it when you come home.

They've taken Blackie to help with the war effort – I expect he will be well looked after and at least your father still has Chestnut to visit his patients. I thought you'd like to know that even your horse is helping the war effort.

I love you and am missing you.
Your Violet xxx

Dear Journal,

No, no, no! Not my proud, spirited Blackie! If people at home only knew what really happens to the horses out here. It's unspeakable! They must have stripped the countryside of horses and private pet ponies. The poor creatures stare around with rolling eyes, shying nervously at unexpected noises. Exhausted and hungry, they are expected to drag heavy wooden carts full of injured men or supplies. Animals don't understand, yet they must wonder why one minute they are being stroked and given titbits as a loved family pet, and the next minute being forced through craters and glutinous mud up to their hocks surrounded by constant screaming, gunfire, and bedlam. My heart just bleeds for them.

And the horses that go to the cavalry … Ah, God. How those idiotic asses living in the past think they can recreate the 'glorious cavalry charge' in a modern war against up-to-date weaponry defies belief! What idiot thinks a man on a horse can compete with machine guns and shellfire? A hundred and fifty horses were sent on a cavalry charge over treacherous ground consisting of holes, decomposing bodies, and barbed wire only to be mowed down like a row of wheat stalks. Just four survived. Four! What carnage. They lie there in agony struggling to get up, whinnying and crying out until someone puts them out of their misery. I just hope Blackie has someone there to stroke his head and offer gentle words before he dies. Magnificent animals sacrificed as cannon fodder. It's wicked.

Hello, Sweetheart,

I've been thinking about you a lot recently. It wasn't really a surprise that Blackie had been recruited. Every family has to make sacrifices for the war. They say they will return them once it's all over.

I hope you like the new-style postcard? One of the other lads gave it to me when I told him it was your birthday. The local women embroider flowers, birds, flags, and messages onto silk which is stuck onto card. I particularly liked this one because it has violets on it – which remind me of you.

All my love, my beautiful flower.
Ned xxx

My darling Ned,

A bit of a stir in the village, because someone shot a pigeon the other day and there was a great hullaballoo when it discovered it was a homing pigeon used for messages. To hear the officer from the Volunteer Corps lecturing us about us not shooting pigeons 'working for the government' would be quite funny if it wasn't so serious. They say you can go to prison now if you harm them! No pigeon pie for a while then!

I loved the postcard. What initiative those women show. If you send more, I will frame them so we can look at them and show them to our children and grandchildren.

I will love you forever,
Your Violet xxx

Dear Journal,

Oh, God, what was I thinking yesterday? I should never have listened to the older men laughing about the 'friendliness' of the local girls or looked at their dirty postcards, but it intrigued me. They mocked me when I said I'd never had a girl. I didn't want to die a virgin, never having known the love of a woman … but last night wasn't love; it was sordid and nasty and I am so ashamed.

I only went to buy more postcards for Violet, but when I saw the red light over the shabby door in the village I recognised it for what it was. I didn't expect to be relieved of a franc and hustled upstairs so swiftly by a fierce-looking Madame. I'd intended to just satisfy curiosity and have a look. Instead, I was bundled into a small room with a single bed, a grubby sheet, and a skinny girl in a petticoat. She was kind, though. She held me and wiped my tears, saying it happened many times and understood that young men were missing home. When I calmed down, she told me to hold my head up high as I walked out of there, so the others wouldn't guess. I am *so* ashamed.

Hello, Sweetheart,

Glad you liked the postcard. Your idea of framing them to hang on the wall when we have our own home would certainly bring back memories. I went to the local village on rest day. It was quite pretty, and the locals are friendly. I tried red wine but would have preferred a pint of cider.

The weather is getting bitterly cold now, so the jacket you sent is proving its worth.

Please remember how much I love you, always.
All my love,
Ned xxx

My darling Ned,

The weather is cold over here too. Some mornings we have to break the ice off the water trough before the horse can have a drink. Well, I suppose it is nearing Christmas.

The newspaper has been advertising gifts to send to the boys at the front, so I've ordered something for you, but I'll keep it a surprise.

I heard the schoolmaster had a telegram about his son Bob the other day. That makes six from the village now. I hope you are managing to keep safe there? I know you all look after each other as much as you can. I miss you so much, and will ask Papa to offer a special prayer for you all on Sunday.

I wish you could come home to me soon,
Your ever loving,
Violet xxx

Dear Journal,

If I hadn't been there, I don't think I'd believe what happened today. How long have we been at war now – about four months? They said the war would be over by Christmas – but of course it's not, and we are at stalemate yet again … between forty to a hundred yards away from the German lines.

No one expected Christmas Day to be any different, with typical thundering echo of shelling, staccato bursts of machine guns, and the high-pitched whine of sniper rifles alongside tense anxiety of continual watching, waiting, and uncertainty.

But on Christmas Eve, the guns fell silent. Christmas Day dawned with an eerie feel in the air; the atmosphere charged through temporary calm. I felt the hairs on the back of my neck stand on end as I heard a singing chorus of men's voices drifting up into the dawn sky from the German trenches …

"Stille Nacht, Heilige Nacht."

Not knowing what to do, we replied with a rousing chorus of "Oh Come, All Ye Faithful". In the following pause, we sniggered when one of our lads shouted out 'Good morning, Fritz!', only to hear, 'Guten Morgen' shouted back.

And to our astonishment, numerous little lights materialized over their trench walls … it was candles! Little candles attached to little fir trees – their version of Christmas trees, I suppose. It was like a dream. One of our pluckier lads filled his pockets with fags, crawled over the top, and slowly stood up. As he walked forward holding his hands out to show he had no weapon, a German appeared from the other side. Before long, men from both sides were in no man's land shaking hands, greeting each other, and exchanging gifts of cigarettes, beer, and cheese. What a surreal experience, face to face singing carols with someone you'd been shooting at only a few hours earlier.

A message came through later that day, declaring that further up the line a similar thing happened, except they played a game of football. Football, for goodness sake! Fighting and killing each other one minute and playing the next. Is this a real war or isn't it? It feels real enough when the man next to you is lying with his guts hanging out because half his body has been shot off.

Why do those stupid men up top insist on war, why? Does it make them feel good? Do they feel powerful? Does it make them feel young and dashing again? Why should I have to die for that?

Hello, Sweetheart,

You're never going to believe what happened on Christmas Day – the strangest thing. Both sides stopped firing at each other, and instead met together in the area between the trenches! We swapped some things like cigarettes and beer and sang Christmas carols. I know it sounds hard to credit, but it's true. They are just the same as us. Then we shook hands and went back to our own sides ready for the war to continue next day as if the ceasefire never took place.

Thank you so much, darling girl, for the Christmas parcel. You managed to pack such a lot! The sweet camp coffee is perfect for this cold weather

All my love, as ever,
Ned xxx

My darling Ned,

I'm pleased the parcel was useful, but it was very surprising to hear about you talking with the Germans on Christmas Day. How did you understand each other? It must be strange facing one another and smiling.

I also heard a strange thing. Apparently, an open letter was printed in an American newspaper, from British suffragettes to the women in Germany and Austria! (It had to be the United States because of the conflict, of course.) I haven't seen it yet, but Alice promised to get a copy for me to read. She said the letter informed the German women that they would look after any of their boys taken prisoner, and hoped they would do the same for ours. They also wished them peace and goodwill. I'm not sure if it's very patriotic to write to Germans and Austrians, but I like the idea of mothers taking care of sons. I'll tell you more once I've read it.

Some more news for you, I'm thinking of getting a job! Lots of girls are getting jobs now, because there aren't enough men. I know you think I'm a fragile little thing, but I'm quite strong really and I'd like to do my bit for the war as well.

All my love in my heart from,
Your Violet xxx

Dear Journal,

I know about women working … there are women out here! They are desperately brave, but I don't like it one bit. They shouldn't be allowed in this wretchedness, but they are stubborn and courageous, and can't be stopped. Officially not allowed to serve at the Front, they set up their own medical units nearby, managing to keep smiling throughout the worst of suffering and despair of wounded soldiers.

It's certainly changed my views. I've discovered women are just as brave and capable as men – and they can do things really well. They not only drive cars and ride motorbikes, but can fix them when they go wrong. That's more than I can do! I thought women were vulnerable, needing men to protect and make intelligent decisions for them. But I was wrong. Oh, how very wrong I was. Mentally they are as strong as us, and where a man would use physical strength, they use initiative and skill. To think I've underestimated Violet all this time. If you asked me about supporting suffragettes now I'd give them the vote gladly.

Hello, Sweetheart,

I'm so proud of you wanting to get a job. After seeing women working out here, I know you can succeed at whatever you choose, although I hope you don't choose a rough occupation such as in a factory. I wish I was there looking after you.

I can't wait until this is all over and I'm home with you again. I was thinking I could ask your father to marry us as soon as I return. Would you like that?

All my love forever, my brave girl.
Ned xxx

Dear, darling Ned,

I was so excited when you mentioned getting married – yes, I look forward to it with all my heart and can't wait until you come home.

Regarding the job, please don't worry, dearest. I've decided I don't want to work in a munitions factory. I like helping others, so I've decided to train as a nurse. It will take about a year, but the best news of all is ... I'll be able to come over there. Yes, really! Are you pleased for me?

All my love forever,
Your Violet xxx

Dear Journal,

No, Violet, No!! This is my worst nightmare come true! The person I love most in the world thrust into the misery, squalor, and desolation of fighting at the Front. What on earth possessed her? Maybe I should have been more honest in my communications – but they'd have only censored it for sure. We are not allowed to tell the truth to those back home.

Oh, God. My beautiful, gentle, kind-hearted, Lettie. Out here. In Hell. What sort of lies are being sent back home? Only two of us left from the Boys' Brigade Battalion – that's most of the village boys wiped out in just a few months.

We are seeing younger boys every day. Recruitment officers turn a blind eye to boys lying about their ages ready to 'do their bit' for the 'glorious war', because they need as much cannon fodder as they can get – and of course they get paid 2/6d for each new recruit. One young lad managed to get through twice; they sent him back the first time.

Oh, Rosie, if you could just know the waste of it, the utter futility of war. So many good people gone and so many more will go. Both sides have it bad. All those young people lost – who will do the work when they are gone? How will the country survive without a generation of men?

Dear Miss Collins,

It is with great sorrow that I am writing this letter, as I'm afraid it brings you very bad news. I regret to inform you that your fiancé, Private Edward Williams, was killed in action. He was bravely helping one of his comrades back to the safety of the trench, but was hit by a bullet. He did not suffer.

I spoke with Ned on numerous occasions and felt I knew him well. He was very proud of 'his beautiful Violet' and it was obvious he loved you dearly; therefore I would like to offer you some words of comfort at this difficult time.

He was a generous, caring, and brave man, and both his peers and the officers thought very highly of him. His sturdy cheerfulness did much to increase morale amongst the troops and he will be missed by all. His last words to me were, 'Please tell Violet I'm sorry.' I cannot do anything to ease your sorrow, but I will most certainly pray for him and maybe it will offer you some comfort knowing that he is in the safe hands of our Lord.

The War Office will send official notification and personal effects to Ned's parents, but he asked me to forward to you any un-finished correspondence. I therefore enclose his journal in which I saw him writing frequently. Obviously, I have not read the contents, but I understand it to be drafts of the letters he writes to you, and trust he would want you to have this.

With deepest regrets,
Yours faithfully,
T.H.W. Rogers
Chaplain
(C of E)

The Leaving Times
Will Macmillan Jones (SDWC)

These are the leaving times
Thoughts apart but still so near
When I leave you at the station
Will you still think of me at night?

These are the leaving times
Suitcase packed below the bed
When I leave you at the station
Will you still think of me at night?

These are the leaving times
I know you have to go to war
When I leave you at the station
Will you still think of me at night?

These are the leaving times
Now the time has come
When I leave you at the station
Have you left me for the last time
Or will you still think of me at night?

Poppies at the Well
Catrin Collier (SDWC)

She heard the sound of water and was waylaid. Worm's Head and the sea were distant, and the afternoon languid. It would take only a moment, and she had until evening, a whole day free. Unimaginable luxury. She turned and climbed the downs, seeking the waterfall she sensed was near, but it eluded her. Perhaps in the next copse of trees ...

'You looking for someone, Miss?'

The man was tall, dark, rough-looking; neither young nor old. She looked no more. Instinctively, she lowered her eyes and backed away, for she was unused to people, only children, and afraid of men.

'No. I beg your pardon, I heard the water ...' Her voice trailed.

'It's not a fall. Here, I'll show you.' He stepped back and moved some bushes. 'I'll not hurt you,' he offered gruffly, sensing her fear.

Warily, she inched forward, then she saw it, a spring gushing out of an old pipe set into a low, dry stone wall.

'They call it "The Well" – Talgarth's Well. It's not mine, though it's on my land. Everyone has the right to draw water here. Not that they do,' he murmured. 'No one comes here any more.'

'Your land?' she ventured shyly, looking around the wilderness that was the downs. 'You live here?'

'Where I'm standing, Miss.'

For the first time she looked past the greenery and saw the veranda. Stone-built, it blended with nature. Only the profusion of poppies betrayed man's artifice. They were everywhere, their full round heads hanging heavy as though their stalks could no longer bear their weight. Here and there a bloom had burst into full crimson. The heralds of summer.

'It's beautiful,' she stammered. 'It looks as though it was meant to be this way.'

'My grandfather's grandfather built it. He carved his name and date over the door,' he said proudly.

She gazed at the cottage, long, low, straw-thatched, built of the same stone that littered Rhossili Down, marking the Norsemen's graves.

'Would you like to see inside, Miss?' he pressed. 'It's much the same as it was when the first Ellis brought his bride here.'

Suddenly she remembered where she was. And the Mistress. The stern, uncompromising voice rang through her mind.

'Never speak to a man, Kitty, unless women are near. Men want only one thing, and once they have it, a woman is tarnished, used-up, despised by the world. Finished.'

Wasn't it true? Hadn't it happened to her own mother? Where would she be now if it wasn't for the charity of the Mistress? The London streets, a tawdry whore to be broken and dead before her time like the woman who had borne her.

Terrified, she shrank from him. 'No. I must go. The Mistress will be waiting.'

'Are you from the village?'

'No, the big house. I help with the children. I must go.'

'May I walk along with you?' His voice was gentle, as though he sensed her fear, and the reason behind it.

She ran. He followed. When she reached the carter's track he spoke again.

'Forgive me, Miss, I know my manners are rough, but I see no one, living at the Well as I do. It's a good life, but a lonely one. I'm sorry I frightened you. Please, will you

18

come again?'

'I can't,' she whispered, her eyes downcast. 'I have to work. There's no time.'

'You're here now.'

'You don't understand. The children were invited out; there wasn't room in the carriage for me.'

'You must visit your people sometimes,' he persisted.

'No. I have no one to visit. I'm from London. The Mistress took me from the Institution. She's been kind. I'd still be there if it wasn't for her.'

'I've always wanted to see London. But I don't suppose I ever will. I can't leave the farm. Besides, there's no reason for me to travel. I went to Swansea once,' he continued. 'With my father. My mother took care of the Well then. Life was good in those days. We were happy. I had my parents. Brothers and sisters too. They all died of the throat fever, five years back.'

'I'm sorry.' She was, truly. She was familiar with loneliness. She knew what it was to have no one to care for, no one to love who did not already love others better.

'You're pretty.'

She fell silent. The Mistress was right. Men wanted to use women, not talk or befriend them.

'I mean it. Would your Mistress let me call on you?' he ventured tentatively. 'I could walk to the hall of an evening. We could talk.'

'I have to work.'

'The children. They must go to bed early.' He was amazed at his own temerity.

'The Mistress wouldn't agree.'

'I wouldn't want to see you alone. The Well is my life, but it's not enough. I want it to be as it was, with a family living there again. Not one lonely man. Will you see me again?'

'I'd like to,' she capitulated hesitantly, encouraged by his sincerity. 'You're not like the others.'

'What others?'

'In London, men came in to the Institution. At night. They never talked, only wanted to …' She stood still for a moment, twisting her hands around the iron bars of the drive gates. 'I was too young, they didn't bother me, but if the Mistress hadn't taken me, my turn would have come. I must go. Goodbye.' She turned and fled up the long drive to the hall.

'Your name. I must know your name,' he shouted after her.

'Kitty,' she called back breathlessly. 'Just Kitty.'

Kitty Ellis would be a good name, he thought that night. And he, like Kitty, slept a little less lonely than he had done in years.

That Sunday he went to church in Reynoldston. He'd been to church before, but only the weather-beaten, clifftop church of Rhossili. The warm, comfortable, sheltered church in Reynoldston was alien to him. He crept in early and sat at the back, leaning against the grey stone wall.

People filed into the church. The curious glanced at him, not unkindly, but he saw only the stares, not the friendship proffered behind them. The vicar walked in slowly from the vestry, holy book in hand, altar men and choir trailing behind, all dressed in white surplices. This was a grand parish, not a windswept one where poverty whistled in on the winter storms.

The gentry from the Hall came in last. They could afford to. Wasn't God's servant also their own? They paid him more than his stipend in the Easter offering. Heads bowed, they glided to their pew, retainers following in their wake like ripples trailing behind fisher craft going out to sea.

Ellis saw Kitty. She looked different. Her long hair was tied in a stiff little knot, an ugly starched calico hat nailed

20

to her head. She wore black, which accentuated all the corners the Institution had chiselled into her frame. When the service was done he followed the carriages back to the hall. He'd made up his mind. He would speak to her Mistress, and ask for Kitty's hand in marriage.

'Kitty, come here.' The butler's voice was leaden with condemnation. 'A young man had the audacity to knock the front door and enquire after you. I sent him packing, but the Mistress will want to see you after evening prayers.'

'Oooh Kitty, you naughty girl. What have you done?' winked Nancy the scullery maid. 'And there's me thinking you were quiet.'

'That's enough, Nancy. The poor girl's in trouble. Kitty, how could you?' Cook's reproach was worse than the butler's harsh words. Kitty burst into tears.

'I only met him once. He seemed nice, lonely like me.'

'I bet he did, men always do. There, there, don't take on so. Listen girl, watch your manners and say nothing. I'll warrant they'll not be too hard on you.'

The Mistress's charity was as rigid as her tightly-corseted body.

'Bad blood will out, Kitty. I regret now that I ever thought otherwise. You will be returned to the Institution tomorrow. The Master's decision is final. You may go and pack. That is all.'

Kitty went, with hot tears coursing down her pale cheeks. She had nothing to pack. The fine uniforms were to stay for the next girl. All she owned were two yellow winceyette frocks. Institution clothes. Hairbrush, flannel, soap, towel – even her underclothes, all belonged to the mistress. She lay on her bed and wept. The children whom she'd loved the most were kept from her goodbyes, and her fellow servants dared not comfort her, lest they too be tarred with her brush.

Then she thought of another. One as lonely as she. She would go to him. She made a bundle of her spare dress, lacking even a cloth to tie round it. There was harlot's blood in her veins; she would not give them cause to call her a thief too. She slipped out of the house into the night. The darkness held no terrors for her that could match those of the Institution. She found the Well, and rested by the flowing water. The sound soothed her, the first lullaby sung for her and for her alone.

He rose as the first fingers of dawn stretched out into the sky. She heard him stir, saw the casement opening, smelt his bacon frying on the fire. Timidly she crept to the door and knocked. He opened it, his dark eyes lighting at the sight of her in her bedraggled state.

'If you still want me, I've come,' she murmured fearfully. 'But I must warn you, I've bad blood in me. That's why the Mistress won't have me at the hall any longer.'

'Want you?' His arms reached out to take her. 'Oh yes, Kitty. I want you.'

They were married that morning. They walked from the Well to Rhossili church and told the vicar that as they were already living under the same roof there was no time for banns, and he, taciturn, silent man that he was, asked no questions. Instead he read the service over their heads, motioning the verger and his wife to stand witness.

No one in Reynoldston knew the identity of the strange young man, and the vicar of Rhossili church was famed for his refusal to speak a word out of God's house.

The Mistress never discovered Kitty's fate.

'Are you happy, my love?' It was autumn. The poppies had long since withered, but Kitty had not missed them.

'Happier than I ever believed possible.' she smiled. 'I expected nothing, and you have given me the world.'

Ellis lay back on the downs and gazed out to sea. He too was used to happiness now. The meal waiting on the table when work was finished for the day. Clean, darned clothes where once there had only been yesterday's dirt-encrusted cast-offs. Thoughts, work, walks over the downs … lives shared.

Kitty lay close to him, marvelling at her summer memories. Of the time that Ellis had left her alone at the Well, and how she, proud of the trust he placed in her, had worked as she'd never worked before. His glorious return from Swansea laden with presents. The first she'd been given. Clothes that would have graced the Mistress's wardrobe. Hairbrushes, not wooden and chipped, but silver and gleaming. Trinkets, jewels, ornaments for the mantelshelf, but most of all, his love. He had changed her. The lost, hungry look had left her face, and sometimes when she looked in his glass she felt almost beautiful.

'I never did walk over the causeway to Worm's Head.' she said as they watched the first of the winter breakers crash against the cliffs.

Ellis took her hand into his own. 'October's not the time. We'll go together. In the summer when the poppies are in bloom, I promise.'

Winter came and went. Nothing disturbed their peace. Old animals died in winter storms, and young were born in the spring to replace them. Then, they had a visitor. The first of the poppies bloomed at his feet, but his news shattered their world.

'They need more men for the war, Ellis.'

'It's not my war, Iestyn, it won't touch the Well.'

'This war will touch everyone, Ellis. If you don't go to fight, it will come. Even to your Well. You must go, boy.'

'Why?' demanded Ellis. 'Why must I fight? I don't

hate enough to fight.'

'You have to go, boy, come now, the sooner you do, the sooner you'll be back. We march to Swansea tonight. Kiss your pretty wife goodbye; you'll see her again before winter sets in. I promise.'

But Ellis wasn't back by winter. Kitty shivered alone in the old cupboard bed at night, and she lived and worked as Ellis had once done. In isolation, with only the wind and the animals to keep her company.

After winter – spring. The poppies bloomed and Ellis returned.

'I'm back, my love. Just as Iestyn said. Have you been lonely?'

'Not any more.' She moved over, making room for him in the bed.

'The Well. How is my Well?'

'We have new calves, more chickens. I put butter out with the milk churns, and there's extra money in the chest.'

'Thank you, my love, for loving this land as I do.'

Kitty wasn't lonely any more. Ellis was with her. Wherever she went he was at her side, helping, talking, loving. Then the postman came with a telegram. She couldn't read. He had to tell her what it said.

'Ellis is dead, Kitty,' he shouted clumsily, terrified of his own emotions. 'He died for his country.'

'Thank you.' She walked away. Ellis was at her side. He comforted her; she had no need of anyone else.

'Poor girl. That's all she said? "Thank you"?'

'Yes. Shook me up, I can tell you.' The postman took a nip of warming elderberry wine in an effort to steady his nerves.

24

'All alone up there. She should move down here to the village. A body needs Christian company.'

'The Ellises were mad to build on the downs. Our family always said so. But then she's a pretty little thing.' The postman put away his flask and picked up his sack. 'Seems to me she must have known what she was doing when she married him. Where did she come from, anyway? The whole Ellis clan were mad. Always were, and always will be, if you ask me.'

Kitty loved Ellis more every day. The nights were best, when she lay next to him in the old wooden bed, listening to the water trickling from the Well. It pleased her to think of the generations of Ellis women who had been lulled to sleep by that self-same sound. But the peace did not last. In the autumn the postman returned.

'He's not dead, Kitty.'

'I know.'

'They found him in a field hospital. They're bringing him back to you. He'll need looking after. He was gassed, you see, he's not what he was, Kitty. I'm sorry.'

They brought a stranger to the Well, and left him. His head was bandaged and he sat awkwardly in a wheelchair. His legs had gone, left on the fields of France for the crows to peck. And she had to tend to this ... this ... whining, fretful being, constantly demanding time and attention of her that should have been her husband's. She had no time for Ellis now. He waited patiently in the shadows, and she lived for the brief moments they snatched together, when the stranger wasn't looking. Ellis was even kept from her bed at night, for the interloper was there, awake, pain-ridden. She could no longer listen to the music of the Well. His noise drove everything from her ears, even Ellis's sweet, loving whispers.

She knew what she had to do. She and Ellis planned it, whispering together in corners when the stranger's back was turned. She waited for the spring to come, the poppies to bloom, then she spoke to the interloper.

'The poppies are blooming; we can go to the sea. It's not far. I will push you on to the causeway. You will feel better for the sea air in your lungs, you may even sleep easier tonight.'

He smiled up at her from his chair and patted her hand awkwardly. She had seemed cold and distant since his return. But then it was a lot to expect. Even from someone who loved you. His disfigured face, his crippled, useless body, his mind constantly wavering from the poison he'd breathed.

They set off for the sea. He felt her presence as she pushed his chair. She was murmuring to herself but he took no notice. It came of living alone, he thought. God only knew he had done enough of it in the past. He shuddered, regretting all the lonely years, and his shattered body. He would recover; the doctors had told him so. Things could never be as they were, but they would get better. They had to. After all they still had one another, and he loved her, and she him.

Not even his mutilated body could alter that.

She pushed his chair on to the pebbled causeway then wandered away, looking for crabs. They were sweet and good to eat. He made her move his chair, just once, so he could look up the downs to the copse of trees that hid the Well. Then he dozed.

The water woke him. It was swirling around what was left of his thighs, cold and clammy, it made his stumps ache. Frightened, he called out to Kitty. It was so easy to wander and forget the time. The tide was notorious. Many had been caught here and drowned. He looked for her frantically, worried lest she be hurt.

Then he saw her, standing on the cliff above him, laughing. Her arms stretched out to a shadow. He shouted, but the wind carried his voice, then the tide took his chair and he saw no more.

They came for her. She knew they would. Their cart carried her away from the Well but she did not mind. The poppies were in bloom, and he was at her side. Wherever they took her, Ellis would come too. They could not take that away from her, no matter what ...

Hanging Washing
Wendy White (SDWC)

He slipped away while she was in the garden,
pegging his damp shirts along the line.
She didn't see him leave or hear the door close,
that softest click the full stop to their life.
She didn't catch his steps move down the pavement,
his hurrying feet that would soon learn how to march.
She didn't watch him wave goodbye to neighbours,
hear his banter, his quick, boyish laugh.

Down the street he strew her dreams behind him –
the wife he wouldn't meet and wouldn't wed,
the children that would never become substance,
the long and joy-filled life he'd never have.
He didn't comprehend he was deserting,
as he stole out on the day that he signed up,
with a lie of extra years upon his proud lips,
an idealist's childlike honour in his heart.

He stripped away her hopes while she pegged washing,
as she'd done at least a thousand times before,
so she didn't have a last chance to persuade him,
plead with him to wait just one year more.
He was impulsive, impressionable, eager,
too buoyed with courage to survive for long.
And he slipped away while she was in the garden.
She came in to find she'd lost her only son.

Dawn at Mons
Di Coffey (external short story competition winner)

It's nearly daybreak and I'm frozen through to my guts.
The snow that began with a flurry of flakes has turned to a
drenching sleet that's soaked my serge uniform. The
sergeant, no doubt dry beneath his cape, stands behind me
and the wooden post that's been cemented into the yard.
His strong, rough hands pull my arms backwards and I feel
the bite of cord wrapping its grip around my wrists, smell
his fag-laden breath, warm against my ear.

'Sorry lad. We'll make it quick.'

Now he's in front of me and for the split second it takes
him to drag a jute bag over my head, I'm eyeball to eyeball
with him. The bag stinks of sour wheat grains that trickle
down my face and make me sneeze. The sergeant fiddles
with something then pats my chest and moves away from
me. I know what he's done. He's pinned a bit of white rag
above where he thinks my heart is. It's a target to aim at.

'Bloody hell, Arthur, you've gone and done it then?'
There's no mistaking the admiration glinting in the eyes of
my young cousin, George, or the reverence in his voice.
'Bloody hell,' he repeats. 'You're going to fight the Hun?'

'Beats swotting for exams.' I pull out my Players and
offer the pack to George, flipping the lid open in what I
hope is a sophisticated gesture. Leaning against the
gatepost to the school's riding stables, I inhale deeply,
savouring the rich taste of tobacco fumes on my tongue,
the smell in my nose. 'Anyway, who says I should have to
go to Oxford?'

'Well, your mother does, for one. Isn't she going to be

29

awfully cut up about it?' George coughs a little and stubs out his half smoked cigarette under his shoe. 'Your father died last year, didn't he?'

I sigh. 'Can't let that stop me. I'm doing the patriotic thing, George. I'll make her proud of me. You see if I don't!'

'But you're only sixteen.'

'So what? I'll be seventeen when I finish my training.'

'You'll still be underage.'

'Oh shut up, George, will you?' I kick, poor-temperedly, at a stone.

'You *lied* about your age?'

'Of course I bloody lied about my age. Now put a sock in it, will you?'

George continues stubbing out his cigarette with renewed vigour. Then he glances towards me. 'So ... um. They'll give you a *real* gun?'

'Can't shoot the Hun with a bloody pea-shooter, can I? Of course I'll have a *real* gun. A bolt-action rifle probably – with a bayonet.'

George whistles softly through his teeth. 'A *bayonet*! You lucky sod!'

Though the loose weave of the jute bag I watch the soldiers across the yard stamping their boots, trying to beat life into their frozen feet, their fingers restless on their rifles. Fear gnaws my bones, forms ice in my bowels, and I begin to shake. I bite my tongue – taste the iron-squirt of warm liquid in my mouth.

Oh my God, they're lining up! Think of something else. Think of anything but those men – those guns. How the *hell* did I end up here? What started it? But I know the answer. It was at school – a couple of weeks before Founder's Day.

The notice board outside the school refectory is plastered

with boring shit about choir practice and rugby matches and the forthcoming Founder's Day which I know Mother will attend. I guess she'll visit London soon, searching for something new to wear to the event.

She's attractive, as mothers go. But not too flashy. She's always had confidence where choosing her clothes is concerned. Less so when it comes to instructing cook which meals to put on the table or even *finding* a good cook, come to that. Things have gone downhill since Pater died. There's no doubt about it, my father was the one who managed our household, albeit behind the scenes. He had the necessary air of authority where servants are concerned, but Mother's too timid to say boo to a goose, let alone demand high standards from the maid or the cook or the gardener. She isn't coping at all well. But she's my mother and I'm very fond of her but when the war's over I intend to take charge of things. Just like Pater.

I conjure in my mind our rambling old house and its mullioned windows and impressive portico – the sweeping lawns that are traversed by winding pathways to hidden-away places where a young child may make a den, ward off tigers; or, if astride a fallen tree, simply pretend he's on a ship, crossing a stormy ocean, battling pirates.

My gaze settles on the poster set to the right on the notice board. The Royal West Kent is recruiting! There's an address in town to report to and that afternoon I skive off from school and present myself to the officer in charge. Thirty minutes later, after filling in various forms and been given a date to have a medical check by an army doctor, I'm well on the way to becoming Private Arthur Harrington of the Royal West Kent Regiment.

The training is exciting. A lot of hollering and bayoneting stuffed dummies dangling from gibbets, fags, and men's talk in the mess afterwards. Talk of sweethearts with apple-blossom cheeks and whores with glossy red lips, and the number of times we'd been laid. And I lie

31

with the best of them with nothing but a seventeen year old's wet dreams as experience.

''Ow about you, Arfur? 'Ave you 'ad your leg over yet? 'Ad a bit of 'ow's yer father, 'ave you?'

''Course I bloody have. Loads of times.' I cup my hands beneath my chest. 'The last one had whoppers on her. Absolute whoppers!'

There's a roar of approval from my mates. We scoff our rations and I walk out to the parade ground feeling like a man who is ten feet tall.

But then we are sent to the Front – to the killing of Germans and the explosions and the hell on earth of mud-filled trenches and gas – and the screams of dying men.

Time and again comes the command, 'Over the top, lads. Up and at 'em.' Day after day, I scramble out of trenches and run towards enemy lines, hoarse with roaring abuse, sickened by death and destruction. On the afternoon before I run away, I stumble over a Hun. I think he's dead but his eyelids flicker open – his eyes widen in fear as he gazes up at me. He looks too young to be on the battlefield but he's lying here, bloodied, with his left arm half blown away – and in his right hand he's holding a pistol that's pointing straight at me. I feel the choke of puke in my throat as I take hold of my rifle with both hands and drive my bayonet into the boy's chest – hear his last rasping breath, see the light in his eyes die – think of a German mother mourning her son.

Then I run. Through the mud and the driving rain, I run. Mile after mile, I run, until I come upon a derelict barn where I collapse onto stinking, decayed straw and lie, whimpering like an abandoned puppy, until exhaustion brings sleep of sorts – and hellish nightmares.

I awake, my mouth dry with thirst and fear, belly empty. Then I hear the tramp of booted feet, the shouts of soldiers. The Royal West Kent's men have come to make an example of one of their own. But I'm not really 'one of their own' because they're not cowards and I *am* – a coward.

A shout goes up. 'There he is. Over there!'

The soldiers across the yard have formed their line. Oh my God, I've started to pee in my pants. It's flowing like lava down my icy thigh. I remember telling Mother how I'd make her proud of me. Proud? Bitterly ashamed more like. Why couldn't I have stuck it out? Died in battle – honourably. Not caught like a rat in a trap, hauled back to a five-minute court martial and sentenced to be shot at dawn. Was it only *yesterday* that sentence on me was passed?

I raise my head and through the rough sacking I see the sleety rain has stopped; the sky is lightening and threaded with streaks of red. 'Red sky in the morning, shepherd's warning' I chant to myself, over and over again. 'Red sky in the ...' High above me, a trio of geese fly west. A solitary white feather flutters down and lands, quivering, on the jute covering my face. I try to blow it away. But the white feather for cowardice persists in staying put.

'*Take aim.*'

I close my eyes and I'm back at home. I'm in our garden, rolling down a grassy knoll, laughing, laughing. And my parents are laughing too. It's my sixth birthday and the sun is shining, warming me. Rufus, our spaniel, is barking in excitement as he chases a rabbit. Cook has prepared a scrumptious picnic for us – cucumber sandwiches with the crusts cut off, and slices of fruit cake and a Victoria sponge. Daisy, the house maid, has laid a white cloth on the garden table and is setting out crockery and cutlery and jugs of chilled lemonade. She places a glass bowl of Mother's favourite roses in the middle of the table. I smell their heady scent and watch Mother turning towards me. She is smiling and all is right with the world.

'*Fire!*'

The Letters
Steve Jones (SDWC)

Some people say the defining feature of an alcoholic is the inability to stop drinking once started. In my experience as a young drunkard and generally worthless man about town this overlooks the heart of the matter. For me, the defining feature of my predilection was I was drunk pretty much all the time, and always when it would have paid me to be sober.

One such time was a mild February day in 1918 when I walked out on South Madison Street into a marching band. I just naturally fell in step with them and went along swinging my arms and saluting. People were actually cheering me. The same folks as wouldn't have helped me out of the gutter on any other day. Even when we marched into the courthouse and there was Judge Witzner all dressed up in his National Guard uniform standing behind a desk I didn't sober up enough to understand what was happening.

He gave me a card to read from and a bible to hold and I did as I was told and signed on the line. 'Congratulations, son,' he said, 'I never guessed you had it in you. You go on home now and pack. You need be at the railhead at eight tomorrow morning.'

I didn't go home. I went back to the tap. When I finally did arrive home my stepfather, Carl, was there to meet me. I've rarely seen a man look more delighted than he did that day.

'I've made you some coffee,' he said. 'We need to get you in shape.'

'In shape for what?'

34

'Damn it boy, you just this afternoon enlisted. Everybody saw you go in and take the oath with all them other fools.'

'Oath?'

He snatched the paper I was holding, smoothed it out, and began to read from it. 'I do solemnly swear or affirm I will support and defend the Constitution of the United States against all enemies, foreign and domestic; that I will bear true faith and allegiance to the same; and that I will obey the orders of the President of the United States and the orders of the officers appointed over me, according to regulations and the Uniform Code of Military Justice. So help me God.'

As he read his voice got faster and jauntier. He finished on such a happy note I found myself laughing along with him, which coincided with wail of anguish from my mother who'd been standing in the kitchen listening.

'I'm in the army?'

'You sure are, Clint, and you have to be on a train to Missouri in twelve hours.'

'They're sending me out of state?'

'It's more than that, boy,' he replied, to a fresh crescendo of sobbing, 'They're sending you to France.'

'Why in the hell would I want to go there?'

'Because you just volunteered and that's where the war is, boy. You're gonna go overseas and fight for the USA and come back all covered in glory.'

'The hell I am,' I said, making for my room, and the bottle I had hidden behind the wash-hand basin. 'Mom,' I called out to her, 'Can you bring me a coffee in here? I don't like the one Carl made.'

Normally this would have provoked him just nicely, but that time he only smiled and said, 'That's all right son, I'll drink this. You lay down and have a rest, you're gonna need one.'

Next morning Carl made sure I got down early to the South-Western Railroad station at West Grove. As I'd expected the platform was crowded with excited farm boys. I knew I'd made a big mistake and I had my excuses ready, hoping some official would be present to whom I could explain matters. There was no one there though, only the station master who wrote us out pre-paid tickets. In the absence of anyone better I told him I wasn't sure about going no more. He said in time of war deserters were routinely shot, but I could make up my own mind. I decided to make the trip, at least as far as St Louis.

The crowd on the train was all in high spirits except for me and a rich kid called Billy-Rae Tolmund who sat morosely opposite me as the South Wyaconda Express swayed and rattled south. People like Billy-Rae would ordinarily have had nothing to do with the likes of me. The difference now was we both had our tickets paid for by the government and was both wishing we was anywhere else.

'You enlisted too then, Clint?' he said eventually.

'I did.'

'Aren't you a bit old?'

'I'm not yet twenty-nine, Billy-Rae, but I've had a hard life. Why, how old are you.'

'Nineteen.'

'Then you must have had it real easy. How old are you really?'

'Seventeen.'

'You got to be seventeen and a half to enlist.'

'They didn't ask to see my birth certificate.'

Then we didn't say nothing for a while, just watched the countryside go by through the window.

'Why'd you do it?' he asked suddenly.

'I was drunk, why'd you think? What about you?'

'I'm running away from my wedding.'

'You're honeymooning on your own?'

'No.' he explained, 'There hasn't been no wedding yet.

36

I don't want there to be no wedding, it'd be my whole life ruined.'

'Is she having a baby?'

He nodded.

'Do I know this girl?'

'You'll know her by name, its Aniela Cobb. Her folks own Cobb's Pharmacy and Diner, and the new automobile place. They got some land as well, they was going to build us a house.'

I thought about this. A tall woman, aged about thirty with a plain, homely face came to mind. 'Goddamn it Billy-Rae,' I said, 'that spinster's my age.'

At first he looked surprised. Then he said, 'No, you're thinking of Jessica Cobb, Clint. She's Aniela's older sister.'

'I am?'

'Sure you are. Aniela was the May Queen last year.'

Another completely different face and body came to mind. 'That's her, that purty little thing is, Aniela Cobb?'

'Yep.'

'She's the one you joined the army to escape?'

'Yep.'

'You got the best-looking and wealthiest young woman in Bloomfield in the family way, and you're running out on her?'

'I guess I am. Do you think I'm doing wrong?'

'I think you're crazy. If I was you I'd have knocked her up on purpose just to trick her into marrying me.'

'I knew you'd say something like that.'

'Why did you ask then?'

'I was hoping for better,' he said.

Although I'd seen him a million times before, this was the first time we'd spoken. I don't recall much more of our conversation on that trip, but I know that's where our friendship got started.

That night we arrived at Jefferson Barracks, St. Louis,

Missouri and was both assigned to Company 'B' of the Fourth Infantry. While we were there the number of recruits rose from about four thousand to over six thousand. We did some drill and such, but mostly this was a holding centre for the real army. We were introduced to it three weeks later when we shipped out to our new camp, Camp Stuart at Newport News, Virginia. Here we were attached to the Third Army of the American Expeditionary Force under Major-General Joseph T. Dickman.

At Camp Stuart we trained hard and lived under military discipline, which I didn't much mind. I was used to being insulted and shouted at. Billy-Rae, being from a more privileged background than my own, found it tough going. Not that it mattered, he and I both knew it was too late to quit.

After a month of Camp Stuart I was in better shape than I had been for years and in April we had the Pass-out Parade. Marching out four abreast we left for Alpine Landing in Hoboken, New Jersey and a packet-boat to Europe. Two weeks later we were in Colombey Dus Eglise in north-western France to be trained in trench warfare.

I'd expected we'd end up supporting some French or British division, but it turned out Pershing had no intention of handing us over to them to get slaughtered. He was quite capable of doing that for himself. At the beginning of June we were moved up to our position at Belleau. This is just north of the Marne River which was more or less the southern edge of the German salient. We mustered at Essomes-sur-Marne. It was here just before we got sent up to the forward line at Château-Thierry that Billy-Rae got the first batch of letters from Aniela.

'How many are there?' I asked him.

'About a dozen, I guess. Should I write her back?'

'Why wouldn't you?'

'If I do, she'll know I'm here.'

'She already knows you're here, dimwit.'

'I mean I'm not ready to go home and make an honest woman of her, Clint.'

'You got a girl back home writing you, Billy-Rae. There are guys here who would do anything for that. Anyway, you can't go home, none of us can. Some of us won't.'

So Billy-Rae read the letters. Then he gave them to me to read, asking if it was some kind of code or a trick as there was no mention of marriage or the pregnancy which had caused him to run to Uncle Sam. For that matter there was nothing at all of a personal nature, just gossip about Bloomfield. There was even a bit about me. It seemed Clint Decker had bravely gone to serve his country when so many others had shown the White Feather.

'You still think I should write back?' he asked.

'Seeing as there's nothing about a jilting or fatherhood here I don't see why not.'

'I wouldn't know what to say, Clint.'

'Just say how you feel, whatever you're thinking at the time.'

'I keep thinking "is the baby gone".'

'I don't think you should write that.'

'Hell, I don't know. You write regular to your mom. You tell me what to write.'

I passed him a letter I'd written to send home, hoping it'd inspire him, but it didn't seem to work out. His spelling was awful and the short letter he wrote hard to read. As near as I could make out he was asking her to send some fruit candy he was partial to. I explained there was a difference between correspondence a boy sent to his mother and the sort he sends to his girl.

'But, it's just what you wrote, Clint,' he said.

'I know Billy-Rae, but I wanted you to get some ideas from it, not copy it wholesale.'

In the end we settled on the obvious solution. I answered the letters and he cleaned my equipment and did some fetching and carrying. At first I worried she'd write something of a personal and private nature between her and Billy-Rae, which would embarrass us both, but she never did. So eventually I relaxed and got into the rhythm of it. I enjoyed writing to her. Me and Billy-Rae did everything together anyway, this was just one more thing. They were 'our' letters to Aniela. I wrote and signed them, but with his name, and we both read her replies.

On the sixteenth of June we were joined up with the Seventh Infantry to relieve the Marines at Belleau Wood. It seemed the Germans had no inclination to quit just because they were facing, 'The Finest Fighting Force on Earth'. Even so, according to the Marine Commander, Colonel Wendell Neville, the enemy was just about beat and only needed finishing off.

It seemed no one had told the Germans this. As soon as we entered the trees two boys we'd marched with for months were killed straight off, and that was just the start. We fought all day and didn't gain an inch but lost a third of our number. From that time on I was resigned to being killed myself.

After the Belleau Woods fiasco, battered and depleted, we were moved back to our trenches at Chateau-Thierry. Periodically shells would strike the foxholes men had dug in the clay banks of the Marne, disembowelling and dismembering them. Not something to be hinted at in letters home, but when writing to Aniela I could give some intimation of what we were going through. Every time we were rotated out to the support trenches there would be a fresh batch from her. We'd both read them and I would answer them as if they'd arrived on separate dates.

Billy-Rae's attitude to Aniela changed. He began to look forward to seeing her again and let on he was worried their child would be put up for adoption. Since she hadn't mentioned anything of that kind in her letters it was hard for me to suddenly introduce it. While we were considering ways the subject might be broached Billy-Rae got wounded. I was sick with dread when I visited him at the hospital in Bézu. His foot was gone and he was very low, but I believed he would be OK. Then blood poisoning set in and four days later, at the age of seventeen and a half, he died.

When the division was next rotated out of the line there were another three letters waiting. Since we'd been buddies they were just automatically given to me. Billy-Rae never had any last words about what I should do. He never had any last words at all. So I did what I'd always done, and answered the letters. I pretended as usual to be Billy-Rae. I guess I expected those to be the last. The news would get back to his parents in Iowa and they'd tell Aniela he was gone. I didn't mention anything in my letters to Mom about what had happened. They deserved to hear of his death properly, not through a neighbour.

More letters arrived. Our platoon sergeant brought them to me. He said, 'I'm guessing you know who sent these?'

I nodded.

'I know about the arrangement you boys had,' he said, 'So I'm giving you a choice. I can return these, or you can have them. What's it to be?'

I took the letters and with some trepidation opened the one with the earliest postmark. It began, 'Dear Billy, It has not rained here for more than a month, but is always oppressive and humid. We have had one tornado, which demolished a barn out by the Fox River. A horse in the barn at the time survived but has become skittish. I am the only person unsurprised by this.

You must send me your chest measurement as I plan to knit you a jersey for the winter.'

In my reply I could not bring myself to tell her what had become of her late fiancé and found myself still posing as Billy-Rae, but being in every other respect honest and truthful. And so it went on. I was never again asked about the letters. They kept on arriving and they was just automatically given to me.

In September the jersey arrived. It was as she had promised, 'dark in colour and made of old wool, but very warm and snug'. By now I had some French and I told her what a beautiful country this would be if it wasn't for the war. In her reply she said we would visit it together after the fighting was over.

By October allied troops had turned back the German spring offensive and reached the Hindenburg Line and it was clear we were winning. I decided if the Lord allowed me to live I would go to college when I returned. I would make something of myself and waste no more of the precious gift I had seen taken from Billy-Rae and so many others.

Then in November 1918 the German army surrendered. It was a strange thing. One day they were there, as full of fight as ever, and the next they'd just packed up and gone. Even so it was March 1919 before I took the train back home to Bloomfield, exactly a year after I'd left. I wrote Aniela before leaving New York Depot. I could not even then bring myself to say I was not Billy-Rae. Instead I told her Clint Decker had something important to say to her.

When I arrived I scanned the platform. Locomotives in those days let out a good deal of steam and smoke. When it cleared a tall, slim, well-dressed woman was standing there holding a package which I knew were my letters.

'Hello, Clint,' she said.

'Hello Jessica.' I said, 'I guess we been corresponding some.'

'When did you know it was me?' she asked.

'It took a while. What about you?'

'From the first letter; that sweet handsome boy was barely literate.'

Her grey eyes looked intently into my face as if seeing

me for the first time, which in a way I suppose she was.

I said, 'At the end, just before he died, he was concerned about Aniela and the baby.'

'There was no baby, Clint,' she said. 'That was a romance invented by a bored, spoiled child who never stopped to think of the consequences of her foolishness.'

While I was digesting this, she asked, 'Did he suffer?'

'Yes,' I said, knowing I couldn't lie to her. 'He was brave though, much braver than I was, and a better soldier. Will you tell Aniela that?'

'I will.' she promised.

'Why did you keep on writing, after you knew he'd been killed?'

'Because I knew you needed me to. I hope my letters were a comfort.'

'You have no idea,' I said, wanting to say more, but fearing I would lose my composure.

She laid a gloved hand on my arm and suddenly I knew what I wanted, what I'd wanted all along, when I was writing all those letters. And I was afraid she would walk away from me and the moment would be lost forever.

I said, 'I am not the man I was, Jessica Cobb. I have changed. The war has changed me.'

She stepped closer and pressed her cheek against mine, holding the bundle of letters against my chest. 'I know that, Clint,' she said. 'You were lost, and now I have found you. You will not be lost again.'

The Passing of Time
Janet Killeen (external poetry competition winner)

Grandfather never seemed quite right
To me.
He was away somewhere else,
Caught on the shivering wires of memory,
Peering through the sights of inward eyes,
His hearing muffled. Sometimes his hands trembled,
reaching for a plate or cup.
But it was years since Passchendaele and the guns
And surely clichéd time had done its work?
It's supposed to heal.
But now I guess
He heard their hollow thunder every night
in the rumble of traffic.
His clay-clumped feet had stumbled away from hell
But then his life dwindled halfway
Out of the ditches dug
For him and all those others
Who took their bodies home
But left themselves behind.

His life was like a shell,
Held to the ear,
Full of the ceaseless iteration of the sea of war.
And I was blind
To it.

The Sunrise
Julie Hayman (external short story competition joint second)

Flanders' bloody fields. And here I am, laid up.

What I really want to do in the future is run a pub, I tell the nurse who redoes my bandages. She's new, I think, just drafted in. Not very old. Eyes cold as the water she washes me in, but her arm is plump and soft and warm when she bids me hold to it as she lifts me up to flannel my back. The effort leaves me panting and I can't speak for a bit.

The Sunrise, I say soon as I can, as she works her way south, lifting up the blanket as she goes and scrubbing underneath. That's our local at home: The Sunrise. I'd like to run a pub like that. There's a woody smell about her, spreading over me as she flannels, and I like it. Lots of the nurses smell faintly floral, of violets or lavender or lily of the valley, but the timbery smell of this one reminds me of the woods I ran in at home as a boy. As a boy! How do you like that? Four years ago was the last time I ran alone there, the moss springy under my feet, twigs cracking, brambles snatching at my coat as I … didn't know that I'd walked straight into … he came at me before I could … *for Christ's sake, for Christ's sake, give me a gasper.*

'You lie still, Private Jenkins,' she says, pushing my shoulder a bit into the camp bed, and now there are two of them over me, the woody one and the one I know as Nurse Johnson, too pretty to be here and certainly too pretty to be looking after me. She has green eyes, does Nurse Johnson, and I spend a lot of time trying to think what sort of green. To say they put me in mind of frogspawn makes them sound ugly, but they aren't at all: it's just that the green is

45

the colour of mucus and with that black dot inside I naturally think of frogspawn. She has a lovely soft line to her cheek and nose, and I wish I had some skill in drawing so I could show her to herself. Her hair's shiny and brown as conkers, with copper streaks where the sun finds it. She has a few freckles on her cheeks, like stippling on a mare's rump, and is tall and straight and lean, and her mouth looks always about to smile though it never does. I love her. I love Nurse Johnson fiercely, as no one before. It's almost worth being laid up to see her moving around the field hospital, almost worth hearing the poor sods moan and gasp and bubble in their throats, almost worth the sight of those wheeled curtains round someone's bed for an hour or so before the bedding is changed and someone new comes in and lays in it and the whole symphony of suffering begins again.

'Should be all right now,' says Nurse Johnson, moving away from my bunk. 'Don't go.' I say, or think I did. The tightness in my chest might have stopped me. Something spurts out of my mouth, and the woody-smelling nurse wipes it away quickly. I feel embarrassed at that. Wiping my mouth like a baby's. 'Washed my tackle yet?' I ask with a straight face, and she smiles. Now, who'd have thought that wintry-faced girl could smile as warm as that?

'You were telling me about the pub you want,' she says, parking herself gently on the edge of the bunk and dabbing at my brow with a clean cloth. Her ice-cold eyes never look directly in mine and I think of staying silent, to force her look at me properly.

'The pub, Private Jenkins, the pub,' she says. 'Think about the pub.'

Which pub? Which pub does she want me to think about? There are thousands of pubs. Does she mean the pub I intend to run, or The Sunrise at home?

The Sunrise, she says, as if reading my thoughts, Think about The Sunrise.

Dad took me there for a pint the day I turned fourteen. Let's have one for Stephen, my youngest, he said to the landlord, jabbing his thumb in my direction, jiggling the coins in his palm to hurry the man along … we were in the fog and then I stepped on mud and it cried out … for Christ's sake, for Christ's sake, oh for Christ's sake … Percy Dodd who never did a moment's harm in his life … splintered, his head half-off his neck …

'Sister, Sister.'

That voice is the woody-smelling nurse's. I see her leaning across me, worried, calling to Nurse Johnson who walks calmly over, her mouth tight and eyebrows suggesting she's cross.

'It's all right, Private Jenkins,' says Nurse Johnson, pulling the blanket smooth over me, and patting it in place. 'There's nothing to be alarmed about.'

I haven't said there is. She beckons the woody nurse to come to the end of the bed, and they both turn their backs on me, while Nurse Johnson says something sharp with lots of spattered s's and tutted t's. I see the lovely line of her cheek, the lovely line of her nose, lit up with a kind of halo by the light coming in through the open flap of the tent some way beyond her. Looks like a sunny day out there. I'd love to have the sun on my skin. If I ask, will the woody nurse let me go outside for a bit of a smoke for half an hour, if I promise to come back in when it's finished?

If you walk alongside the stream then cut across Broken Bridges and past the ringed bull in the pasture to your right and continue along for half a mile, you come to The Sunrise. It's got beams and a big old fireplace with inglenooks, and it smells smoky and welcoming. There are logs in the grate all year round, blackened and stiff and laying one beside the other, like the hundreds of limbs we had to march over and poor old Percy Dodd in all that mud.

'Try to lie still, Private Jenkins,' says the woody nurse,

still wiping the sweat from my forehead. 'It won't hurt so much then.' Something trickles out of my nose and onto my lip and my tongue licks it up.

Just next door to The Sunrise is the house where Emily Grainger lives and what's funny is that, if you sit in the garden of a late summer evening in August, like that evening I turned fourteen, you see her father's sunflowers poking over the top of the wall, nodding at you. Emily thought it a fine thing when I told her I'd joined up. 'You'll have such a lot to tell me when you're back, Stephen,' she said. 'I'll be waiting.'

Can't recall what colour Emily's eyes are. Frogspawn green, I'm thinking.

The sun is gone and it's dark. There's a deep ache in my chest as if a painful sigh is caught there, unable to escape. I'm thirsty. The woody nurse appears with a sip of water for me. 'Here, take this, Private Jenkins,' she says, putting her left hand behind my neck to help me but not trying to lift me higher this time. 'What's that bloody thing doing there?' I ask. The curtains-on-wheels is two beds along. 'Push it away,' I say, 'It should be four beds along.' The man in one of the beds next to it has a handlebar moustache and is sitting up reading a book in the lamplight; the man on the other side is lying with his arms crossed beneath his head, staring up at the ceiling of the tent, softly whistling a tune. His leg pokes out from under the covers; the bandages stop short of where his foot should be. 'Move that bloody thing,' I say, meaning the wheeled curtains, and I don't recognise the harshness of my voice.

My rifle's held across my body and I'm trudging along pulling one foot and then the other out of sucking mud and the tin hat's bobbing on my head like a bloody float on a stream and I need the woody nurse to mop my brow because the sweat's dripping in my eyes and stinging so that I can't see anything but the volcanoes erupting around

48

me, and in all that smoke I didn't know that I'd walked straight into No Man's Land and the Hun, he came at me before I could think, his face white and frightened, and I pointed my bayonet at him and his jacket bloomed horrifyingly red and I trudged on over him, over the thousands of arms and legs and ribs in the mud, feet slipping this way and that, passing by some dear soul crying, *'For Christ's sake, for Christ's sake, give me a gasper.'* We were in the fog, me and Charlie Betts trudging on side by side, and then I stepped on mud and it cried out, *'for Christ's sake, for Christ's sake, oh for Christ's sake, help me,'* and it was Percy Dodd who never did a moment's harm in his life, his body splintered, his head half off his neck, and how could that be?

'... and lead us not into temptation, but deliver us from evil, for thine is the kingdom, the power and the glory for ever and ever. Amen.'

The chaplain's voice, a good fella. Shouldn't be out here. Too soft. The war's torture for him.

A wagon must have fallen on me, I can't breathe. 'Move the bloody wagon,' I say, but the woody nurse says, 'Hush.' and strokes the hair off my forehead.

'I am the resurrection, and the life: he that believeth in me, though he were dead, yet shall he live ...'

All my pals like the chaplain. He's a good sort, wouldn't harm a fly. We all go along to his services.

It's dark around my bed and I wonder why. My eyes aren't working very well, but I think the tent's closed in on me and I'm the only patient in it now.

'Won't be long,' says the woody nurse.

'Sssh,' says Nurse Johnson, 'Hearing goes last.' Raising her voice a little, she says, 'You'll go to sleep soon, Private Jenkins.' Her voice lowers as she orders, 'Talk to him.'

'My dad runs a pub,' says the woody nurse, her voice trembling like she's at a funeral. 'It's called the Ring O'

Bells.'

I love these lies.

'Light,' I say, I want a light, but nobody hears me.

For Christ's sake, for Christ's sake, oh for Christ's sake, help me. Woody arms are holding me down. Help me. Percy Dodd who never did a moment's harm in his life, his body splintered, his head half off his neck, we left him in the mud and trudged on, taking the rifles from across our chests and aiming at the heads that bobbed over the parapet like sunflowers over a garden wall, just that far away, as a light burst over us, brilliant as the sunrise, and I rose into the air and flew backwards, away from the noise and the red-blotched foreheads and the head of Percy Dodd half off his neck and landed in the wood looking up into the frogspawn eyes of Emily who sat heavily on my chest, lovingly whispering, 'Private Jenkins, Private Jenkins, Private Jenkins.'

Friendly Fire
Ann Marie Thomas (SDWC)

'Friendly fire' they called it.
How is it friendly
to shoot your own side?

'Friendly fire' they called it,
mistaken identity.
Why not stop to find out?

'Friendly fire' they called it,
still a noble sacrifice.
Nothing noble about a shot in the back.

'Friendly fire' they called it.
Who do you hate
when the enemy is your own side?

'Friendly fire' they called it.
Still dead.
Still gone.

Just War
Robert Kennedy (external poetry competition joint second)

War is the work of many hands,
              A form of mass reduction;
                          One colour available:
Black.
Not Brooke nor Rosenberg,
        Not Owen or Sassoon by hell,
                 Could call my brothers
Back.
Now they`ll never be old men
             With knots in their laces.

War is the work of backroom boys,
        A Haig or a Bomber Harris;
                One flower in blossom;
Poppies.
Not "FTSE UP", nor "Wounded down",
            "Hero`s welcome" or hymn,
                 Could make them any less
Puppets.
Now they`ll never be gardeners
             With earth in their fingernails.

War is a collector of young men,
        A tax-excusal man;
               One payment overdue:
Life.

No TV reporter in camouflage,
               Nor economist pinned by his stripes,
                    Can redeem their interest-free loan:
Eternity.
Now they'll never be sons of angels –
               Damn your euphemisms anyway.

Unreserved
Gail Williams (SDWC)

Pulling the rough khaki collar closer, Sergeant Richardson huddled down in the stinking mud. It hadn't stopped raining in weeks; hardship and annoyance had ploughed permanent lines across his face. Rain collected on his forehead and ran down his patrician nose.

Beads of rain hung on his eyelashes. Back home *his* girl joked about his long lashes, but here, they were at least a defence against nature's assault.

He wished for a greatcoat; they all did. 'It's summer,' the quartermaster said, 'you're going to Flanders, boys, a nice little holiday in the sun.'

The sun; he'd forgotten what that was.

Soaked to the core, his feet ached and itched, a telling combination as he sat in his funk hole. He'd have to get the MO to check it out tomorrow, once they were rotated out of the trench again.

At least the artillery bombardment had stopped as nature took over the attack. God had forsaken them. If they went over the top, keen-sighted Germans would stop them. They couldn't get their fallen comrades from no-man's land. As Richardson remembered what they'd found last time they'd gone out, he closed his eyes.

What he saw were images of Jack, his best friend since they'd started school. His eyes had been gone, the peck point tears made it clear the carrion eaters had already plucked them away. His flesh was putrid, mottled blue and swollen. When they'd picked him up, the skin of his bloated stomach has burst, releasing the stench of decay, the first stage of liquefaction. Jack had been taken away, but his image, and the foul reek stayed. No-man's land stank unremittingly, and now another waft from another decomposing skin bag crept with mindless cruelty across the air to molest his nostrils.

Unable to stomach the stink in his nose, the memory forever etched behind his eyelids, he opened his eyes.

He looked down the line. All he could see before the traverse cut off his view were two riflemen, Bert Thatcher and Billy Edwards. They too squatted, in shallow funk holes cut into the side of the trench opposite the fire-step. Like him they were cold, damp, and miserable.

The only sound was the splat splash of the constant rain. Even the wind had taken the day off in this world of brown and grey.

'Help!'

The weak cry expressed a need they all felt. For a year they'd been posted on and off the front line, living in fear.

'Please, help me.'

Had he spoken aloud? The words had sounded clearly in the air. He looked to his right; Billy looked back, looking concerned.

'Please, God, help me.'

Springing to his feet, Richardson peered through his periscope. Raindrops plinked off the brim of his helmet. Someone was out there. Eyes wide, he searched through the fall of rain and rise of splash. Then he saw it. The movement of an arm.

'Help!'

Harry! No! It couldn't be. But it was. Even distorted by pain he knew Harry's voice. Harry, Jack, and him, the three musketeers. Not that he'd ever read the book, but Jack had told him enough to get the gist. All for one and one for all. It was what they'd always stood for; it was why they were here together.

Richardson side-stepped to the nearest ladder; he wouldn't let Harry down. He was two rungs up when a hand landed heavily on his back, heaving him back into the trench where he found himself face to face with Captain Watson. Bert and Billy blank faced behind him. Snapping to attention, Richardson saluted and looked dead ahead, over the captain's head.

'What do you think you're up to, Richardson?'

'Harry Shoesmith is out there, sir. He's alive. I'm going to get him, sir.'

'No. You are not. You know what standing orders are.'

'But he's alive, sir.'

'Yes, and that's no-man's land, son. You stick your head up there, you're dead. Visibility isn't good, but the Germans can see enough to kill a man.'

'But sir –'

'No.' Watson cut in. 'No buts. We'll go for Shoesmith under cover of darkness. Here.' He thrust an envelope into Richardson's hand. 'A runner gave me this. God knows how it got in the despatch bag, but it's addressed to you. You'd just as well take it.'

He watched the officer walked away, boots splashing on the waterlogged duck-boards. Bert and Billy melted back to their posts. Neither looked happy.

Glancing at the letter he recognised Rebecca's handwriting, but the address was already smudging so he slipped it in his cartridge pouch where it would be safe from the rain. He'd read it later.

Rebecca Fletcher.

She was the girl next door, literally. They'd known one another so long, they were the same and yet so very different.

Rebecca's family had moved into the street in 1898. It had taken a while for rumour to spread but the accepted wisdom was that Mrs Fletcher had been a lady's maid down south. When she had fallen foul of a certain gentleman, Mr Fletcher, then an under butler, had been persuaded to marry her and the terraced two up two down next to the village bakery in a northern town had been the persuasion. Mr Fletcher had been fortunate to get a job at the steelworks, doing their accounts. But all the same, the Fletcher family held themselves a cut above. Mrs Fletcher was never seen with a hair out of place. She always wore a hat and carried gloves. Rebecca was brought up to be a lady.

He'd been smitten with the blonde angel from the moment he'd noticed her. She would have been around ten, he twelve. He'd always known she was there, but that summer was the first time he really saw her. She was beauty and grace. Her button nose was adorable. She was perfect. He'd wanted her for his own from the start; though even he believed he wasn't good enough for her.

His family were grafters. Workers. That was what they did. His great-grandfather had opened their bakery and every generation since had been bakers. His mum worked the shop, so it was up at five for him, Dad, and his brother, bake the bread, make the cakes, knock off around ten or when everything was clean. Then they would go their own ways.

David was taught the sales and business sides of the company, in preparation for taking over eventually. But no one had any expectation for him, so he just did more deliveries. The butcher and the grocer used his strong back to get the shopping out to those who ordered.

As the pair grew up, Mr and Mrs Fletcher became less impressed with their daughter's liking for a baker's boy, but their disapproval hadn't changed her feelings for him. She had teased him, he'd pulled her pigtails. Slowly the relationship had grown, advancing to the occasional kiss, nothing more; it was important to save themselves for marriage. People said he was just 'her bit of rough', even Harry and Jack laughed at him for that. They said they'd grow out of it, but it wasn't like that. She was his and he was hers. This was love and they would be together forever. No reservations.

Then war came, and later conscription. His brother had argued reserved occupation status, his absence would cause *'Serious hardship ... owing to ... business obligations'*. Delivery boys could not do the same.

And now, now he sat in the trench and clenched his teeth. He heard Harry cry out again. He thought of Jack. His body under a blanket, being taken away from this hell for the last time. It was wrong, a dead man safely behind the line while a man in need of medical help was left in danger. What kind of man would allow such a thing? His hand moved to his pouch, to the letter. Not the kind of man who could look a girl like Rebecca in the eye ever again.

He had to get to Harry. *Standing orders.*

Disobedience like this might get him court marshalled. Probably would. That would only end one way.

It was Harry.

Delaying till night could cost Harry his life.

Sod the order.

Surging to his feet, Richardson raced up the ladder and over the parapet. German bullets flew towards him, sending plumes of mud near his feet. He held his hands wide and open, obviously without a weapon.

His heart hammered, adrenaline coated his throat, that foul taste of metal and fear. His bowels felt uncomfortably loose but that was a common sensation out here, and Harry was more important. More important than Watson's orders.

Bullets hit the ground around him. Even through the curtain of rain he knew they were only warning shots, as he opened his hands and gestured to the still moving man. Calling out in broken German, 'Medizinische hilfe!'

One of the medics had taught him that on his last break from the trench, he wasn't sure he'd got it right. 'First aid!' he said instead. Whether he said the German right or if they understood the English, he didn't know, but the bullets stopped.

He found Harry, as he'd expected, ten yards out in the cover of an old shell hole. Offering words of encouragement he assessed the wounds, the mask of agony, Harry's deathly pallor.

All the time talking soothingly he gave Harry dry biscuits. Harry clearly welcomed the sustenance and kept back the pain of movement. Richardson offered sips of water from his canteen, hoping it would help with the shock, while he used supplies from his pack to dress Harry's wounds. The blood was mostly clotted, some scabs breaking and oozing as the wounds were covered.

Having done all he could, Richardson cradled Harry's head, raised him up, and offered him a sip of rum from his hip flask. Seeing Harry shivering, he stripped off his jacket and laid it over Harry's torso, covering the wounded arm.

'I'll be back at dusk with a stretcher team, mate. You hold on, we'll get you as soon as we can.'

His undershirt already soaked through, Richardson crouched low, dodged craters and barbed wire, bodies and body parts as he ran back to the trench.

Watson was waiting, his square jaw clenched. Richardson looked down the line; no one else was in the area. He drew himself up and saluted, ready for the inevitable.

'Do you,' Watson's voice was low, his jaw locked, 'know what I now have to do, Sergeant?'

Richardson swallowed. 'Yes, sir.'

'Where's your jacket?'

'I left it over Harry, he was shivering.' Richardson saw some reaction in his commanding officer, but he wasn't sure what it was.

'I cannot condone disobedience.'

'No, sir.'

'Which is why this didn't happen. Understand?'

Richardson blinked, not at all sure he did. He frowned

and for the first time looked at the man in front of him instead of the officer. 'Sir?'

Watson moved an inch closer. 'You should be shot for what you just did, why the hell you weren't shot by the Germans I do not know. If the other men were to find out about what you've just done, there would be mutiny, I can't risk that. But you're a good soldier, and I need more like you instead of the conscripted children that they keep sending. Only Thatcher and Edwards know what you did today and they are under orders never to reveal it, and now so are you. When the stretcher bearers go up tonight, you go with them, you get to Harry first, retrieve your jacket, give no sign of what happened. Understand?'

'Yes, sir.' Richardson wondered if God was watching after all. 'Thank you, sir.'

'I'm putting my career on the line with yours here, Richardson, you'd better never put another foot wrong.'

Grateful for Watson's unexpected latitude, and the fact that the rain suddenly ceased, he retook his position. Bert and Billy returned; they didn't say a word.

With nothing else to do, he took the letter from his pouch, smiling at word from his sweetheart.

The words blurred before his eyes. Not from rain this time.

She said she was sorry. She was going to marry William Harker, a senior clerk at the steelworks. Oh, to have had a reserved occupation. She said she was sorry. He wasn't sure he believed her.

'Richardson.' he heard the captain's deep voice behind him, 'let's finish saving Private Shoesmith.'

He gathered with the others. There was no fear now, reservations were in the past. Under cover of darkness the captain led the way over the top. Striking out Richardson went straight to Harry, careful to obey orders to hide his earlier actions, then it was back where they'd come from.

The men poured back into their trench. Richardson

stood and watched as Harry was carried away for proper medical attention. Finally he knew. Knew without a doubt. He wasn't a baker. He wasn't a delivery boy. He was worth more than any man cowering behind a reserved occupation. He was a soldier.

He huddled down in the cold rain and stinking mud. He had a job to do.

Bringing Billy Home
Alison Leighton (external short story competition highly commended)

The brown paper parcel sat ominously on the kitchen table. It had been there for several days and its very presence seemed to suck the life out of the room. Gwen stared into space, neither looking at the parcel nor the dishevelled kitchen that she normally kept in such pristine condition. To anybody looking in on this domestic scene, they would have seen a woman whose dress was unkempt and whose demeanour looked slovenly. But outside appearances can mask a terrible sorrow, and Gwen was fighting an internal battle that she wasn't sure she was going to win.

With eyes too red from crying and exhausted from lack of sleep, Gwen tried to remember when her nightmare had begun and realised it had been a week since the telegram had arrived. It had been thrust without ceremony into her hands, and then she had been left standing on the doorstep, bemused and yet naively ignorant of what its contents might hold. Having never received a telegram before, Gwen had tentatively turned it over in her hands before carefully slitting open its contents. In doing so Gwen's life had changed forever. Its message was stark and beyond the bounds of any mother's comprehension:

'Private William Davies was sentenced to death for desertion and shot on September 20, 1916'.

Time had stood still as Gwen had tried and failed to take in the dark contents. Like any mother, she had been convinced that the telegram had been sent to the wrong household, but her son's army number was printed at the

62

top of the message along with his regiment. The words death and desertion had smashed into her heart as if she herself had received the bullet that had killed her son.

On that first day, sitting in the dying warmth of her kitchen, Gwen had found the word coward popping into her head. She didn't understand its significance initially or why it bore any relation to her grief. Cowards were men who didn't fight and ran away from their responsibilities. She had been proud when her husband Alun had volunteered soon after the war had started and shocked when her son Billy had volunteered, underage a year later at the age of seventeen. She remembered him standing at the kitchen door with the sun at his back on the day he left; her handsome boy full of heroic zeal and enthusiasm for the war effort. 'Don't cry, Mam.' Billy had said. 'I'll be back before you know it. I may even come back with medals on my chest. I'll write when I can but don't worry about me.' And with that he had marched off down the road with his schoolboy friends Davy and Ian.

It was this memory, searing in its clarity which had started the tears that had turned into an ocean of grief. Gwen had realised that for all his bravado, somebody somewhere had labelled her son a coward and he had been shot unceremoniously by his own men, and buried with the same lack of care, in a land so far away from home. She knew nothing of his crime as the telegram had revealed little, except his fate. Gwen searched her heart for a way to bring her son back to her. Standing, she reached up to the mantle shelf and pulled down a well-worn letter from behind the clock. Carefully unfolding it, she began to read it as she had done so many times before Billy's death. This time though each word and nuance seemed to carry extra weight and meaning.

September 17, 1916

Dearest Mam,

How are you? Hope you are coping on the farm without me? The weather's been blazing hot here. Hope you've have had the same and you've managed to get the hay in. Have you heard from Da? I'm not feeling my best at the moment. Sadly Davey Jones was hit by shrapnel yesterday and didn't make it. Mam, it's hard here and I have been feeling under the weather. Nobody understands that and I've got myself into a bit of trouble. Felt really ill today and when the sergeant told me to join a scouting party in no man's land my legs wouldn't move and I later hid in a reserve trench. They caught me and I've been thrown in the clink. No idea what's going to happen now but don't worry, Mam, I'll explain to them. Sorry I won't get paid for a while though while they sort this out so can't send any money home.

I am forever your loving son,

Billy

While the letter made it clear that Billy had been ill, it told Gwen nothing about why her son had been branded a coward. What happened, Billy? Why did nobody speak out for you? Why did nobody understand? You were never a coward, Billy. It wasn't in your nature. Around here they'll think you deserved it if you were a coward, and I can't live with that. Oh, Billy, I need your Da here now.

Gwen's eyes took in the ominous package on the table yet again. It came to her with sudden clarity and a calmness that had eluded her for days, that if Billy wasn't a coward then neither was she, and she owed it to him to open the parcel. Gwen gingerly untied the knots in the string, and with shaking fingers, unwrapped the shiny brown paper and looked at the objects that were all she had left of her son. There was the photograph of her, Alun, and Billy at the seaside the summer before the war began. It showed them posing stiffly for the camera, but the simplicity of such a day seemed a world away from everything that had happened since.

She looked at the other objects. They seemed a paltry representation of a life; a shaving kit, a cigarette case, a watch, a diary, and what appeared to be a letter. She picked up the shaving kit and turned it over in her hands. When Billy had left home he had hardly been shaving at all. With a deep sadness she realised he had left home a boy and died a man; but barely that. She brought the bristle brush up to her nose in the vague hope that she would be able to smell something of her son, but was only met by a musty, pungent smell that turned her stomach.

The sight of the watch almost stopped her beating heart. It had been meant as a twenty-first birthday present as it had belonged to Billy's grandfather and was worth quite a lot of money, but both Gwen and Alun had decided if their son was old enough to go to war then he should have it sooner. Billy had argued with her about it, saying that he would never be able to look after such a lovely timepiece while wading through mud, crawling on his belly through shell holes, and dodging bullets. Gwen had grown really angry at the time and berated her son for making the war out to be far worse than it would be. Billy had finally given in and packed the watch in his bag. How ignorant could she have been? Her son had experienced horrors no man should have seen and paid the price.

It was nearly impossible for Gwen to pick up her son's diary. He had always kept one since being a young boy, and she knew the details in this epistle might tear her apart and leave her unable to carry on. With trepidation she opened it at the last entries, which she noticed did not contain any information after her son had been thrown into jail.

September 10, 1916

The shelling has been going on for weeks. Dead bodies are rotting in shallow graves and lying out in the open in no man's land. It's terrible watching your comrades die. We had two twins with us in the regiment and one got hit by a sniper bullet today right through the forehead. They had to cart his other brother off with shock. Just got back from the medical station myself earlier. They say I am fit for duty again. Can't say I feel ready. Bit sick of this bloody war at the moment. Feel so tired.

Gwen paused and realised that Billy had never told her that he had been so ill as to be hospitalised. Skipping a few days she came to when Billy's friend had died.

September 16, 1916

Bloody awful night. Shelling never stopped and my nerves are in tatters. We hadn't gone far up the trench before we came across four of our own lads lying dead. Their heads had nearly been destroyed by a shell. We had to scramble over the poor bastards. Turned my stomach. One of the worst sights I have ever seen. We were given the task of burying them while the bloody Jerries were still shelling us. Felt at my lowest ever here today. Things had just quietened down a bit when I heard Davy had been hit by shrapnel further down the line. Got permission to go to him but he didn't stand a chance. Had ripped out his stomach and all I could do was hold him while his life seeped away. He called out for his mam. Brought tears to my eyes.

Gwen could not read on as her own tears overwhelmed her for a few minutes as she envisaged her son holding on to his dying friend. But then, whilst the last of her willpower was still intact she opened the letter, which turned out to be her son's last words to her and the world.

Dear Mam and Da,

The Padre has given me a pen and paper so I can write to you and he has promised me you will get it. I don't know what to say. It didn't work out. They didn't understand. I've been court martialled for desertion. It all happened so quick. They didn't even let anyone speak out for me at the hearing although one of my doctors said he would. So this is it. I'm so sorry I let you down. Don't cry for me, Mam. Remember your son as you loved him most in those sunny days before the war. I am going to my death unafraid but don't know what this war is about any more.

Always your loving son,
Billy

Through her sobbing, her broken words echoed off the kitchen walls. 'Oh Billy. My poor boy, my poor, poor boy. I can feel your pain. You weren't a coward. They just made you go through too much.' Gwen slumped in her favourite chair by the fire but there were no flames to warm her and she was doubtful she would ever feel alive again.

As the day's light began to fade and the last vestiges of the sun cast shadows on the kitchen walls, Gwen heard a knock at the door. She had no energy to answer it or any desire to see anybody so let the knocking go on. Moments later the door opened and in the light from the setting sun she saw her son again as he had been when he left home in his army uniform. 'Billy!' she cried out, 'You've come home.'

'No, Mrs Davies, it's Ian, Billy's friend. I'm home on leave.' Gwen rose to her feet and without a word walked to the door and wrapped Ian in her arms. Ian was the first to speak. 'I am so very sorry about what happened to Billy. I had to come and see you. You have to know that Billy wasn't a coward. He was one of the bravest men I ever knew and the best friend any man could ask for.'

Gwen searched Ian's face for any sign of dutiful pity which would have influenced his visit. Seeing none there she invited him to sit in her husband's chair and had barely sat down before Ian began to speak. 'Me and Billy joined together, trained together, and fought together. He was better at it than me. By that I mean he was braver. He was always calming us down before we went over the top; that's when we're sent to attack the enemy trenches. One day we got hit really badly out in the middle of no man's land and we ended up in a shell hole. There were two of our company who were badly injured and would have died if Billy hadn't been such a hero. Twice he braved the shelling and carried these men back to our lines on his back. The mad bugger then came back for me but a shell exploded nearby and he was knocked unconscious. I managed to drag him back to our lines but he was out cold for days. As soon as he came round the bloody doctors sent him back to the front. He wasn't ready and then it was terrible for him to see Davy die. We could all see that but our commanding officer didn't give a damn. He shouldn't have had to face no man's land again for weeks and none of us blamed him for not wanting to go. They should have listened.'

Gwen reached out and grasped Ian's hands in her own. 'Thank you for coming, Ian. I can't tell you how much this means to me.'

'That's not all, Mrs Davies. I've brought a few letters from the lads that all say the same. It will make you proud to read them and know he was your son. Albert's sent something. He was one of the lads that Billy saved. Says there was never a braver man and he will be forever grateful for what Billy did that day. Read them when you feel able to, Mrs Davies. It may make you feel a little better to know that so many people are glad that your son was part of their lives. I know I was and Davy too.'

Ian placed the letters on Gwen's lap and headed for the door. He was stopped by Gwen's words. 'Bless you, Ian. You have brought my Billy home. You have given me my son back and nothing is going to take him away from me ever again.' As Ian closed the door, Gwen leant forward and put a match to the logs and paper in the fireplace. She wanted to feel warm again. She lay the letters to one side, wanting to read them once she had destroyed the travesty of a story that she had known was not her son. With a steely determination she took the telegram from its place at the back of the kitchen drawer and ripping it into the smallest of pieces, threw it onto the fire and watched it burn.

Tearing Back Centuries
Jean Moir (SDWC)

My darling, I am well. (But deeply tired.
 I cannot share with you
This searing cold; the guns are mired
In thigh-deep crystal snow.
 We try to dig, with ice-bound bumbling hands
In rough and brittle sands).

The other day we found something, my dear,
 Lodged in the wintry sod.
 ('What blinking idiot left a fish-can here?'
 'No sir, it's not ... Good God!')
 With cat-like rasping strokes Knox prised it free –
Tore back a century.

We washed, we sanded, burnished the rough steel
An aide-de-camp, perhaps?
 Surveying the Chateau, wood, village and hill,
 Preparing battle maps?
 'Look! Here!' Knox touched our crest stamped on the
back
'Sir, this will bring us luck!'

(What charms, what gods protect us? Weary days.
 The men are drained, torn, cowed.)
 I smiled. 'En garde!' I parried winter's haze
And Boney's ghostly crowd.
 Along the trench the laughter rippled out,
 And then a hearty shout.

'Hurrah, the tenth! Hurrah, the tenth!' My love,

Did he like me once pine?
His sweetheart in a muslin gown and gloves?
God willing, you'll be mine.
This talisman, I'll wear it in the fray,
And on our wedding day.

Keep the Home Fires Burning
Jean Moir (SDWC)

Do not imagine me, my Frank
As when we danced, hushed, with shy love,
At the summer ball. Oh, remember that!
But picture me in thick-ribbed woollens, slacks and boots,
Pulling my sledge to the little wood.
It's hushed, no bird-song
Only my crunching feet and shadowing fleeting deer
Or crack of icicles in winter fastness.
Sudden shouts from the parade ground – our stable yard.
Our hunters are all gone to the front.
I stack my wood.

My gowns are all sealed up,
My "glorious golden locks" shorn off,
My Emma went to take her brother's place
Behind the plough, but cannot take his place
In all our hearts.

Or see me in my uniform –
My cocky hat and cheeky grin
Whistling, yes, as I drive my truck
Or ferry generals, Father's friends.
He writes, too sparingly. But sometimes
I have to drive an ambulance for troops.
Oh my dearest! Come back safe, come back well!

And now I'm in a warm red skirt and top.
The kitchen's hushed; only the soft fall
Of sleepy embers and quiet snowing.

I push back brother's French books,
Sister's sewing. Oh my dear,
Shall we be married your next leave, in spring?
I long for you.
May your sword protect you,
As will my love always.

The Poacher
Maggie Cainen (SDWC)

My mouth and nose are full of feathers choking me, making me cough as I wake up from sleeping in Farmer Smith's hayrick. I was used to feathers after plucking all the game I'd shot to feed our large family, but I hadn't been out poaching lately.

'I know you Sam Snell, you idle layabout, why aren't you out fighting in the war, you big lummox?'

My throat's too dry to reply but I open my eyes and recognise Lady Mary Slavin from the big house who'd tipped a pillowcase full of feathers all over me.

'Why aren't you in uniform, you big coward?'

Because a soldier's pay won't look after my ten little sisters, mother, and grandmother, that's why, I thought. I make far more poaching fish and game on all the big estates like yours.

She was a pretty little thing was Mary, but full of airs and graces. Normally she went past me with her cute little nose up in the air but not today. Today was 'pick on any non-uniformed lad day' and I was her target.

Whilst she bestowed her disgusted looks I leapt up, grabbing twin handfuls of the feathers, and stuffed them down her high-necked blouse.

'Get off me, you big oaf.'

She made a half-hearted attempt to get my hands out of her blouse but the next thing I knew she'd pulled me down in the hay. Her hands ripped off my shirt as she flung herself on top of me. I felt her lips teasing the skin along my shoulders and then she seized my mouth. She was passionate, her nails tearing the skin from my back. She

74

wasn't the first girl I'd kissed, and they'd all been more than willing, but I'd never tussled with one who smelled so good or who was so uninhibited. Hours later when we pulled our clothes back on we spoke for the first time.

'I ... we ... I don't know what to say ...' That was Lady Mary, usually so full of herself stumbling over her words as she blushed crimson in the setting sun. 'We'd better forget about this, Sam ... I must get back.'

'Just a minute, Mary, don't go yet ... didn't you enjoy it? That was fantastic. When shall we meet again? Look, you're going to be all right, aren't you?'

'Not have a baby, you mean?'

'It might happen.'

'Does it matter? Don't you know I've been pushed into marrying some titled, chinless wonder next week ... before he goes off to war?'

'Oh Mary, I'm so sorry. Have you actually met him?'

'Of course, a couple of times ... his father was in the same regiment as my father. His estate adjoins ours. He's just left Eton's Officer Training Corps ... he really loves himself ... stinks of cologne.'

Tears trickled down her face and I felt deeply ashamed. She was only a young lass and didn't deserve that. No wonder she'd flung herself at me.

'Is that why you're throwing feathers at us village lads?'

'I'm so bloody fed up, Sam. I hardly know him ... the Honourable Julian Smythe-Henderson ... I've been persuaded to marry him ... so he can have an heir to his estate if he dies in the war. Just like a bloody brood mare ... wouldn't I laugh if I'm pregnant already with yours?'

'Come on, Mary. What we did together was something special, I'll never forget it. Don't talk like that, don't spoil it now. But you don't think Honourable what's his name might notice you're not a virgin?'

'I doubt it. I'm not sure he even likes girls. He's never touched me … Not once. He hasn't stopped drinking since he was commissioned … he'll be far too drunk to notice a thing.'

'Mary, promise me you'll tell me if … you know … you're having a baby. Come on, let me see you home safely across the fields.'

I turned out with everyone in the village the following week to watch Mary leave the local church arm in arm with a skinny, black-browed Guards Officer. It sickened me the thought of that oaf with my beautiful Mary, it turned my stomach. The next day I signed up. I wanted to put a good distance between me and the tempting, passionate Lady Mary.

Ypres in a field hospital. Midnight. About fourteen months later.

'Go on, Sam … don't stop there. We're all friends here. You've been a soldier with us for over a year now. What happened?'

'First off the Honourable Julian copped it six weeks after arriving in France just like a lot of the young subalterns. Next, I find out Mary had given birth to two sturdy, blue-eyed, blond boys nine months after her wedding.'

'What did her new aristocratic, black-haired family say to that?'

'What do you think? They had to make the best of it. "They're the image of your maternal grandmother, Mary. You know she was a blonde, blue-eyed baby too. Look they've both got your chin, darling."'

'Have you been home since then, Sam?'

'Come on, Pete, you know I have. I only got back last week. I met the nursemaid in the village with them. They look just like me. I had to bite my tongue to stop shouting out, "They're mine, can't you see?" I had to get out of the village fast before anyone else noticed.'

'So that's why you cut your leave short, Sam ... and volunteered to be tested again as a sniper. You know how dangerous that is. They always go for the officers and snipers first.'

'Well, I did know so I'd deliberately missed a few shots when they first tried us out, Pete, but I scored several bulls this time. I've been a crack shot all my life ... loads of practice. Lots of practice dodging the gamekeepers too.'

'Don't we know about your shooting. Without all those rabbits and pigeons you kept shooting for us we'd have starved!'

'Don't forget the rats, Pete ... made the trenches a bit more comfortable for you lot, didn't it?'

'Come on, Sam, no one actually eats rats ... do they?'

'They do in some of the trenches. They haven't got me shooting up half the countryside for them. Bringing them rabbits and pigeons to eat. You never know, they might be desperate.'

'So why're you here in the hospital again, Sam, if you've only been a sniper a week?'

'Got clipped by another bullet capturing that machine gun, didn't I?'

'Bloody show off. Snipers are usually hiding miles off ... what do you mean?'

'Well first our officer copped it ... nice bloke he was too ... knew all our names. Then my mates, the other Pete, Lou, Harry, and Bert all went down, so me and my twin Eric moved in close to finish them off ... the bastards.'

'Hey, someone says you're up for a gong for that machine gun business ... Is it true?'

'Yep me and my twin Eric.

'Was he wounded too?'

'Copped a Blighty one, upper thigh wound.'

'What about you?'

77

'Nicked my collar bone …bullet went straight through. Good job it was the right one.'

'What d'ya mean? You need your right to shoot your rifle.'

'Not if you're left handed you don't, haven't you noticed we're both lefties, me and Eric?'

Two days later, same field hospital, 2 a.m.

'Sam, Sam, wake up, you're making a hell of a din, man. Shouting out "Mary" all the time … none of us can sleep.'

'Sorry, Pete, I can't bear it. They're my kids … not honourable dead what's his name's. All I got was one tumble in the hay, she'll never spare a glance for a common soldier like me.'

'Listen, there's nothing you can do about it now. Try and sleep … do you want a pill? Just concentrate on getting fit … so you can knock out some more Hun machine gun nests for us.'

Same Field Hospital, Ypres. Eight weeks later

'What, you back again, Sam? You must lead a charmed life. Now look here, my colleagues and I are fed up with patching you up, can't you keep out of trouble for a bit?'

'Sorry, Captain, I'll try harder.'

'I should think so. I heard in the mess that they want to give you a Military Medal this time, you heard anything about that?'

'Who cares about medals? Wouldn't mind a bit more pay or double rum rations … you couldn't put a word in for me, could you, sir?'

'Cheeky devil. I'll see what I can do. What about a spot of leave instead … that do you?'

Same Field Hospital, Ypres. Two months later

'Welcome back, Sam. How was Blighty?'

'Hi, Harry, my old mate. You're an orderly now? I thought you were done for way back.'

'Well, I couldn't carry on fighting, not with my gammy leg. It's not bad being an orderly, and I still get paid. So how're things back home? See your kids at all?'

'I certainly did, right chips off the old block they are too. With our Eric limping around the village a bloody hero, everyone can see the resemblance. Luckily for me someone started a rumour that the old squire was a bit of a lad, so no one's surprised.'

'Jammy bastard. So you're going to stop trying to get yourself killed now?'

'Yes and no. I only came to say goodbye. Didn't you know they're making me an officer? They're sending me off to train snipers.'

'Train 'em how to get killed or wounded like you, you mean? How many times have you been in here?'

'Only three – just scratches. You've got to have a lucky rabbit's scut like me … so I've brought a few back for the men.'

'Bye, Sam, stay lucky. Stay in touch, see you back home, man.'

After the war, back in Sam's village

'Good morning, Lady Mary. There's a young man to see you. Our local hero, actually he's the one of those twins who got a Military Medal in the war.'

'Thank you, Patsy, show him in please.'

'Well then, Sam, this is a surprise, welcome back. Quite the hero, I hear.'

'I wouldn't know about that, ma'am, but I hear congratulations are in order, two fine, healthy sons!'

'Sam, you old fraud, I've missed you. I might have known if anyone would survive that mayhem you would. I heard they made you an officer too. Come and meet my boys, see what you think of them.'

'Two lovely boys, you must be very proud. Oh I forgot, my condolences, ma'am. I heard about the sad death of your husband.'

'He died serving his country. Now, what can I do for you, Sam? I imagine people will be falling over themselves to offer you a job. Not many soldiers get a Military Medal and survive to tell the tale. How can I help you, Sam?'

'Eric, that's my twin brother and I, we heard you were looking for gamekeepers, ma'am. Any chance of you considering the pair of us, do you think?'

'Splendid idea, Sam. I can't think of better men for the job. I heard you were a crack sniper in the war, rushing about taking out German machine gun nests. Tell me, this twin of yours, Eric. Is he identical to you?'

'No, ma'am, he's the ugly one.'

'You liar, Sam, even your own mother says she can't tell you apart. Can he shoot as well as you?'

'Have you been talking to my mother, Mary?'

'Of course I have. I could've died waiting for you to get in touch. I was worried about you.'

'Oh, Mary, so you do care after all. I've missed you so much, you're all I thought about all through that horrible war. I imagined every single German I killed was attacking you and the babies.'

'Sam, you're wonderful. See my estate manager and he'll sort out a job as gamekeepers for the pair of you and perhaps you can help train my two sons to shoot when they're a bit older too; they're going to need a good male role model and I plan on seeing a whole lot more of you, Captain Snell!'

'It'd be a pleasure, ma'am.'

Kites
Alan Bryant (SDWC)

It was Corporal Willis who found the man. He marched him back at gunpoint to his unit, an Australian anti-aircraft machine-gun team. They were camped in a shell-shocked farmyard in the middle of Picardy, in the middle of 'the war to end all wars'. The seven other men in the gun crew sat on the wall of sand-bags around the Vickers machine-gun and watched them approach.

'Look, Sarge,' said Evans, one of the men. 'How did he get here? He's gotta be a pom, they all think they're Lord bleedin' Kitchener, don't they?'

The sergeant looked across at the man. He wondered why anyone in their right mind would be wandering around the shell holes of the Somme as if to enjoy the air.

The man's age, the sergeant guessed, could be anywhere between thirty and fifty. He had short brown hair, and wore a tan tweed jacket and plus fours. His shirt was cream silk topped with a maroon cravat, and his glass-polished brown brogues were far too clean and expensive for the surrounding battle torn terrain.

'Tie his hands, Evans,' said the sergeant.

The man clamped his hands together and surrendered them forward to oblige. Evans bound his wrists together with a piece of rope. He gave it a final over-tightening flourish to signal his contempt for such an open display of sartorial exhibitionism on a battlefield.

The sergeant took a deep breath that, along with the air of gun-smoke and farm sewage around him, almost drew in his moustache. He looked the man in the eye. 'If you are a pom,' he said, 'why are out here dressed like you're on the way to your golf club?'

The man smiled, showing both rows of even, cream-white teeth. 'I heard that you Australian chappies were in the area,' he said. 'It's such a glorious day I thought I would stretch the old legs and call for a chat. An old school chum of mine actually visited Australia once but returned to England because he missed the weather. Mind you, he also said the place was full of misfits and thieves. I'm sure he was jesting. He was always such a wag.' And the man gave another broad, even-toothed smile.

He could have been addressing a table of guests at a stately home. He was pleasant, personable; if his hands had not been tied, the sergeant thought, they might have been helping him articulate in gentle, flowing movements.

The sergeant turned to Corporal Willis. 'Hark at this pommy tit talk,' he said. 'Just like one of those bleeding Brit aristocrats. So, Corporal Willis, where did you find this.' he paused for satirical effect, 'person?'

'Sitting at the bottom of that hill, Sarge,' said the corporal, and pointed his rifle at a small grass covered mound a hundred yards away. 'He had a picnic hamper, offered me a scotch egg.'

'It was actually a very fine fois-gras,' said the man,

'It looked like a mashed up scotch egg,' said the corporal.

The sergeant leaned into the man's face until an inch away, and snarled his words. 'Picnic? The only bit of grass left in the bloody Somme and you want to have a bloody picnic on it. You must be a bloody pom; no one else would be so stupid. You bloody pommy twonk.'

The man gave only a naïve smile in reply.

The sergeant walked around the man, inspecting him up and down until he came back to face him again. 'Papers?' he said.

'*The Times* normally,' said the man, 'and the *Sporting Life*, when one can get a copy these days of course.'

The sergeant now roared with the intensity of a man who could kill a kangaroo with one bite. 'Your papers,' he said, 'your identity papers.'

'Sorry, Sergeant,' said the man, raising his tied hands to wipe the spittle from his eyebrows. 'They must be in my other jacket. I'm always forgetting them.'

The sergeant took another deep breath. His search through the man's pockets found nothing. He looked around the farmyard at the few remaining buildings left standing after the pummelling from all sides. Most of the old stone walls stood now with a leaning and precarious uncertainty. 'Corporal Willis,' he said, 'put him in that shed over there.' As he spoke, his voice got louder with each syllable. 'Stay with him. If you lose him I'll have your stripes.'

'He won't get away, Sarge,' Corporal Willis ushered the man towards the small building with a reminding dig from the butt of his rifle.

The man started to walk then stopped with an unexpected turn that made the corporal walk into him.

'Get a move on, mate,' said the corporal.

The man did not move. He stood with his head cocked to one side. Slowly, he lifted his tied hands. One finger was pointing to the west. 'Do you hear that, Corporal?' he said.

The corporal shook his head. 'All I hear is those sodding cannons day and night.'

'Listen,' said the man, 'it's aeroplanes, quite a few of them. I would say they were Sopwith Pups, they must be the Royal Flying Corps. Do you know what that means?'

'Yes, it means they're going to bomb the crap out of the Kaiser. Move on.'

'Possibly,' said the man. 'But what else does it mean?'

'How would I know?'

'It means that if the RFC is up there, the Germans will soon be up there looking for them.'

'Well I can't hear them. So move on, now.'

There came a reminding shout from the sergeant.

'Get that man in that shed before I drag you both in there and lock the two of you up.'

'He says he can hear planes, Sarge.'

'Get him in there now or you'll both be hearing angels playing bloody harps.'

'Yes, Sarge. Come on, you, move.' And he pushed the man into the shadowed interior behind the open shed door.

The sergeant, a pragmatic soldier, sent Evans to collect the man's hamper.

The shed was built of white-washed stone and topped with a clay tiled roof, typical of the area. Now it stood sad, fearful, cowering in a corner of the yard. Some of the tiles had shivered off and smashed to the floor to lie in defeated terracotta shards.

Corporal Willis had been brought up on a farm in the Australian outback. To him, the shed looked as though it had previously been used as a hen house. Inside was a rough wooden partition fence, about shoulder height that cut the interior in half. In this fence was a low wooden entrance door which could be bolted. The corporal reckoned this could have doubled as a small sheep pen for winter use. The old stonework was unstable and the wooden partition even more so with large gaps between the planks. To Corporal Willis though, it would serve its purpose. The lock up area would be in the sheep pen behind the partition, he would remain on guard near the entrance door. At least he would stay dry if it rained.

He stood back as the man went in, and pointed to the low door. 'Open that,' he said, 'and get in. Get to the back, stand where I can see you, and face the wall.'

'I can't crawl through there,' the man said.

'Get on the floor.'

'I'll ruin these trousers.'

The corporal cocked his rifle. When he raised it to his

shoulder there was an edge of panic in his voice. This was the first time he had pointed a rifle in anger at anyone. 'Get in,' he said, 'or you won't be needing trousers any more.'

'How demeaning,' said the man, and shook his head in slow dissent. He was not angry, but sounded more like a patient parent trying not to scold a persistently naughty child. In eventual submission, he went on his knees and crawled through, all the time voicing mild protestations regarding the possible effects of chicken droppings on tweed.

Inside the small enclosure, he stood upright and faced the far wall. He stood looking through a hole that served as a small window. His tied hands reached up to it to pull away a clump of weeds that part obscured the view of the war-pocked fields outside. As he stared out, he said to the corporal behind him, 'If you don't mind me asking, Corporal, what made you volunteer to come halfway around the world to fight someone else's war?'

Corporal Willis hesitated, wondering if he should engage in conversation.

The man sensed the reason for his hesitancy. 'We may as well chat,' he said, 'it will be rather boring for both us locked up together in silence.'

'Well I'm not the one locked up, mate, am I?' said the soldier.

'Aren't you?' said the man. 'So why don't you leave?'

The soldier did not answer.

'So tell me,' said the man turning to face him, 'why did you come halfway around the world?'

Corporal Willis gave a non-committal shrug, lowered the gun, and un-cocked it. He reasoned with himself; the man was tied up, locked up safely, they may as well chat. 'I was born in Britain, South Wales, some place I can't pronounce,' he said. 'I reckoned maybe I owed the old place something. I still have family there, somewhere.'

'I was in South Wales, somewhere, as child,' said the man. His voice lightened, as if to look for pictures in his memories.

The soldier's head raised and set at an angle that betrayed his apparent disinterest in the conversation. He looked at the man's face, but his head was in the way of the hole in the wall and the daylight behind shone through to give him a bright, haloed effect and a slight blinding to the soldier's eyes. 'So, how did you get here?' he asked him.

'I just happened to find myself here,' the man said, and he took a step forward, his voice lowered to almost puerile secrecy. 'Tell me, corporal, did you ever have a kite?'

'A what?'

'A kite; you were a small boy, weren't you? Didn't you have a kite? You must have had a kite. I did. I used to fly it in the hills of South Wales. Lots of hills in South Wales, crunched with bracken, black, sliding with slag.' His words drifted off again as if trying to capture days of a different life. 'Didn't you have a kite?' His voice was almost a whisper.

'Maybe.'

'Mine was red,' the man said. 'What colour was your kite, Corporal?'

The soldier paused, 'Can't remember,' he said.

'Red? Was it red?'

'Might have been.'

The man moved forward again, his head still haloed against the light. He stopped and stared at the soldier a few seconds. His voice stayed low. 'Isn't that a coincidence, same place, maybe even the same kite? I say, seeing as it's such a small world, do you think we could be related?'

'Us? You are kidding me, mate? I don't think I'm related to anyone with a lah-di-dah accent like you've got.'

The man took another step forward.

The soldier raised his rifle. 'Just stay there,' he said.

'Don't come any nearer.'

'You won't shoot me, Corporal. I know you won't. Besides, I'm locked in here, my hands are tied. You're out there with the gun. But I know you won't shoot me.' He smiled with broad, good humour. There was a chuckle in his voice when he next spoke. 'Tell me, Corporal, can you dance?'

'Dance?'

'Dance, you know, "Waltzing Matilda" and all that. You Aussie chaps are always singing "Waltzing Matilda", aren't you? Can you dance? The thing is, the ladies love a man who can waltz. They want to be swept off their feet, you see. Do you have a girl, Corporal, back home?'

'Never mind what I've got back home.'

The man stopped smiling and gave a polite, understanding nod. 'You don't have a girl do you?' His eyes sparkled with mischief. 'Tell me, Corporal, have you ever had a girl? I mean, you know, have you – had – a girl?'

The corporal took a step nearer but stopped himself short of the partition. The man was deliberately provoking him. 'Listen, pom, I don't want any more shite from you. Keep it shut from now on, OK?'

'Watch my feet,' said the man, almost in a whisper, and with his tied hands held out in front of him he danced with a slow effortless movement in the small space. 'One two three, one two three, are you watching, Corporal? This is the waltz. Easy isn't it? You'll have all the girls running after you if you learn this. It's so easy.' He stopped a moment and turned to face the soldier. 'Do you still have the kite?' he said.

'Have the ...?'

'I don't,' the man said. 'One day I took it up the hill, high up, really high. It was so windy that day, perfect, what a day. I let the kite go and waited till it was as high and as far as the string could take it, and I watched it bob and dive about. It was wonderful. You have to judge things sometimes. Life is all about equilibrium. What goes up, and all that? Don't you think, Corporal?'

The corporal did not answer; confusion evident in his silence.

The man spoke again. 'You should have seen the kite. It bobbed and weaved and wobbled and dived. And when it went up, I knew its next move would be down. And as it went I picked up a stone and threw it at the kite. The stone went straight through it. The string snapped and the kite dropped to the ground.'

'Why would you do that?'

'I never went to retrieve it. I left it lying where it landed.' The man turned to face the window light. 'Nothing lasts for ever, does it?' He spun round again to face the corporal. 'Or does it?' he said.

'You're nuts,' the soldier said.

The man danced and twirled again with his arms out in front of him. 'I can teach you to waltz.' he said. 'Dancing could change your life. And you have only one life, don't you?' He stopped again and looked at the soldier. 'It all depends on how long that life lasts doesn't it? But you wouldn't want to live for ever would you? Not really, not for ever.' He turned to look through the window again. 'Or would you?' he said. 'Would you want to, for ever?' And he danced again.

The soldier stood back, the rifle lying like a docile pet in his arms.

The man glided behind the partition, turning, twirling. Then he stopped, and in less than a second thrust his tied hands through a gap in the wood slats. 'If you untie me,' he said, 'I'll show you how to hold your partner.'

The soldier froze then recoiled against the door, raising his rifle as he did so. 'Don't you try nothing, mate,' he said. Tremors vibrated through his words.

'It's a very romantic dance; erotic even,' the man said.

'You may be a nutcase but I'll shoot you. I will.'

'I do apologise, old man, I never meant to frighten you. And you are frightened, aren't you?' The man took his hands from between the planks and gave a reassuring smile. 'Don't worry, I promise I'll look after you. Now, let's start again, watch my feet.' And he danced again, but only a few steps before he stopped mid-movement. His head tilted back. 'Listen,' he said, 'you can clearly hear the Sopwiths now can't you? And those others with the harsher engine sounds, they would be German Fokkers. They're about to meet.'

The soldier looked up as the sound of a motor screamed low overhead and a shadow swept across the holes in the roof. Seconds later a bomb blast shuddered through the ground and a few more tiles slid to shatter on the yard floor. Machine-gun fire from his unit was thudding in his ears as the airplanes exchanged fire with the gun crew outside. 'Get down,' he shouted, and flung himself in a corner to crouch in a foetal position as another airplane skimmed them and another bomb landed near the machine-gun station. His hands covered his face as if trying to hide his whole body from battle, as if trying to transport him to a place of peace.

The man stood upright and watched through the gaps in the roof as the aircraft roared above. 'Oh wouldn't you love to fly?' he said. And he watched as the sounds faded away. 'They'll be back in about a minute,' he said. 'Let's surprise them.'

Corporal Willis took his hands from his face and looked up at the partition. The man stood facing him, his hands untied, free, his arms spread wide. The soldier scrambled about the floor looking for his rifle.

'Here it is,' said the man, and he pulled back the rifle bolt.

When the soldier looked again the gun barrel was pointing at him. 'Jesus, please don't shoot me, please,

please.'

The sound of the aeroplane motors came screaming at them once more. Machine-guns spat their abuse through the sky. The man smiled to show his cream-white teeth again. As the airplane tore the sky apart above them, he pointed the rifle up through a gap in the roof. He took quick aim, and fired once. The aeroplane flew off, machine gun bullets chasing it until out of range.

The soldier lay shivering as he watched the man pull back the rifle bolt again. He saw the man smile, he saw him tilt his head back, and as another aeroplane roared low over the shed, he heard him laugh. But, to the soldier, his laughter held a strange note that, though it showed some odd pleasure, it was without humour, with purpose, and radiated a consuming loudness that drowned out the scream of the motors and deadened all other sound.

The bomb exploded at the rear of the shed to demolish it in a single, final hit.

When the corporal opened his eyes he saw a face looking down on him. 'Don't shoot me, please. Please don't shoot me,' he sobbed.

'Don't worry, son,' the sergeant said, 'We're on the same side. You were lucky today, son, very lucky. There's no sign of that pommy bloke. I reckon he must be scattered all over the Somme by now; whoever he was.'

The men pulled their comrade from the rubble and helped him across to the shelter of the machine-gun sandbags.

'Sit there, Willis,' the sergeant said. 'I think we got one of them. Evans has gone to look.'

Evans came running back, breathless with excitement. 'Sarge.' he shouted. 'Sarge, you won't believe this.'

'Don't tell me,' said the sergeant, 'We've just shot down the Kaiser, the war is over, and there's jam for tea.'

'Nearly, Sarge,' the soldier said. 'We've just shot down Baron Von bloody Richthofen, the Red Baron. He landed the plane in that field over there, then he went and died.

'Von Richthofen?' the sergeant said. 'Red von Richtofen?'

'Bloody right, Sarge, you should see this plane, it's red and his name is painted all over it. We got him alright, he's dead as dinkum. Shot through the chest, single bullet, in one side, out the other.'

The men cheered and shook each other's hands.

The sergeant took off his hat and banged it on his knee. 'Bloody hell,' he said. He turned to Corporal Willis who was sitting on the floor hugging his rifle, eyes of blank fear sunk in an ashen face. 'We'll be famous,' he said, 'except for you of course, Willis. You went off hiding in that shed with the toff, didn't you?' He reached for the man's hamper, picked out a small jar, and offered it to Willis. 'Here you are,' he said, 'a consolation prize. That's the last mashed-up scotch egg in France that is.'

On April 21st 1918 Germany's ace fighter pilot Baron von Richthofen was shot down and killed on active service. Controversy over who was responsible for his death continues today.

Sleep, Baby, Sleep
Fiona Riley (SDWC)

I know I'm supposed to hate the Germans, but I can't. Hearing my pals screaming abuse across the ravaged patch of stinking mud separating our trenches makes me sick to my stomach. There's not much land between us, and I have nightmares that the Huns, as I've been told to call them, will tunnel through and kill us all.

How I even got here I can't remember clearly. A few months ago I was working on a neighbour's farm in Devon, desperate for my conscription papers to arrive. Training passed in bombastic bravado and now here I am, cowering at the bottom of a soaking, mud sliming, rat-infested trench. I don't know what I'd been expecting when I joined up, but it wasn't misery, terror, and downright boredom in equal measures.

'Get some sleep while you can, lad,' Sergeant 'Baldy' Smith nods towards the slight indent he's made in the wall of the trench. 'May still be warm.' He laughs without humour and moves off to check on another soldier. I push myself into the wall. It's freezing and the rain hammers on my new tin helmet, but I'm grateful for it; some of the older soldiers are still wearing cloth caps.

Convinced I'll never sleep in these hellish conditions, I try to block out what's happening around me and push my thoughts to happier times. Mother was widowed when I was a baby, but by the time I was three years old, she had married Max Petersen; a widower with a two-year-old son, Erich, who became my greatest friend.

Papa (he said Stepfather was too formal) came from the ancient town of Regensburg in Bavaria. He brought Erich to England after the death of his wife and took the position of family doctor in Axminster shortly after. He and Mother were very happy together and our two families bonded as if it was always meant to be. Erich's mama used to sing him an old German lullaby, 'Schlaf, Kindlein, Schlaf' (Sleep, baby, sleep), and Papa taught us in both German and English so she would never be forgotten.

Erich and I were as thick as thieves, always together, rambling around the countryside or playing near the River Axe, even helping farmers at harvest time. People used to joke they got two for the price of one. We were very close, and I believe I couldn't have had a better brother. Although Papa retained his strong German accent, Erich spoke in the same pirate-like Devon dialect as the rest of the village.

We spent many family holidays in Regensburg with Erich's grandparents and relatives. They came often to Devon and fell in love with our narrow lanes and quaint cottages. These were happy times and Mother and I were always treated as part of the family.

Then came war, and, with it, the end of our idyllic childhood. At first nothing much changed, then slowly but surely it began. First the odd looks, then whispered conversations as we passed by. Friends of Mother and Papa began avoiding them, crossing the street so as not to get drawn into conversation. Erich came home from school a couple of times with a black eye, and fewer patients visited Papa's surgery. Propaganda ensured that Papa and Erich went from being welcome in the village to enemy aliens. Papa was no longer allowed to attend town meetings and Erich's scoutmaster, our next door neighbour and family friend, expelled him from the troop. A brick through the surgery window was the final straw. Feeling ostracised and threatened, they fled back to Germany in fear for their lives, and our safety.

I don't hate the Germans, but I do hate the shovellers of

propaganda who tore my family apart.

I'm getting drowsy and feel myself nodding off. As my eyes close, I see my mother's face and remember her words as I left. *Come back to me, James, I can't lose you too.* I mumble my promise into the sodden French soil.

'Petersen.' Strong hands shake my shoulders. 'Private Petersen, wake up.' Baldy Smith's voice is low, but the look on his face brings me to attention. He nods towards the top of the trench. 'We're going over. Wait for the order.'

My legs turn to jelly and I'm sure I'm going to be sick. Several of my pals are standing near me, rifles at the ready, bayonets fixed, waiting to climb the ladders to no man's land. We know how bad it is out there. So many men dead already. No one believes they will come back alive. Not one of us is over twenty and we are terrified beyond measure.

I don't hear the order, but mayhem erupts as my battalion climb, scramble, and fight their way to the top of the trench. Momentum pushes me over the top and on to the fetid, muddy battleground. It's pandemonium, men on both sides screaming, running, shooting, stabbing, shooting again. Body after body falls to the ground, young men of both sides, fighting a war fuelled by someone else's hatred.

Stumbling around in blind panic trying to get back to the relative safety of the trench, I trip over a body. Swearing, I scramble to my feet and make to run away. An agonised moan stops me in my tracks. Dropping to the ground I get closer. He's German; about the same age as Erich. A new terror rips through me. I hadn't thought about it before, but Erich could be out there somewhere. We are brothers united by love, torn apart by geography and the thought that I could be fighting my own brother one day brings me fresh horror.

He's dying. We both know it. He beckons to me.

'Komm, bitte?' I know I shouldn't trust him, but he's not going to spring any surprises. 'What do you want?' I ask in German. His eyes widen in surprise and he gives a faint smile. Pointing to his stomach he says, 'Es ist schlimm?'

'Yes, it's bad. What do you want me to do?'

His belt buckle is inscribed with the words '*Gott Mit Uns*' – God is with us – and I can't help thinking that, today, He isn't.

He looks at my rifle, and then at me. We could have been the only two soldiers on the field as the battle around us fades into the background. I stand over him, bayonet resting lightly on his chest. We stare at each other for a long moment, then he smiles and nods his agreement. Sobbing, I push my bayonet through his unresisting body.

Someone is singing 'Schlaf, Kindlein, Schlaf' – Sleep, baby, sleep.

I realise it's me.

Mons Avenue
Dawn Smith (SDWC)

There's a black spot on my paper round. I've been bitten by two dogs, attacked by wasps, and chased by nutters on bikes, all in the same street. And I only started the round last year. My dad says there's a black spot on the A46 on his way to work. He doesn't know the meaning of suffering.

Mons Avenue. All the streets round the old barracks are named after battles, like Marne, Somme, Arnhem – and Mons. Mr Stevens at number 10 told me he fought in one.

'I'm living in the wrong road,' he said. 'Here I am in Mons Avenue, but by rights I should be round the corner in Anzio Crescent. I don't suppose the council would move me, eh?' He sometimes chats when I take round his *Evening Echo*. He hasn't got a wife, and his dog died. He put a sign in his window this year that says 'Lest We Forget'. I thought he meant his dog at first.

We're doing World War One in history and I said I know someone who fought in the war. Mr Jenkins took the piss.

'Oh, we've got a psychic in the class. Had a séance lately, Matthew? Or is it time travel you're into? Oh no, you can't have a time machine, or you wouldn't be late for class. Ha ha.'

I learned quite a few things in that lesson. Loads of men got killed in World War One and anyone who didn't die is dead now. The streets round the barracks are named after two different wars and Mr Stevens was in the second one. And Mr Jenkins isn't funny. But I knew that anyway.

I also found out about two valleys at the battle of the

Somme called Sausage and Mash. And a poison gas called Mustard. I told Dad and Simon, next time we had sausages for dinner.

'What are you on about?' said Simon, looking at me as if I was a turd.

'That's what they're called.'

'So what? You think that's funny?'

'I never said it was funny.' But I couldn't stop smiling. The more he was mad at me, the more I couldn't stop. It was like when my nan died last year and I kept wanting to laugh at the crem, even when Dad started crying.

'What is it then?' said Simon. 'Hilarious?' He gripped his fork in his fist and some spit came out of his mouth. I could see it on his lip.

'No. I was just saying.' I put my head down and ate some potato.

'Saying what?'

'Nothing,' I muttered.

'Give him a break, Simon,' said Dad. 'He didn't mean anything.'

'Stupid little prat.' Simon threw his fork down on his plate and went out the back door. Some of his gravy had splashed on my hand so I licked it off. Dad sighed.

'He can't help it,' he told me. 'It's hard for him, being back.'

I shrugged. Simon's been out in Afghanistan. There was some kid in the street who turned out to be a suicide bomber and two of Simon's mates got killed. He gets flashbacks, or something. And everything pisses him off.

I wasn't hungry any more, so I took my plate to the sink.

'What, you not having mustard?' said Dad, holding up the jar and putting on a stupid grin. I gave him a smile back, but not a big one, and shook my head. I started washing up while Dad ate the rest of his dinner, then I washed his plate and the pans while he dried. We didn't say anything, but he stood next to me while he wiped, then we both put the pots away, moving round each other and passing stuff, weaving in and out like an ace team.

Simon was drunk when he got back that night. I heard him come upstairs and go into his room, banging against the walls like someone moving furniture who wasn't very good at it. Then it went quiet and I waited, trying not to breathe. I couldn't hold it for long, so I let the air out really slowly and felt the heat coming back off my pillow. Then he started.

If I told Simon I heard him crying at night he'd smash me in the face. Maybe kill me. But he must know I can hear him. Dad built the wall to turn one big bedroom into two small rooms when we moved here, after Mum died. You can hear snoring and coughing and everything. When Simon was at school he used to sneak fags upstairs and I could hear him clicking the lighter. Then the smoke would start coming through a gap at the top of the wall. I used to stand on my bed and try to suck it in. But he doesn't smoke any more, not since the army.

The night of the sausages, he started doing big, blubbing sobs, worse than usual. Loads of snot and dribble, like a baby. I knew it was because of his girlfriend. They were supposed to be getting married when he came home, but she changed her mind and gave him his ring back. Her sister's at my school and she told me. I hoped he wasn't going to cry like that every night because it kept me awake. I put my head under the pillow and tried to scrunch up my ears the way I could screw up my eyes. But it didn't work.

The next day was a Tuesday. I remember that because the *Echo* was doing a World War One supplement on the first Tuesday of every month, and if you didn't put it inside the main paper before you pushed it through the door, it rucked up. I sometimes forgot. Mr Stevens came down the path after I'd delivered his paper, and shouted from his gate.

'I can't read this, young man,' he said, waving his mangled copy of *Those Who Served*. I couldn't blame his dog because it was dead, so I went back and gave him number 12's copy.

'Thanks lad,' he said. 'I've been waiting for this. All about the Battle of the Somme.'

'Sausage and Mash,' I said, without thinking. Then I felt a bit stupid. But he gave me a smile.

'That's right! The two valleys. You've been learning your history.'

'A bit.' I shrugged. 'At school.'

'Good, good. So they told you about our local pals regiment, who lost half their men on the first day?'

I shook my head.

'Then you need to read the paper, my boy.' He waved the supplement at me. 'Five hundred chums dead in a day. It's all in here.'

I felt a bit nervous but I really wanted to ask him something, so I stayed by the gate. He was smiling at me so I thought it would be OK.

'Did any of your mates … I mean your friends … die in the war? I mean your war?'

'Oh yes,' he said, not smiling any more. 'It's what happens.'

'Did it …' I couldn't think of what to say next. I wanted to ask him if it did his head in and turned him into a nutter, but I couldn't ask him that. I could feel myself going red.

'You all right, lad?'

I shrugged. 'It's my brother. He's got back from Afghanistan. He's not the same.'

Mr Stevens nodded. 'It's what happens.'

'But you're all right?'

He laughed. 'Well, I'm all right now.'

'So ... he'll be OK?'

He put his hand over the gate and squeezed my arm.

'Give it time,' he said.

I was surprised because he squeezed me really hard and I didn't think he'd have that kind of strength any more. I thought about the bruise I was going to get. Another black mark from Mons Avenue.

'I'd better get going.' I told him.

'All right, lad. You take care.'

I nodded and walked off. I didn't give a copy of *Those Who Served* to number 12 because they were a young couple with a little kid and I didn't think they'd care. When I posted it through number 14's door, their dog ate the paper as usual, but they were an old couple with a young kid and I didn't think they'd care either. I couldn't help it, when I walked up the road I counted 'Care', 'Not care' at every door. But then I didn't care much either, did I? Except for Simon.

When I'd finished my round, I went home through the woods where Simon and I used to go with our bikes. It's four years since he joined the army but some of our stuff is still there: an old rope tied to a branch, a rusty shopping trolley with nettles growing through it. Simon pushed me down the hill in that. I've still got a scar on my forehead. He was a good mate, back then. We were always in trouble.

We had ham and chips for dinner that night. Normally, Dad would have put mustard out because he likes it with ham, but the jar wasn't on the table. I knew I shouldn't say anything. Simon looked like he'd been kicked in the face. He'd been crying again. But I was mad with him for blubbing in his room while I was out taking the papers round and Dad was driving through a black spot and then making chips. I was mad with him for coming back and

100

making everyone else take the blame. I was mad with him for loads of reasons I couldn't even remember. But mostly for not being Simon any more. So I said something.

'What, no mustard?' I asked my dad, with a stupid, fake grin.

Dad didn't answer. He looked at Simon and then made a face at me. Shook his head.

'Goes with ham as well as sausages,' I said. Then I waited a couple of seconds. 'And mash.'

Simon slammed his fist down on the table, with his fork still in it.

'You trying to wind me up?'

'Nah,' I said. 'That's too easy.' I put a chip in my mouth and chewed it.

'Matt!' said my Dad, urgent but quiet, like Simon wouldn't hear it. Simon was just looking at me, his face getting redder, showing up the blotches round his eyes.

'Say that again,' he told me, in his 'dangerous' quiet voice. I ignored him and ate another chip. I knew it would wind him up more if I stayed quiet. 'Say that again!' he shouted, leaning out of his seat to get his face closer to mine.

'Nah,' I said. 'Don't feel like it.'

'Matt! Please!' My Dad was almost begging. I could feel anger filling me up, like a football being blown up with a bike pump. It made me dizzy.

'You little shit!' said Simon. He tried to grab me with one fist across the table but I got out of my chair and stood by the door. I felt like I was bursting.

'You're the shit!' I told him. 'You're been one ever since you got back. That's why your girlfriend chucked you.'

'Matthew!' Dad only ever used my proper name when he was mad with me, and that made me even more angry with Simon.

'And that's why you're a cry baby who blubs all night!'

101

I yelled. Then I ran out the door.

I knew it was going to be bad when he didn't swear at me. I thought he'd come out shouting and try to grab me, but he didn't. I went for my bike and he went straight to his car. I watched him get in, then I looked at his face. Something about it scared me. I started pedalling, fast as I could.

I made it to Mons Avenue before he got me. I thought he'd try to run me down, so I was pedalling on the pavement. He drove next to me, sometimes a bit ahead, looking at me in his mirror. I thought about going into someone's house, calling the police. But then there was this woman in front of me with a pushchair and I had to either get off the pavement or stop. So I stopped. Simon left his engine going and his car door open and just ran at me. I didn't have time to turn the bike round. So I dropped it and ran. I thought I was fast, but Simon caught me in about five seconds. I watched the first punch coming like it was in slow motion and my heart was pumping so hard I could hear it banging in my chest. Then I felt the fist hit me and I heard a scream and knew it was me. When the second punch came I was on the floor with my hands over my face, trying to curl my legs up, feeling my mouth fill with blood. Simon's fists kept coming down on my head. My heart went faster and I thought I was going to die of a heart attack. Then suddenly the fists stopped, and I could hear Dad's voice.

He wasn't talking to me, and I couldn't hear what he was saying because the blood was still making a noise in my ears. Then I heard him closer.

'Matt!' He said. I could feel his hand on my head and then he was trying to uncurl me, get my arms away from my face. As soon as I moved I saw Simon, kneeling next to Dad, breathing really hard, a weird look on his face. I tried to put my arms up again, but Dad held my wrists.

'It's OK,' said Dad. 'You're all right.'

I didn't feel like it was OK. Simon leaned over me and I was sure he was going to punch me again. I tried to wriggle back, but he just stared down like he wasn't really seeing me. Behind him I could see the woman with the pushchair, watching, and the man from number 16 with one of the dogs that bit me, and Mr Stephens.

Then Simon put his hand on my forehead. I flinched, but he just left it there, like he was taking my temperature or something. It seemed so weird that I stopped struggling and looked at him. I could see Mr Stevens move behind him, put a hand on his shoulder. Dad let go of my wrists.

'You're OK,' said Simon. Then he put a hand on my chest, like he was checking my heartbeat. I didn't move. He knelt there for ages, one hand on my head and one on my heart, looking at me with something missing from his eyes. 'You're OK.'

We all drove down to London when Simon went back and stayed overnight near the airport. It didn't feel like the first time, when we'd taken him to the airbase. That day, he couldn't wait to go. He'd been with his mates and he was like a kid going to camp or something, not like he was going to war.

This time, he was quiet. Calm. Like he'd made up his mind to go, and that was that. We took him to Heathrow to catch his plane. He wasn't going with the army this time. He'd got a job as a security guard out in Iraq.

'Like a chauffeur with a gun,' he said. 'But without the cap.'

He wasn't like the old Simon, but he was OK. He talked to me like I wasn't a kid and gave me £20 before he went through for his flight. It's weird, because I thought I'd be scared for him like I was the first time. I was only ten then, and I kept saying to Dad, 'He won't die, will he? He's not going to die?' But this time I wasn't scared, and even though I'd miss him, I didn't want to stop him going.

It seemed right, somehow, him going back.

He'd taken me for a burger a few weeks before he left, after telling us about Iraq. Said he wanted to explain.

'I don't fit,' he'd said, screwing up his eyebrows as if he was trying to find the right words. 'I know it sounds mad, but living here, normal life … none of it makes sense.' But he didn't need to explain. I got it.

He turned round and waved as he walked towards the gates and gave us a big grin. For a second, he looked like the old Simon. Anyone seeing him would think he was the same as before. But we knew different. Me, Dad, Mr Stevens.

Some people, cousins and neighbours and stuff, thought Simon was mad going back.

'He's done his bit,' they said. 'He can get on with his life now. Why's he trying to get himself killed?'

They don't get it. On the outside he might look the same, but he's a different shape. People think men like Simon can just come back and get normal jobs, marry their girlfriends, watch telly. But they can't, can they? I mean, they got broken. How can they still fit?

Tug of War
Joy Tucker (SDWC)

The shot rang out in the last hour of 31st December, 1918. I still wonder if it echoed in the hills. When I have imagined that breaking of a scene of peace I have always thought of it as a picture hanging on a wall, doing no harm – and suddenly having its glass shattered, its frame twisted, its contents flaring and burning away to ashes. I have passed down the story of that night to three generations of family now in the hope that they will remember what war can do to people and to a family. I also hope they will pass the story on. I can do no more. It could have been any family, anywhere – gathering to celebrate a Happy New Year – very probably their first Hogmanay together after the increasingly weary years of war and all its evil effects.

Imagine my scene of peace – a grey stone farmhouse surrounded by fields in a nest of Scottish hills sloping up to a rocky crag. I remember it was snowing – soft pale flakes, like falling stars against the darkness of the kitchen window. And inside the farmhouse preparations were underway for the bringing-in of a traditional Hogmanay. There was a good fire, candles, a table laid with the best glasses, bottles of ginger wine and whisky, a plate of cake and shortbread.

Then, the family – Annie Murdoch, my mother, polishing the brass ornaments which usually sat on the mantelpiece – a war-horse, and heads of some of the famous and infamous characters of war – Lloyd George, Kitchener, Haig, Marshall Foch. At twelve years old the youngest of the family, I was helping her. My sister Meg was sitting in a rocking-chair, wearing black and looking as sad as she had been for the last two years when she learned that Robbie, the young man she loved and was going to marry, had been killed in France. We three were waiting for the men of the house to come in from the yard – William Murdoch, my father, my two brothers, Tom and Matt – born in the years between Meg and myself. Tom and Matt had only been back from their wars for a couple of weeks.

Those were strange weeks – so different from all my expectations. My brothers seemed almost different people – older naturally, but even the way they spoke was different, and they treated each other as strangers. Tom was not the teasing, joshing big brother he had been. His words seemed curt and somehow rough and he walked with a limp and had to use a stick for support. He had spent many months in a military hospital after his time in the trenches. We knew very little about his injury – and any questions put to him on that subject were not answered. He did not look like someone who would buy the pretty embroidered foreign cards which he sent to our mother. Only his messages inside the cards were war-like – 'Still killing Huns' clashing horribly with the muslin frills and pastel stitching of 'To my dear Mother' on the outside. Both boys signed their letters in the same way – 'from your loving son'.

Matt's letters were brief, telling us that he was fine, thanking us for knitting socks, and asking if Tom was all right. They were scribbled on pages torn from exercise-books, arriving in cheap brown envelopes and postmarked H.M.P. followed by the name of whichever prison he was in at the time. I knew them all – Barlinnie, Winchester, Wormwood Scrubs, Wakefield, and I shocked the village school-mistress by suggesting that a map of British prisons should be hanging alongside the classroom war-maps of Belgium and France, so that we could all see where the

Conscientious Objectors were.

Most people around us were shocked by the thought of 'Conchies' as they were called. Someone scratched 'Hang Conchies' on the farm gate. And for a while, amongst the letters from the boys, there would be envelopes from those who sent white feathers – usually anonymously, occasionally adding their names, or words my mother pencilled over before I could read them – so presumably swear-words.

There must have been many arguments and discussions in the family before I was allowed to know exactly what was going on – early in the war when Tom signed up to join the army or later when Matt had to present his case as a pacifist to a tribunal in Glasgow and subsequently was arrested and taken away in a Black Maria like a common criminal. On both occasions my mother cried. As time went on I began to understand. We had all been brought up to look at both sides of most questions and to accept that people were entitled to their own opinions, and suddenly here was a real life-and-death example for Meg and me to chew over.

'It's like the way it was when the pig was killed, remember?' she explained to me. 'You would put your head under a cushion so that you couldn't hear the screams; Matt used to go to his room and read, but Tom would be right there watching, even helping.'

'What did you do?' I asked.

'I prayed,' was her reply. But when Meg had become engaged and her young man volunteered to fight she wasn't as sure in her views as she had been. When poor Robbie was killed she stopped having discussions with me altogether.

'Whatever are they doing out there? It's after eleven,' my mother suddenly asked, looking at the clock. 'Your father always likes to polish his mother's candle-sticks himself, just for luck. That reminds me. Meg! Did you put out the ash-can? It's bad luck if there are ashes in the house at midnight! Do you hear me, Meg?'

'We wouldn't know what to do with any bad luck here, would we?' Meg replied, rocking her chair noisily.

'Nor sarcasm,' Annie said. 'Let's try and make it a good New Year for the boys.'

'At least they're alive!' Meg snapped back.

'I'll do it,' I said, and afterwards wished I had not offered.

The men came in through the front door, stamping the snow off their boots and bringing a rush of cold air with them. At the same time I came out from the scullery waving the book which I had found in the outside-bin while emptying the ashes.

'Look!' I called, 'I've just saved Matt's autograph book – it must have fallen into the ash-can!'

I brushed the leather cover of the book, dropping ash on the table, and suddenly both my brothers were shouting; Matt yelling that someone had taken the book from his room, Tom grinning as he stated that the ash-can was the best place for it. My father joined in the shouting, and it felt like years before with the boys fighting over a football and my father having to intervene. 'For goodness sake!' I thought you were men now!' he said.

My mother decided to start pouring drinks even though it was not midnight, and everyone sat down. I was hoping that it might turn out to be a good family evening after all.

'I'm going up to put a decent jacket on for Hogmanay,' William announced. 'What about you, Meg? Maybe leave off the black tonight – to help you feel better?'

Annie added, 'I expect the Robertsons will be first-footing us soon – you'll surely want to be looking nice for them, Meg? Anyway, I'm going to get ready.'

'I told you, Mother. I saw them the other day,' Meg

called after her. 'They're not coming this year.'

Tom laughed harshly.

'Well, well. I wonder why that is? Not even young Jenny?'

Meg stepped in, 'They're not coming, because they are missing their son Robbie who was going to be my husband, and you know that very well.'

'But not even Jenny!' said Tom.

He leaned over towards Matt, prodding him with his stick.

'Were you not walking-out with Jenny, Matt? Before you turned yellow?'

He prodded Matt again.

'Don't do that!' Matt warned.

'She gave him a white feather,' Meg said. 'She's not worth bothering about.'

'I might bother about her myself, now that I'm home,' Tom teased, and raised the stick for another prod at Matt, who grabbed it and threw it across the room.

His autograph book fell on the floor, and as he bent to pick it up, Tom tried to pull it out of his hand. 'You and your stupid autograph book!' Tom sneered, limping over to pour himself another whisky. 'What's so special about it?' he asked.

It was as if a dam had burst as Matt answered.

'It's the only thing I have brought back from my war,' he said, 'because it is the only thing that is real. It's full of kind, civilised, sensitive words from good men – men who were my comrades, men who were treated like scum, castigated, mocked, described as the lowest of the low, worse than any other kind of criminal ever sent to a stinking prison. Simply because they didn't want to kill. Read it, soldier. Read it and learn.'

'I wouldn't touch it with a barge-pole,' Tom said, beginning to slur his words, 'You think you had a hard time – do you think the trenches were sweet-smelling? Do you think that we liked living like rats, with rats, and being sniped at if we lifted our heads high enough to breathe in just a few gulps of fresh air? And even the air wasn't fresh any more – when they tried to gas us. Can you describe in some of your sensitive soppy words what it is like to see men dying from mustard gas, or a bullet in the brain?'

Another dam had burst with Tom's words. The boys had even made Meg stop rocking her chair, and she too had words to say.

'Can't you two just be glad to be alive, to have a life ahead of you?' she pleaded.

'But don't you see, Meg, that it has all been for nothing?' Matt said, 'Young men throwing their lives away. There's a quotation in here,' he opened the autograph book eagerly and read aloud, '"the paths of glory lead but to the grave". That's what your Robbie was doing. That was his path.'

Meg looked stunned. All she could say was 'Jesus Christ, Matt – Jesus Christ!' She sat very still and closed her eyes, as if she only wanted darkness. Her hands were shaking.

Tom, who had recovered his stick, stood up and pointed to Matt's book.

'All right, brother – so that's what you brought back from the war – I'll show you what I brought back. Come out to the barn. Come on.'

Matt hesitated. 'We shouldn't leave Meg like this.'

'Our little sister will stay with her – won't you, little sister?' he said to me. 'And I can hear Mother and Father coming downstairs. It's nearly next year.'

'We heard shouting and decided to wait until it stopped,' my father said, as they both came in, looking smart in their Sunday clothes, 'and Meg dear, we are ready for the New Year. Look – no black.'

110

'Where are the boys?' Meg asked, as if she had been asleep.

I told her they had gone out to the barn.

'They always used to finish their fights in the barn,' my mother spoke fondly. 'Meg dear, will you go out and tell them it's time to come in.'

'Yes, of course Meg dear will go.' Meg said, actually smiling as she stood up, singing 'Goodbyee! Goodbyee' as she left the room.

My father laughed 'You know, I think Meg is feeling a little better now that the boys are back,' he said.

My mother nodded and went back to her polishing.

It was quiet in the kitchen, the only sounds the crackle and occasional hiss of the fire and the clock ticking the year away while we waited for the chimes.

I don't remember hearing the chimes, for while I was watching the clock came *that* moment, the moment when the shot rang out, breaking my scene of peace and fracturing our family.

Time blurred then, after my father had run to the barn shouting, 'They must have a gun out there. Stay here with the child, Annie,' and then gone to fetch the village policeman. It was still blurred when Tom and Matt told us how Meg had taken the gun from Tom and killed herself.

Later, I asked my mother, 'Why?' as she sat at the table, her head bowed.

All she said was 'It's what war does to people' and, as an after-thought, 'There were ashes on this table at midnight.' sweeping her hand across the surface as she knocked all the polished brass heads to the ground.

To Wilfred Owen in Chelsea Physic Garden
Lynne Lomond (SDWC)

(On his last leave, the war poet Wilfred Owen sat in
Chelsea Physic Garden, reluctant to leave and return to the
front, where he was killed shortly afterwards, just before
armistice day.)

Here in this garden midst the herbs you sat
reluctant, loath to take the train which would
transport you back to Flanders Field and death
so soon, amidst the poppies, cups of blood.

Your words convey no patriotic flame,
but anguished anger at the wastage wrought
by agonising death in mud and blood,
they cry for what those lost years might have brought.

What would your verses say had you lived on?
Or through your death have your embittered words
carried more weight and moved the warring world
closer to making ploughshares out of swords?
You could have spent your final days amidst
the healing poppies in this place of peace.
Instead you chose to face death in the hope
that glorifying war would one day cease.

Those We Leave Behind
Gail Williams (SDWC)

Looking out of the back door, there wasn't much for Colonel George Randolph to see. The rain had stopped though the cloud cover remained, hiding the moon and its light. The house was quiet now, the brandy had been warmed and drunk, the cigars smoked, memories shared with laughter and tears. Now their guests were gone and the family was tucked up in bed. The back door, which it was Grace's tradition to open on New Year's Eve, was still open.

He pulled in a deep breath and leaned against the jamb. So this is 1919. A year for peace and hope.

Upstairs, Agnes was settling down with Patrick, her husband of two months. Agnes, his reason for getting through the Boer War; coming home to see his blond cherub was the thought that had kept him going. That homecoming was everything he'd dreamed it would be. The small, curly-haired girl was hiding behind his angelic Grace. Agnes had peaked out warily, all wide-eyes and uncertainty. Then she'd looked up at him, remembering the tall dark man from his few short visits during the war, and that little pout had turned into a beaming smile. She'd run to him. He remembered the feeling had filled his heart as he filled his arms with her, then Grace. Then finally little Stephen had stepped up, to shake his hand.

A smile curved his lips.

Stephen, four years older than Agnes, he was the spit of his father, tall and dark. Very upstanding and capable. George had been so very proud when Stephen had decided to join the army. His heart had been ready to burst too see

Stephen, in full dress uniform, pass out of Sandhurst.

Lieutenant Stephen Randolph had looked glorious, undefeatable in his immaculate uniform as they had both left the house, heading out under orders in the summer of 1914. The pride had only grown as George heard more of his son's actions, his heroics, even as he himself had seen more of the new styles of warfare. He had kept that feeling for his son in his heart, as his own hopes for the future faded under each new horror he witnessed. He'd been proud when he'd heard that Stephen had returned from the Battle of the Boot, though he hadn't heard how badly the boy had been wounded until it was too late. Pride. It was a feeling he had desperately clung to as he stood with Grace and Agnes at Stephen's funeral.

The funeral was the first time he had met Patrick, the man who had become his son-in-law. An engineer by training, Patrick worked in something he was careful to never quite define, but George suspected he was working with the Royal Air Force. Importantly, Patrick wasn't a military man, and for that George couldn't be more thankful. Agnes would never have to worry as Grace had, while her husband was away, never knowing if she would wake up a widow. She would never know that pain of that infernal BFPO telegram. Patrick would never have to see or experience the things that had stolen not only George's son, but the faith and hope from George's soul.

When George had returned that last time, the spring of 1918 had been in full glory. He'd seen Grace standing in the doorway, Agnes at her side, very much as they had been in 1902, but everything looked different. He'd walked up the path, battling the tears, the absence of joy in his heart, as he welcomed the women in his life into his arms and held them tight. The colour of the flowers was beige. The sky was grey without a single cloud, and the sun was pale in its glory.

For a long time after his return he had tried to transform

114

from solider to husband. Ex-soldier now. The war was over and he had resigned his commission.

Too late.

All too often he found himself sitting in his living room chair, watching the men under his command slog through the terror and destruction, stepping over their fallen comrades to fight an enemy for an inch of land. An inch that was instantly surrendered as each side returned to their own dug-outs. What was the point? He didn't understand this form of fighting. The drone of war in the air. The rattle of tanks over scorched earth. It was beyond his control and his understanding, the separation of attack and injury worried him. How far would Man go if he didn't have to hear the enemy scream, feel the rush of another's blood staining his clothes, weapons, and hands: watch men dying?

Swallowing the lump in his throat, the bile rising from his stomach, George blinked at the night and checked his pocket.

All present and correct.

The week after he had returned, he had stood in their bedroom and seen Grace in the front garden; she was talking with Nigel Abbot, the butcher. He was a good man, and Grace was smiling up at him, doing that thing she used to do, brushing her hair behind her ear. She had looked happy. Happier than he'd seen her in a long time.

A very long time.

He had been away too much. Abbot was a good catch, a nice match for his perfect Grace. He tried to see the problem. He knew there should be one, but he didn't feel it.

Life had been him and Grace for so long. Outside of the army, it was the only life he knew. Yet he had stood there and known he wasn't the man for her. She deserved so much better. She deserved to be happy. She deserved to be with Abbot.

He had tried to be the husband he should be, the husband he used to be. But it wasn't the same any more. He could tell Grace was different too. The only explanation he had for her not at least moving out of the bedroom was that she didn't want to upset Agnes.

Every night they lay down together, but the love they still felt wasn't sufficient to span the chasm that had opened between them. Though their hands would meet, hold tight beneath the covers, they simply weren't close any more.

They did what they could, for Agnes's sake; when they were together as a family, George felt more like himself, but he wasn't the same. When they visited Stephen's grave, Grace would cling to him, he would remember all the times they were together, times he had been there for her, when they had made Stephen and Agnes. All the pain of the war had been bad, but the pain of outliving his son was worse. Grace didn't say anything, but he knew she felt it too. There was a light missing from her eyes.

The only time that light came back was when Agnes had tripped over herself trying to tell her mother that Patrick had proposed and she had accepted. George had known it was coming. Patrick had spoken to him the previous day, asked his permission. The decision had been easy. Patrick would provide for his daughter and there seemed to be a true meeting of hearts in the match. Of course he'd given his permission. He wished he'd felt the pleasure he should have felt on the occasion. He just wished he could feel anything but this devastating emptiness.

George looked up at the empty sky. Affinity assailed him.

In those last few days Grace had seemed tired, distant. He should have realised, understood. But numbness had overtaken him.

He would close his eyes and the memories, the

116

nightmares, would return. He would sleep and the dread would drown him. Fear clamped his lungs, horror clawed at him, pulled him into the graves of the untold number of men and boys he had left behind. The men, women, and children; the innocent dead whose cold, decaying eyes would look at him with the blame that he felt at his core.

Paralysed and unable to call out, he would wake, coated in a cold sweat. The damp would soak his pyjamas, the sheets. Grace was very tolerant, never complaining if he disturbed her, but the distance between them had grown.

That was why.

After one particularly gripping, fearsome nightmare in late August, he had woken, gasping for air, desperate for oxygen. Desperate for human contact he had reached out and taken Grace's hand. At first he had thought her lack of reaction was simply because she was asleep. Then he'd felt the dampness of her skin, the cold clammy dampness. The grave cold had registered. He'd turned and switched on the light, turned to his beautiful wife.

Her skin was grey.

Denial.

He'd seen this before. He understood immediately.

Denial.

He called her name. Denial. The tears rolled down his checks. Denial. He called her name. Denial.

He didn't need confirmation. But he stood, pulled on his dressing gown, called the doctor. Denial.

Diagnosis.

Denial.

Spanish Flu.

Denial.

However diminished he was, that, he had felt. Grace, the love of his life. Gone. It should have been him. This wasn't fair. Another innocent life lost.

Agnes had been devastated. He had held her for hours, listening to the crying intensity of her feeling, wishing that he felt the same depth. He just wasn't capable any more. He had loved Grace more than anything, but he was incapable of it now.

Now he stood beneath the New Year's night.

It wasn't the only 'new' in his life.

Today, over dinner, Agnes had announced that she was with child. He should have been overjoyed. He should, at least, have been happy. He was happy – until his incredible daughter had said that there was every chance that his grandchild would be as brave and as good a military leader as he was.

He knew then.

He knew that while he had saved his family from the invasive forces of foreign powers, he could never save them from the unmistakable truth. He wasn't a coward, but he was a murderer.

He was a soldier.

He had killed all the right men. Or the wrong men.

He didn't know.

How could he?

He stood away from the jamb and stepped out into the night.

He patted his pocket.

All present and correct.

Grace.

Agnes.

His grandchild.

He couldn't face the prospect of that new human becoming what his grandfather was. What had destroyed the child's uncle.

Everything George loved. Everything he needed. Everything he remembered feeling. All gone.

Taking the bundle he had prepared earlier, he carefully closed the door. The earlier rain beaded on his polished shoes, soaked through the lush fabric of his dress trousers. Colonel George Randolph moved away from the house.

Across the immaculate lawn he felt the damp invading his dinner suit, he paced until he reached the treeline. With military precision he laid out the tarpaulin he had brought with him. He stood to one end of it. He took the revolver from its hiding place.

He checked the cylinder.

One bullet.

It was all he needed.

Sound and Silence
Stuart Randall (external poetry competition joint second)

One hundred years of grainy film
has seared the images into our brains:
helmeted, rifle-clutching men
going over the top to charge
across a dislocated landscape.

Or the staggering figure
of a Tommy in a trench,
bent almost double beneath
the dead weight of a wounded comrade,
shattered earth showering down.

But these are silent movies;
artillery's deadly roar unheard,
exploding shells struck dumb,
machine guns' deadly scything mute
on this soundless battle ground.

We are deaf to the screams
and frantic cries, the whistles,
moans and groans of dying
men and horses.
all is silent as the grave.

Silent, too, the men who returned,
their nightmares too real to be shared.
They'd said goodbye to all that,
tried to pick up the broken threads of life,

banish bombardment of the mind.

And how do we remember them?

With marching bands,
shouted orders, bugle blasts,
old soldiers trudge to 'Tipperary'
and speeches infiltrate the gaps,
Silence drowned by hymns and organs.

The Sniper
John Keenan (external short story competition joint second)

I'm due to go back soon. My wounds have healed. I'm sitting waiting for transport and remembering; memories twisting, turning, and confusing. They are mostly dark and bitter, but not all.

Thinking back to the start, things began to change the morning the footballer got sniped.

Kent was tall and an ex-professional footballer. He was always making footballs out of stuff ... string, brown paper from parcels, anything, and then he would show off his football skills in the trenches when things were quiet. He was clever with the ball, but slow thinking.

He had got one of the lads to throw him the ball and he would jump and head it back. On his third jump the bullet went cleanly through his head.

Sergeant Higginbottom was there in a flash, but there was nothing to do but swear and curse the Hun sniper, just a few hundred yards away across the filthy slimy hell that was no man's land.

I held back.

'Look after number one. Keep your head down and don't volunteer for anything ... nothing, not even if it looks like a good thing. The army don't do nobody any favours.'

That was my Uncle Eddy's advice when I signed up for the BEF in France. I was just a few steps ahead of the Bobbies. I was no hero.

If Mr Boche left me alone then I wasn't about to give him any trouble.

Eddy looked after me when my dad died falling through the roof of some big house he was robbing. He was not much of a burglar. Eddy was into all kinds of rackets on the Merseyside docks where we lived and he showed me plenty on getting ahead and out of the slums we were brought up in.

Me and my best mate, big Phil. Phil signed up when he heard where I was going.

'What have you got there, Jimmy?'

This was two days after Kent the footballer got hit. We were having a brew up and I was taking some 'special' items out of my pack.

'Woodbines and real coffee.' Phil lowered his voice to a whisper. 'You got a racket going, Jimmy?'

'No roll-ups for us, mate.'

I passed him a shiny new packet of cigarettes and watched it disappear into his tunic pocket. Proper fags were as rare as a shirt with no lice.

I was putting into practice everything that Eddy had taught me. I had the quartermaster's clerk in my pocket. Phil and I got all the cushy chores.

Corporal West looked after me, as long as I kept him supplied with little treats. I knew he was sharing his good fortune with the sergeant, not that he would ever admit it.

Phil was never like me really. We were kids together but he had a job and used to train for boxing. He was good too. He never got into the rackets, but somehow we still had this thing … we were mates.

He never refused my treats but I found he was giving them away to the other blokes.

Then there was the time a new recruit fainted as he waited for the signal to go over the top. He was only fifteen … lied about his age. Phil got the corporal to stand him down and he took his place.

When I cursed him for a being a fool, he looked at me with those big eyes and said, 'Jimmy, all we got in this bloody hell hole is our mates. Me, you, and all these other blokes, we have to look out for each other.'

I just didn't get it, not then.

Then a few more lads got sniped, and everybody was talking about the sniper. The word came down from Intelligence, who got it from agents in Berlin, that he had won an Olympic medal for sharpshooting. His name was Luther Schmidt and he was a German hero. Apparently he had a tattoo on the back of his hand. It was a sniper rifle over a bull's eye target. He was adding bullet holes for every kill. Seems it was almost covered.

That didn't bother me, until … until one day we were being inspected by some fat fool from HQ, who was wetting himself and couldn't wait to get out of the trenches and back to his three-course lunch.

Phil was a good soldier. When the sergeant yelled at him to make room for the officer's big gut he instinctively jumped up onto the firing step to make way.

The sniper got him with one clean shot.

I went a bit mad after that. I was on a charge for cursing and threatening an officer … the fat fool. Then I 'acquired' an officer's binoculars and spent every minute off duty staring into no man's land and trying to spot that bastard sniper, me and a hundred other blokes. That was another charge.

Then the rats … they never bothered me before, they had their job and I had mine. But I got it into my head that they were chewing their way into Phil's grave and eating him up. I couldn't stand it. I went around killing them … with my boot, the butt of my rifle, whatever came to hand. One night I was caught by a sentry making my way back to the rear to check on Phil's grave. I could have been shot for that, but the sergeant said it made no sense to accuse me of desertion when I was volunteering for every dangerous duty I could.

'Let him get it out of his system,' he said.

I just wanted to kill as many German soldiers as I could and die trying, especially the sniper.

Perhaps I would have gone completely mad but the other lads looked after me. They shared their stuff and they talked to me ... and they listened.

I must have done six or seven night patrols when the inevitable happened. We were close to the German forward positions when we were caught in a routine flare. A machine gun opened up and two lads were killed instantly. I was hit twice and ended up at the bottom of a shell hole. I think the rest got back to our lines.

It was then that things took a turn.

I came around just as the first low shafts of sunlight gleamed through the morning mist. Then I saw him. The muzzle of his long rifle was wrapped in khaki cloth but it must have slipped and reflected the light. He was crawling to his position just a few yards from me, heading for a burnt out gun from some earlier attack. He was wearing sniper camouflage and was virtually invisible; but not to me.

I had lost my rifle but I still had my bayonet. I had a bullet wound in my thigh and my head was covered with blood but my mind was clear. I knew what I had to do.

I waited until he had settled into his firing position and for the morning bombardment to begin.

The din was deafening but I was used to it, and it suited my purpose.

My bayonet slipped into his body where the neck joined the shoulder. He was aware of me at the very last second ... too late.

I stared at his slumped body and then I turned him over.

I felt anger ... rage. I wanted to shout and curse him ... ask him, why ... why?

He was a little older than me. He had a long, angular face and some spasm of violent death had twisted his lips into a sneer.

'You are a fool,' he seemed to say, 'this is war.'

I hated him. I looked at the boastful tattoo on his right hand and took a deep breath.

When the attack came from the British lines they over ran me and had put up smoke. I managed to crawl back to our trench ... just about conscious.

They took me to the First Aid dug out. Sergeant Higginbottom was there when they unbuttoned my bloodied battle dress and I heard their gasps as they took out the tattooed hand, badly butchered at the wrist.

'Phil, it's for Phil,' I was mumbling. The sergeant put a calming hand on my chest.

'You're for the hospital, my boy,' and to the men, 'I'll take charge of that,' reaching for the white, blood-drained claw.

I'd intended to bury that bastard's hand in Phil's grave but the top brass had other ideas.

The rumour was that it was delivered in a polished wooden box to the German Brigade HQ. The regimental insignia of the Lancashire Fusiliers was carved into the top.

There was no note but the message was clear. The sniper 'hero' from Hell had been returned to his origins.

I am on my way back to the Reserve HQ. The lorry turns into the yard.

The regiment is at rest at the moment and I see the men from my unit waiting. There is Sergeant Higginbottom and Corporal West, but there are many more men ... some new recruits, strangers, and they are all cheering ... cheering me.

Bloody fools, eh.

Aye, but still, it feels fine ... really fine.

Trouble Comes in Threes
Carl Morris (external short story competition highly commended)

Lieutenant Morgan sat as still as a stone. Watching. Waiting. Waiting for the hour to come and to lead his men away from the relative safety of the British trenches and across no-man's land. As his men prepared in practised silence, Morgan marvelled at the matter-of-fact manner in which they went about their preparations, as if about to take part in nothing more adventurous than a football match. The reality was starkly different, of course, as the men blackened their faces with pieces of burnt cork; making sure that not an inch of pale skin was visible in the muted shadows of darkness. They checked each other's kit for any noticeable signs of noise – a strap buckle to be tightly wrapped in a strip of khaki cloth; the removal of unnecessary tin, steel, or brass that might jangle or catch on something – all swaddled or collected and stored, as men made the wicked transformation into shadowy wraiths.

The men called him 'Dai Eyes', Morgan knew, due to his propensity to stare off into the middle-distance when deep in thought, or when focused on the million and one things that he so fastidiously covered before risking the lives of his men. Of course, they did not call him this to his face and not just because he was an officer. No. The men respected Lieutenant Morgan because he came from them – he was not *one* of them, least not any more, but sprang forth from the same hard, unforgiving, blackened earth as his men.

Lieutenant David Morgan had enlisted as Private

Morgan at the onset of war in 1914 in a carnival-like recruiting drive in his home town of Swansea. Since then, the war had swept its dispassionate hand in a wide, sweeping arc across humanity and ravaged all beneath its reach. Many had answered the call to arms; now many lay dead. Morgan had survived and risen in the ranks on a tide of blood, sweat, and tears. He was not a man to lay low or shirk, but neither was he a man to make flamboyant displays of bravado. Morgan was a soldier through and through and although he had been an electrician before the war started, he could not imagine living any other life than the one that claimed him now. Make no mistake, Morgan was not a merchant of death or a lover of war, nor did he bask in the glory of saga-style tales of martial bravery, but he was a soldier and, as the passage of time was revealing, a damn good soldier!

Trench knives were checked for their ever-present edge and blackened with a single sheltered flame. A soft rustling of movement could be heard as men adjusted clothing and made space in their small packs for the weapons of war. Spare magazines were issued, clunking against each other as they were passed around. Each man began carefully arranging his own pack so nothing rattled or clinked. Wooden truncheons and morning stars – solid wooden shafts topped by a steel ball adorned with wicked metal spikes – were slipped into belts and straps; instruments of murder that would be at home in the melee of a medieval battlefield. The men had forgone their wide-rimmed steel helmets in favour of tight fitting woollen hats that completed the spectral facade of a head that was cloaked in darkness. Only the whites of their eyes and the teeth that might be bared would split the coal-black face of death that each man sported, waiting for the time to visit Fritz.

As Morgan observed the men around busily preparing for the tense night ahead. Corporal John Jones, known as

JoJo to his mates, was busy honing the edge of his shortened stabbing blade with the battered steel fist guard, humming in a low, merry fashion. Close by was the Corporal's long standing friend Corporal Harris. Harry was the sombre side of Jones, a ferocious looking man as hard as toughened steel and the two together were a formidable pair – both behind the lines and in the midst of battle. As Morgan watched, Jones broke into a broad grin and winked at him as he passed Harris a sawn-off shotgun, which he casually stuffed into his webbing belt. Morgan smirked back, amused at the vagaries of war and thought it sadly strange to find such unity and equality at last; here, in the middle of nowhere and with no one to see or care about its simplicity.

The night had shrunk to the size of a halfpenny piece as the rolling clouds shrouded the darkened landscape in sleep. The odd tremulous star dared to breathe its life upon the brooding earth below, but was rudely pushed aside by leaden clouds as night became absolute. It was time and Morgan got to his feet, loping slowly along the trench and tapping each man on a shoulder or cap-covered head. Silence roamed freely as the men all stood with knees bent and shoulders straight, ready for the command to go.

Standing crouched low in the forward sap trench, Morgan quickly checked his own vital pieces of equipment. He slipped his hand into his pocket and found the cold brass knuckles within, sliding his fingers into the holes and making a fist, before releasing his grip on the comforting weight. He checked his worn leather holster, curling his fingers around the smooth wooden handle of the heavy Webley revolver tucked inside. Slipping the firearm out of the holster a few inches, Morgan snapped the revolver firmly back into place – these were the battle rituals that he instinctually went through before releasing himself fully to the ways of the combat soldier and the mission ahead.

Morgan and his party of three men stood in line and listened in stone silence. Everything was as still as the grave as Morgan gave a barely perceptible nod of the head to Private Rees to 'stay put' and the three nebulous shapes poured over the parapet and oozed into no-man's-land.

As the small flicker of light poked through the deep blanket of night, the bolt action Mauser jerked violently and hammered into the shoulder of Obergefreiter Kreuz. The loud report echoed into the distance, as darkness enveloped the scene through the sniper's optical sight once more. That's the third foolish soul tonight, thought Kreuz, as he flipped back the bolt and ejected his third empty shell of the night. Will they never learn? he mused.

Kreuz had been a silent observer since midnight. Creeping out from his temporary home in the burned out hulk of a tank, he had returned to the dilapidated farmhouse on a slight rise next to the woods. Easing himself up into the eaves, he would remove a single slate and settle in for the night. It was his third night here and the hunting had been good. The Tommies weren't too bright and had shelled, mortared, and shot at anything that looked like it might house an enemy sniper, but with little reward – he was still here and he was still killing. It was quite simple, really – the British, as with all soldiers, liked to smoke. Bored on sentry duty or just nipping off for a quick smoke in the dead of night was almost ritualistic for soldiers on both sides. However, the inky cloak of darkness was no shield for a single, determined bullet. Such was the accuracy and ease with which an accomplished marksman, like himself, could send a bullet to a mark by almost will alone. All it took was a brief pinprick of light as a match was struck to seal a man's fate. To be precise, it took three tiny sparks: one to draw his attention; one to help measure his aim; and the final tiny flare of light to signal the brain to tell the finger to ease the trigger. To make matters easier, the psychology of the average soldier was a simple one and, as such, very easy to read. The soldier looked for safety in numbers. It is an animal instinct of all prey and especially the hunted. If they just went to smoke alone, then there would not be the opportunity to hunt so efficiently at night. Instead, each individual sought out his pals and unknowingly brought themselves death.

'Nicht bewegen – don't move,' breathed a ghostly voice into his ear.

The feel of cold metal pressed to the back of Kreuz's neck froze him into place and a chill ran down his spine. The slow click and roll of the chamber rotating – the almost imperceptible scrape of a bullet slipping into place – caused a cold rivulet of sweat to run from his temple.

'Easy there, Fritz; wouldn't want to shake my hand now, would you?' whispered a voice over his shoulder. 'Harris, signal Private Rees that the cat has caught the rat, will you, and give him a break from burning his fingers for the rest of the night.'

With his hands still on the rifle, the finger still poised beside the trigger guard, Kreuz continued to stare through the optical sight. There! One, two, three sparks simultaneously flared up – enough light produced to reveal the features of a soldier, who was grinning and waving back at him.

'All secured and ready for the off, sir,' said another voice.

As Kreuz felt the pressure of the revolver barrel on his neck remain, he knew the hunt was over. He felt a firm hand grab him around his leather webbing belt and pull him slowly to his feet.

'Den Kopf wenn sie Englisch sprechen?' the voice asked. Kreuz nodded his head, slowly. 'Gutter, junge. Then let's see those hands out wide, Fritz, fingers spread and up you get.'

As Kreutz was hauled to his feet, he was turned around slowly, still holding his arms out wide with his fingers spread, as ordered. He was faced by a demonic vision of three men; each of them blackened from head to foot and grinning broadly.

'He don't look too happy, sir,' said a brutal looking man who was holding in one hand what looked like a shotgun that had been hacked off almost to the stock and, in the other, a short stave of wood with two inch spikes of steel protruding from the top and sides.

'I imagine he feels quite stupid right now, after his recent successes and all. He's probably also wondering why he's still alive, as well as how he managed to get caught in the first place.' The man who spoke was clearly in charge, as he stared directly at Kreuz with a blank look that left the soul feeling cold and alone.

'Orders is orders, mate and HQ want a trophy – and guess what Fritzy, you've just become the prize.' The officer stepped a little closer and spoke to the sniper in a voice full of menace and as cold as the steel grey eyes that bored into him. 'Tell you what, though, promise not to mount your head above the fireplace, what with you being the great hunter and all, just wouldn't seem right, really.'

The men to either side of the officer chuckled with the irony of it all. 'As to how we caught you, well … third light unlucky, right? First muzzle flash, we found you. Second flash, we tracked you. Third flash, we were standing right behind you and you didn't even notice. Golden rule of hunting, Fritzy – relocation, relocation, relocation!'

A chill ran down Kreuz's spine. All he wanted was to leave this place and these men as soon as possible.

Lieutenant Morgan spoke to his two comrades, never taking his eyes of the sniper. 'Tie him up, then, nice and tight and we'll be on our way.'

At the Cenotaph, Whitehall
Joy Tucker (SDWC)

I have been listening
to the sounds of silence,
standing in a misty rain
on a grey November street,
late flowering
with a blossom
of scarlet poppies.

I came here to remember,
to think of death and duty,
of young men dying,
of pain and suffering
and women crying;
to stand head-bowed
in a silent, mourning crowd.

But these pavements are packed
with living, breathing people,
walking, talking, waiting
like some nervous flock,
for a clock to strike a reminder
of one more eleventh hour
to a war-worn world.

Sad music drifts with the mist,
'Nimrod' brings tears to my eyes
and someone behind me sobs,
while from a line of leafless trees
starlings rise in a chattering swirl.
I realise there can be no dead silence
for the living, and whisper my thanks.

Remembrance
Anthea Symonds (SDWC)

Iris opened the front door; outside the freezing rain which had persisted all day was turning slowly to snow. London snow, falling with a grey viciousness. It was only just gone four o'clock but it was already turning from dusk to evening. The yellow light of the street lamps picked out little piles of frozen slush in the gutters. On the pavement people hurried by, heads down against the barrage. How different it had been a year ago; November 1918, the armistice, the year the war ended. Then the streets had been filled with cheering hysterical crowds shouting and singing.

She turned to the woman who was buttoning up her, shabby, shapeless, black coat in the hall behind her.

'Snowing again,' she said.

The woman raised her head, her dead eyes looked through her. 'You're sure it was him and he's all right, he's happy?'

'Oh yes it was Michael all right, he had a message for you didn't he?'

The woman's face was a mask. She pulled on her hat until it covered her forehead. Then she opened her large, scuffed handbag and took out an envelope which she laid on the hall table.

'Thank you so much Mrs. Tavistock-Langley,' she said, 'I feel better now, the money's all there.'

'He saw you there last week, after the service, watching the parade, he was there too, marching with the rest.'

The woman tried to smile but her badly fitting teeth just joggled in her mouth. She stepped out into the foul evening. Under the light outside the tobacconists next door Iris could see her friend waiting for her. They linked arms and walked slowly away towards the bus stop, their heads close together.

They usually came in twos. All women. Over the year she had been doing this lark she had only once had a man come to one of her séances. Pulling her cardigan close to her, she went back inside. There was an hour before the next one. She lit the gas mantle and poked the fire.

The sheer blank misery and hopelessness of the last one had unsettled her. Why should it?, she wondered. She'd been doing this now for the past two years. It was easy, well, easy compared to the jobs she'd had in the past it was. Waitressing had been the hardest. On your feet all day, always smiling and constantly burning your hands on the handles of the teapots. But when she first worked in the tearoom it had been bliss compared to the factory. The buses had been the best. But even then you were either too hot or too cold and running up and down the stairs played hell with the backs of your legs, but there had always been people to talk to and have a laugh with. Especially the soldiers, she'd enjoyed flirting and laughing with them.

'Hey, miss, you going to clip my ticket?'

He'd had a cheeky grin that one, a right Jack-the-lad. Got the bus every day at the same stop, she'd gone for a drink with him, they'd kissed and held hands. For all his chat, he was quite shy, she'd made up her mind that the next time she saw him she'd let him do what he wanted. He was on 'French leave' he said, he'd see her next time, he'd get on her bus. He never came again.

The clock struck the half hour, plenty of time to get ready for the next one. She heard the front door open and footsteps go up the stairs. The new lodger was home, the one who'd taken the upstairs front room. She worked in an office somewhere, one of the new 'business girls' as the

135

papers called them. They had never spoken, just nodded to each other in the hall. Iris remembered that she had gone out to the remembrance parade last week, dressed in a black suit, carrying a bunch of flowers.

Since the service, she had been rushed off her feet with calls. The papers had been full of it, the 'great silence' it had been called, the crowds had been ten deep all down Whitehall. Everywhere the traffic had stopped, there had even been a silence in Streatham, miles from the centre. Then that story had appeared in the *Daily Mail*; a medium had reported seeing and photographing a column of the dead marching down Whitehall each carrying their name on a placard in front of them. After that she had to turn them away. Today she had seen five women and it was not yet five o'clock. That would be ten pounds she had got today. Ten pounds! It would have taken her three weeks to earn that in the teashop.

The last woman's mask like face flitted across her memory, her whisper,

'He was all I had. His father died before the war.'

People were already saying that everything in their life was dated by 'before the war' and 'now it's over'. The woman had looked like the last century, she had noticed that too. It was as if there were two tribes now, those who were 'before' dressed in the old way, and those like her in the upstairs front, with shorter skirts and hair were already in the next. But upstairs front had lost someone too, she remembered the suit and the flowers, but had nevertheless moved into the 'now it's over' tribe.

What about me? Am I a 'before' too? I'm already thirty-two, unmarried, and unlikely to be now there's no men left. Wonder how old upstairs front is? Bit younger than me but not much. Looks younger because of her clothes and hair and she's had an education. Not like me, left school at twelve and out to work as a tweenie in that horrible house in Crouch End. But then she doesn't earn ten pounds a day, does she? Wonder how long it took the last one to get the two pounds for a consultation? But she got what she paid for didn't she? Suddenly she felt bone-tired; just one more to see today, then rest, open a bottle of stout.

She was thinking too much, she told herself, pull yourself together. The gas mantle hissed, she turned it down and lit the candles, they would just about last the day, must have candles to set the scene. The door knocker clanged three times, she pulled herself up: just this last one to go.

Over the top! She straightened and went to open the door. The snow had now turned to sleet and in the yellow light it fell in straight lines on the two women who stood there. They both had large black umbrellas which blotted out the light from the street lamp. Department store types, she judged, the ones that looked you up and down judging your worth as you went in. Made you feel scruffy.

'Mrs Tavistock-Langley?' The darker and taller one of the two was the first to speak, 'My friend here, Mrs Wilson, has an appointment with you.'

She spoke with a shop voice, carefully practiced to sound her aitches clearly. They were both still in their business clothes, dark suits, skirts just below the knee, fitted coats, strap shoes with a heel, and the new hats which looked like upturned dishes on their heads. The other one, the one for the consultation, was younger, fairer, rather pretty, she looked nervous and her hands were constantly twisting, she wore a wedding ring. Married and working – a young widow.

Iris was uneasy, they made her feel like those department store assistants always did. She forced her voice to sound strong and authoritative, she looked straight at the dark one.

'Perhaps you would like to wait here while I consult with Mrs Wilson.' She gestured towards the hall chair and opening the parlour door, she directly addressed the fairer woman, 'In here, please, Mrs Wilson.'

'Do you want me to come with you, Cyn?' The dark one asked her without looking at Iris.

Iris said sharply, 'I think it's best if I see Mrs Wilson alone.'

Still the younger woman did not speak but she turned and went into the parlour. Iris closed the door and pointed her towards the chair.

'Please sit down. Now, did you bring something belonging to the departed as I asked?'

'Yes, I brought this,' she drew from her handbag a small oblong box. 'It's his darts. He always played with this set, wouldn't use any others. Took them to all the matches.'

A darts player, went out a lot to pubs with mates, probably a drinker.

'What was his name?'

'Jack. He was in the London Rifles, joined up with a load of them from the darts team. He was reported missing in June 1916.'

'Have you heard anything more?'

'No, that's why I've come to you. Missing, believed killed it said. Some have had letters telling them that they're buried in such and such cemetery but I've heard nothing. It's the not knowing, it's been over three years now. He must be dead, mustn't he?'

After her previous silence the words seemed to fall over themselves to be said. The shop voice faltered tripping over the last aitch.

Iris looked directly into her face. The eyes anxious and pleading but with no trace of the unutterable grief she had grown to expect. She saw fear overlaid with hope, but not grief. She had known there was something different about

138

the two of them when she had opened the door. This one needed Iris to tell her that he was dead, not happy in a better place, but never to return, dead.

The woman rushed on. 'The papers had a report the other day of some soldier who had been reported missing believed killed, but he had turned up. He walked all across France and came home to his family. The army does make mistakes, doesn't it? I've got to know.'

Her voice trembled slightly and she swallowed. The silence between them was touchable. She rushed on again, the words falling from her,

'Then someone at Pontings told me about you.'

'You're there, are you?' She was right, they were Kensington shop girls.

'Yes, I used to work there before, they were so good when Jack went, offered me my job back for the duration. My friend who came with me, she works there too.'

'Have you any children?'

'No, we had a little girl but she died just after we got married. Scarlet Fever, it was. Didn't have any more after. Jack wasn't that bothered, he had his job at the docks and he liked to be with his mates and his darts, but I'd have liked another one; it would have been company for me. Just as well we didn't, though, as things turned out.'

'Now the war's over will they keep you on?'

The woman hesitated then looked straight at Iris, her eyes narrowed, she took on a more confident air,

'Well, as a matter of fact a chap at work wants to marry me. He works there too, in the office. He was wounded early on and demobbed with a pension because of his leg. If we do get married, we'll have that and his money and there's this government dowry too.' Her voice which had softened and steadied, now became raised and anxious, once more she appeared on the edge of tears.

'But I'm still in the dark about Jack. I can't stop thinking that he might come back'.

Iris returned to the thoughts that had engulfed her earlier as she had sat by the fire waiting for the last one to arrive. The woman's words battered her. Iris understood. Here was one of the luckier ones, a survivor, she would have a husband even if he was a cripple. She had moved to the 'now it's over.' It was the 'before' she wanted dead and buried. Before the war and Jack, before the lonely marriage and the death of the child. The war had rescued her.

Iris stood up and stretched out her hand.

'Well let's see what we can see shall we? I'm sure we can get a message from Jack.'

Wooden Shoes
Steve Brodie (external short story competition highly commended)

The pigs were feeding. They snuffled around Rose's legs, the deep grunts of the sows and the high-pitched squeals of the piglets in happy harmony. It would soon be that time, the time Rose dreaded and the time Rose lay awake at night looking forward to with silent screams of excitement. The time of day that she couldn't bear but couldn't imagine living without. Sure enough, Mrs Hargreaves appeared at the end of the pig pen.

'It's nearly eleven thirty, Rose,' said Mrs Hargreaves, 'tea urn time.'

Rose shut the pen gate behind her and knocked the filth off the bottom of her clogs by kicking the bars of the pen. She took deep breaths, hoping no one would notice how flustered she was. How flustered she always was at this time. She counted to herself, one, two, three, four ... and then set off up the dirt track to the farmhouse. Sometimes she counted to ten. Sometimes all it took was one.

The animal pens were three hundred yards from the main building. They'd been recently built. It was an arable farm by birth but in times of crisis, and war was the ultimate crisis after all, a nation needed milk, meat and cheese in its belly. There were still arable fields between the pig pens, chicken coops and cow sheds, and the farm buildings. In those fields, men were reaping the hay required to see the animals, well, some of them, through the winter. Those men were the enemy, German prisoners.

He was there, near the fence. She didn't know what excuse he gave. She did know it was the most well

141

maintained fence in all of Wigan. Maybe, after she had gone by, he gave it a kick to give him an excuse to repair it. She put her head down, deep red flooding her cheeks and blood roaring lion-like in her ears. He leant on the fence and in heavily accented English said, 'Hallo, little vooden shoes. How are you today?'

She'd already taken in his form, his face, his shock of blonde hair while walking up the path. Now, she stared doggedly at her clogs, carefully placing one foot after another, pleading with her liquid knees not to give in. She looked up to check that he was still watching her. He was and his face broke out into the warmest smile she had ever seen. She did not think it were possible, but her heart beat even faster. She permitted herself a little smile and walked on.

Mrs Entwhistle, the farmer's wife, was waiting for her in the yard at the back of the farmhouse. Hot tea was steaming in a milk urn. There was a jug of milk balancing on top and seven sturdy white mugs hanging off hooks on the back of the small, two-wheeled trolley the urn was sat on.

'Have you run?' the farmer's wife inquired.

Rose stammered that she hadn't, it was a warm day and the pigs had been particularly lively.

'It's a shock for you spinners, working the land, isn't it?' said Mrs Entwhistle. 'Do you the world of good getting fresh air in your lungs. Have you heard from Cyril since he went back?'

Rose felt waves of nausea at the mention of Cyril's name. Guilt, she realised. Usually no one asked how your fiancé heard from Cyril since he went back? There was a jug of milk balancing on top and seven sturdy white mugs hanging off hooks on the back of the small, two wheeled trolley the urn was sat on.

'A letter,' said Rose. 'He seems in good humour.'

Rose thought back to Cyril's last visit. The chirpy

extrovert, her young fiancé had signed up straight away, seeing the war as a way out the grim drudgery of the Lancashire coal fields, had been replaced by a silent man. The stillness around him created a barrier Rose could not get past. He drank all of his money and smoked furiously, as if he resented the presence of oxygen in his lungs. On the day of his return to the front, while walking in silence alongside the canal on the way to the railway station, he had pushed Rose to the ground and methodically started to push up her skirts. 'No!' Rose had shouted, shoving him away. 'Not like this.' He had stared at her, through her, beyond her, and walked off to catch his train. He apologised in a letter. 'It's strange,' he had written, 'Here in the trenches I am myself, the man you know, a cheeky chappy. At home, surrounded by the fixtures of normal life, the realisation of the peril while I'm over here overwhelms me.'

Rose pushed the cart back towards the animals' pens. The German was still there, leaning on the fence.

'Just tell me your name, little vooden shoes.'

She said nothing but just as she was past him, she looked back and smiled. The small trolley, diverted from its course, hit a large pebble on the path and one of the wheels came off. Mercifully, the tea urn stayed upright. The German leapt over the fence, collected the errant wheel, and began to screw it back into place. He was so close to her. Rose marvelled at the small golden hairs on the back of his neck and watched fascinated as a trickle of sweat raced from his temple, past his ear, and down to his collar. The wheel fixed, he stood up and their faces were inches apart. Rose, conscious that she must smell of pig, breathed in the hay scent surrounding him and stared into deep blue eyes.

'Rose,' she said.

'Wolfgang,' he replied.

Seconds passed but to Rose it seemed a lifetime.

Neither moved. A voice, the guard, shouted 'Oi, Wolfgang, get your bosch backside back in this field.' The moment was broken. Rose thanked him for his trouble and continued down the path while he vaulted the fence. Rose had never felt so alive.

The farm girls drank their tea clustered around the trolley and urn. 'I need to take most of the pigs to the slaughterer,' said Mrs Hargreaves. Rose was horrified. She'd fed these animals, cleaned them, even tickled their backs. 'Who wants to help me?' Four of the girls said they would but Rose couldn't face seeing her little charges die.

'Very well,' said Mrs Hargreaves, 'Rose and Mabel can stay behind and store the hay bales in the barn.'

It wasn't an easy job. The dust made her sneeze and the hay pricked at her arms. With Mrs Hargreaves out the way, Mabel saw a way to escape for the day. 'It's my time of the month,' she told Rose. Rose was sure she'd said the same not ten days ago but she acquiesced to the girl leaving and promised not to say anything to Mrs Hargreaves.

Later, she was struggling up a ladder carrying a bale up to the barn's loft when she heard a noise at the door. She dropped the bale and turned round, expecting Mabel returning for something. It wasn't Mabel though. It was the German, Wolfgang.

'Hello, little vooden shoes,' he said. 'I have been ordered to bring up more bales from the field to store. It seems you are in charge here. What would you like me to do?'

Rose sat on the ladder step and regarded him carefully. She turned and climbed up the ladder. Once she had reached the loft, she sat, swinging her clogs to and fro.

'I'd like you to leave the new bales outside for the time being,' she said, 'and I'd like you to close the barn door behind you.'

He looked disappointed but walked out of the barn and

144

began to close the door.

'No,' said Rose, 'I meant for you to stay inside.'

The house Rose lived in with her parents and brother shared an outside toilet with three others in their street. Rose was inside the toilet and could hear her brother, Albert, outside in the small yard. He had been drinking.

'I've been in The Bird Inth, and …' he slurred. 'Met one of them guards watching over the Huns working at the farm. Said he'd noticed one of our lasses, *our lasses*, getting right friendly with a German. Said this lass were about twenty, slim, auburn hair, brown eyes. You wouldn't know a lass who looked like that, would you Rose, *Would you*?' Rose felt her stomach heave again though there was nothing else to bring up.

She opened the door and faced her brother. He was still black from the pit, coal dust entrenched deeply in the lines of his face. Rose subconsciously wiped her mouth and her brother's eyes flared with sudden realisation.

'It's not only you they're referring to, you've got yourself knocked up, haven't you?' he hissed. 'How's Father going to take that? A Bosch bastard in the family. Oh wait … hang on … he didn't … he didn't force …'

Rose's cheeks reddened and she couldn't look him in the face.

'No,' she said, 'It were me that chased him. After Cyril's last leave, I just wanted some joy, some love, *summat else*!'

She thought of her father who still worked down the mine though his lungs now rasped with the sound of emphysema. He was a quiet, dignified man and the shame she would heap on his family would most likely kill him off. Her eyes filled with tears. Her brother was hopping with rage. At one point he raised his foot and Rose could see he wanted to plant his heavy pit boot into her stomach.

'There's you and your Cyril,' he said, a sob catching in

145

his voice, 'Both got Germans trying to screw you. Well I'll tell you this. The guard I met was an evil piece of work. Said he was looking for any excuse to bag himself a Bosch. Frustrated that all his prisoners were happy with their lot, out the war, getting fed and the other guards treated them as mates ... you've just handed him his excuse. This news'll be all over Wigan in no time and he'll hear of it, you can be assured of that. And when he does, he'll visit merry hell on your kraut. The poor sod will wish he'd have caught a plumb one at Ypres, you mark my words.'

'What can I do?' Rose wailed, 'what can I do!'

Albert calmed down and seemed to sober up.

'We'll sort this,' he said.

Albert took her to a house a couple of streets away. Rose didn't know who lived here. The front step wasn't as scrubbed as others in the street. The windows seemed darker. He rapped hard on the door and after a pause, a short, ill-kempt elderly woman appeared. She said nothing, just regarded them.

'This'un needs sorting and sorting sharpish,' said Albert and turned on his heels and left Rose behind. The woman stood aside and gestured for Rose to enter. Rose found herself in a parlour stocked with growing herbs and earthenware jars. The room smelled pleasantly sweet.

'I'm Evelyn,' said the woman. 'Sit yourself down. How far are you gone, dearie?'

Rose sat on a wooden chair and then burst into tears.

'Six weeks, I think,' Rose sobbed. Evelyn put an arm around her and Rose felt comforted.

'Don't worry,' said the older woman, kindly, 'no poking, no gin baths. I need you to brighten yourself up and go and buy me some flypapers. We'll need quite a lot so it might be better to visit more than one shop.'

The following day, Rose took the short train trip to Leigh, where she was unlikely to be recognised, and bought flypapers from two different shops. Evelyn was pleased when she returned to Wigan and set a large pot to boil on an old rusting cooker. Rose was puzzled but Evelyn told her they were making fly-paper soup. The water boiled and Evelyn skimmed the scum off the top of the boiling liquid and decanted it into a small white jug. Eventually she seemed satisfied and took the pan off the heat.

'What we have here in this little jug, Rose, is arsenic. It's the ingredient they use to kill the flies. I want you to add a couple of drops of this to your food. Make sure it's just a couple. It shouldn't do you much harm and you won't taste it but it will bring on the solution we desire. If nothing happens after a couple of days, increase your dose but be careful. Too much of this and ... well ... anyway, you be sure to let me know how things turn out.' Rose gave her a hug.

Rose went back to her house and began making a broth with some shin beef she'd bought on the way and vegetables from her father's allotment. Her brother had been on an early shift and she could tell from the sweet and sour smell of alcohol that he'd been drinking again.

'Same pub,' said Albert. 'That guard were there too. He's got the Parry brothers involved and you know how mean them lads are. They were whispering but I picked enough up. They're looking to take out your lad at the weekend and they're going to make it nasty. Parry brothers have got hold of some dynamite from the pit head. I'd tell your chap to try to scarper. Better getting shot than what these lads have in mind. I know he's the enemy, but no man ...' his voice trailed off.

Rose tried to imagine what her life would be like after the war. She'd be with Cyril, if he survived the trenches, the Cyril from his leave, not the Cyril she first knew, and he would go back down the pit. She thought of her mother, joyless and ground down by the hard life of a miner's wife

147

and looking twenty years older than her age. That was Rose's future. Wolfgang would probably be tortured to death, shot or, if he managed to survive, back in his homeland with a woman who wouldn't be carrying the ghost of what might have been in her belly for the rest of her days. Rose felt a blackness like a yawning abyss in her soul. She finished making the broth and set off for the farm.

None of the other girls liked stacking the hay bales and with most of her pigs gone for bacon, Rose had the run of the barn. As Wolfgang was the German selected to deliver the hay, she also had the run of him.

'Hello, vooden shoes,' he sang as he opened the barn door.

'Hello, Wolfgang,' Rose replied. 'I've a treat for you today. I've made some lovely broth for us to share.'

Back at the house, Albert's mother had found the white jug.

'Do you know where this came from?' she asked. Albert didn't and asked what was in it.

'Nothing,' his mother replied, 'whatever was in it has all gone now.'

The Schoolteacher
Rosemary J Cortes (external poetry competition highly commended)

The turret clock is chiming. Now my company of children
Will fare through field and furrow to their homesteads in the vale,
With scrimmages and skirmishes, while I collect the workbooks,
Place chalk beneath the blackboard and the duster on its nail.

And musing in the twilight, while around me night birds whistle,
I feel your presence by me and believe I touch once more
Your shorn head with my fingers, as we linger in the arbour,
And lavender and roses bleed their sweetness round my door.

My chief among ten thousand, when you looked forth at my window,
I gladly would have left my home and classroom in the dell,
To join the ranks of battle, without counsel or conscription,
To change my quiet harbour for your tent in Neuve Chapelle.

Are you marching to the thunder of cannon and torpedo,
Or driving screaming horses through the mud of no man's land?

Biding sleepless in the trench in the witching hour of darkness,
Would you brave the wraiths and smile if you had me close at hand?

Our lives here in the valley still pulsate to the old measures:
Deeds domestic, seeds of kindness that neighbours try to sow.
My part in battle lies within the book, the word, the lesson,
For I aver that hearts of oak from little acorns grow.

Not mine to ask the wherefores of our young men shot to glory,
No vote or clout possessing, but each day my scholars hear
Of lambs that lie with leopards, in the dawn of that new morning,
When men make swords their ploughshares and forsake the warrior's spear.

The Last Sentry
Peter Martin (external short story competition highly commended)

He was awake before the hand touched his shoulder. A crunch of a foot upon the frosted mud on the trench floor as the figure bent down beside his funk hole. The moon was bright and the snow clinging in patches to the wall of the trench reflected the cold light. It had made an attempt to melt under the sullen winter clouds earlier in the day, but as evening fell the skies had cleared and a polar chill fell along with the moon's stark shine. Layered on top of each stacked sandbag and on the peak of each timber post, frost and ice sparkled in the unchanging white glow.

'Come on, move over, mate, my turn now.'

Corporal Lane's gruff voice was unsympathetic and impatient as he propped his rifle against the frozen trench wall and pulled an extra blanket over his broad shoulders in preparation for sleep. It was more tiredness than noise discipline than lowered his voice to a growling whisper. His stint on watch was over and he intended to waste not a moment of his chance to rest.

Private James clutched the blanket tighter and steeled himself for the cold. His woollen hat was drawn down over his eyes to the bridge of his nose, and his scarf up over his mouth to the edge of his nostrils, yet still he couldn't feel the numbed tip of his nose. A rough slot carved in to the side of the trench and supported by crude wooden posts, the funk hole was cramped and cold. The collection of blankets piled on the couple of hard planks that separated the floor of the hole from the earth beneath did little more to keep him comfy than did the corrugated iron sheet wedged against the roof. It was barely high enough to lie sideways in, and his booted feet protruded from the end of the earth cavern. The fraying, perforated old blanket that had given the slightest air of privacy to the den had been pulled aside by Lane, who, having now adjusted his headwear in to a similar configuration to James, was preparing to roll his substantial trench-coated mass into the funk hole without further delay – and, apparently, regardless of whether its current occupant had yet gathered the courage to emerge. James sat up and heaved himself off the hard planks as Lane sat down beside him and rolled in to the space in a single motion, vanishing in to the shadow of the hole and pulling the old blanket across his body. A shuffle and a muffled cough followed briefly before his friend settled rapidly in to silence.

James stood alone in the trench. His well-adjusted eyes could make out much in the moonlight, and with nose stinging and eyes running from the sharp air, he shuffled his way towards the firestep a few paces along the trench. Avoiding the duck-boards that had turned from sodden wood to frozen bars of slippery ice, he dug his booted feet into the narrow, crunching channel of half-frozen mud running between the boards and the back wall of the trench. Rifle slung over one shoulder, gloved hand bracing him against the earth and timber posts on the rear wall, his feet ground and slipped on the frost-hardened slime and earth.

As he rounded the corner of the trench to turn towards the fire-step, one foot fell unexpectedly lightly on soft, spongy fabric. Quickly stepping back, he glanced down, expecting to be sworn at by a sleeping comrade, but was surprised to see a square foot of neat, clean carpet stretched over the floor of the trench in front of him. He stared at it for a minute, his muddy boot mark staining the pile of the cloth – it must have been found in a house and bought along by a carrying party to line the trench floor. A shame he hadn't borrowed it as a small mattress for the funk hole.

Sighing again with tiredness, he continued his shuffle towards the firestep. Here, the front wall of the trench had a step hewn in to it, allowing the sentry to climb three feet above the trench floor. He placed the butt of his rifle on the step and leant the heavy muzzle and long, rattling bayonet gently against the front side of the trench. He was too experienced – perhaps cynical – an old soldier to feel nervous about his head emerging over the parapet, but he nonetheless stepped up quietly and carefully, gently raising his eyes over the uppermost sandbag.

For all his experience, a glance in to no man's land never ceased to raise a sense of awe and gravity. Beyond the frosted sandbag, confused tendrils of barbed wire sparkled in the moonlight, adorned with a stubble of delicate ice crystals. The shell-scarred land beyond stretched in to darkness towards the German trenches, hidden some five hundred yards distant behind the gentle slope of the land. Silent in the stillness of the night, countless hundreds of the enemy lay, sleeping cold and uncomfortable. Somewhere, also, stood their sentries, and perhaps, just perhaps, somewhere in that littered confusion of crater and rubble, crept a sniper or a raiding party, slipping slowly forward to find British blood. His eyes and his ears strained and searched the black horizon beyond, the steam of his breath drifting away through the twisted wire.

That crude wasteland that extended beneath the shivering dome of stars, he mused, was the gap between two warring empires, between two ways of thinking, between two alternative futures for mankind. Frank James was a patriot, and for all the cold and discomfort he protected a stoic belief that he and his friends were here for a reason. His gloved hands felt their way up and over the sandbag, and he tantalised himself with the thought that his fingers were hanging over the very frontier of civilisation itself. He was the last sentry on the fighting edge of the Empire. Beyond in the darkness lay …

He stopped in surprise as his fingers reached dry, painted wood. Not cold or frosted, but a neatly cut bar of fine timber, painted white with glossy paint that glowed steadily in the starlight. He had seen all manner of debris used to line and repair the trench, but that really was odd. Perhaps it was found in that old farmhouse a couple of miles back, or maybe …

'Frank?'

The voice called out from no man's land, a high and distant call, like a boy. Without thinking his hands snapped down to heave his rifle from its resting place, and flung it to his shoulder in a single reflexive motion. Leaning back to balance its weight, he thrust the muzzle through a gap in the wire and squinted over the sights in to the darkness beyond. His thumb instinctively ran over the safety catch, forcing the oiled lever forward. The weapon was already in its cocked position, and the undimmed steel of the exposed bolt gleamed silver in the moonlight, protruding past his face in stark contrast to the blackened metal of the rest of the Lee Enfield. Its mass against his body was reassuring as his heart pounded and adrenaline surged. His eyes flicked left and right across the dim horizon.

'Halt! Who goes there?' he whispered harshly.

In the chilled blackness, his straining eyes settled on a smudge of yellow light. He brought the squared iron sights of the rifle round sharply to bear on it. The pale, flickering glow wobbled unsteadily between the dark posts of the gun-sight. Showing a light? In no man's land? Someone must be mad.

'Frank? Frank, are you alright?'

The whispered voice again called from the emptiness beyond the wire. His breathing quickened and his heart pounded with panic and confusion. It was a woman's voice. He tightened his grip on the rifle, depressed the

154

trigger until it was a hair's breadth from its firing pressure. Distant beyond the rifle the light hovered, framed in the rifle's sight.

'Who goes there?' he shouted, the tension pressing his face against the wooden butt of the Enfield, the fear cracking his voice.

The light – a light on a post. It was a gas lamp, glowing warmly beyond the trench, its light reflected on the neat, painted timber of the window frame on the edge of the sandbag. His aim shivered and tears of incomprehension and despair welled in to his eyes.

'Who – goes – there? Damn you, I'll shoot!'

'Frank – Frank!'

His wife's gentle hand slipped up and over his shoulder, and he turned sharply from the bedroom window, eyes wide with fear, panting for breath. He looked at her eyes, awake with concern and love. The beautiful features, that precious photographed face that he had stared at through so many months in the line. Soft lips that spoke of safety, of warmth, of comfort. Shining fronds of scented hair hanging limp over her forehead. His wife, his Edith, mother of his child, his best friend in all the world. A vision of peace, of beauty, of salvation. He turned and grabbed her and held her tight to him, burying his face in to the shoulder of her soft, warm silken dressing gown as her arms extended calmly around him. Sweat and tears soaked in to the fine, smooth fabric as he gave muffled sobs, and she clutched her arms around his weeping frame, holding him still and protected as the fear and delusion melted away.

Outside in the lane, the gas lamp flickered in the gentle breeze of a May night, shining through the opened curtain in to their comfortable little bedroom. It was 1921, and, holding Edith's hand as they descended the stairs for cocoa, Frank James stood down from another sentry duty.

Second Skin
Dawn Smith (SDWC)

If they had bound my eyes
and led me across the ground
I would have found you,
drawn by the scent at the back of your neck.
Muddied or soaped,
liced or unbitten,
warm or stiff-dead.

But they didn't.
They wrote, quite politely.

Then the boy came from the regiment.
I can't call him a man.
Soft growth on his chin, just fledged,
raw from scraping in cold bowls on steel mornings.

I asked if they had found you face down.
His eyes grew round. How did I know?

If I had told him I noticed the change in scent
from the back of your neck
while out in the garden, nose to the coast,
he would have fled.
Witched.

So I smiled, said there was a fifty-fifty chance;
and led him to a bed.

Bewildered by my need to breathe him in

he lay quite still,
almost an infant curled upon the sheets.
His hair was damp.
There was salt between his shoulder blades.
His soft, strawberry birthmark seemed sweet.

I rolled away,
sucked air out of the room.
I wondered when, in politeness,
I could ask the boy to leave.
I had no clue about such things.
But he slept.

I crept to your old cupboards,
grabbed soft handfuls: shirts, vests.
Buried my head,
Touched sleeves, collars.
Failed to weep.

Old friends looked down from dusty shelves
but didn't judge.

The Purple Poppy (A tribute to animals of war)
J.J.Moffat (SDWC)

Recruiting for the First World War was something pigeons, cats, dogs, and horses were not prepared for and neither were the glow worms or the slugs. Millions of animals were taken from the comfort of their homes to join the army. They marched beside soldiers, bewildered, frightened, and without choice.

In France, trenches soon became infested with thousands of rats, breeding young ones and spreading disease. And so it was, 500,000 cats were employed as ratters. Many a man welcomed these creatures, not just because they killed the rats, but they raised morale which helped temporarily to relieve the stress of war. Quite often, when the sound of the guns blasted above them, the cats lay with the dying soldiers.

Above the trenches, come rain, wind, or snow, soldiers on horseback raced to the front. Over a million mules and horses had been deployed from Britain alone, with the rest being shipped from North America at a thousand per week. Eight million horses died during the Great War, mostly from war wounds; foot rot, influenza, ringworm, starvation, and gangrene. Hunger was a major problem, so sawdust was added to their food to slow down digestion. And despite all their efforts, these brave animal soldiers of war, often succumbed to the relentless bombardment and suffered from debilitating shellshock.

Once again, when threatened by mustard gas, the army turned to animals for help. They tested many of them for the detection of gas but they all failed, with the exception of the innocent garden slug. Why, may you ask? Exposed to mustard gas, the slug closes its breathing aperture, so protects its lungs. Recruited immediately and without training, they were marched to war!

Back in the dark, dank trenches, winter loomed with the promise of being the coldest that France could ever recall. Soldiers struggled to read their maps and letters from home and morale was low. Then along came an enormous army of glow worms. Not your average soldier by any stretch, but they proved their worth by joining the ranks and living in jam jars. It seemed that nothing could escape this terrible war!

Soon, the trenches, built from sandbags and wood, were occupied not only by soldiers, but cats, glow worms, slugs, and dogs. It is no wonder that typhus, dysentery, and cholera soon followed. The unsuspecting dogs, once someone's pet, were trained as messengers and enemy detectors whilst others became mercy dogs on the battlefield. Carrying medical supplies in a box attached to them, these brave canine soldiers sought out the wounded and dying. Sitting beside the bloodied men, their cries merged as one.

Americans didn't use dogs, until they discovered a stowaway on board one of their ships. That dog, 'Sergeant Stubby' became the most highly ranked and decorated service dog in military history. Around a million of these dogs died in action.

The war was not only being fought on the ground, but up in the sky where pigeon 'spies' flew between France and Britain and frontline trenches. Strapped to them were messages, vital to the soldiers. These amazing birds (100,000 of them and probably more) fought the enemy falcons, released by the Germans in the battle of the sky. These birds of prey could bring the pigeon spies down when all else failed.

And so this bloodiest of wars, with a total loss of more than nine million soldiers, not counting civilians and the animals that supported them, ended at 11 o'clock in the morning of the 11th day of the 11th month in 1918. But for the animals, their war was far from over.

The National Archives in Kew, London, tell a sad tale of thousands of animal 'soldiers' left behind at the end of the war, in the hands of Belgian and French butchers. The same thing happened after WW2. Churchill was furious when he heard of their plight and arranged for their safe return home.

In November 2004, Princess Anne, the Princess Royal, unveiled the Animals in War Memorial in Hyde Park, London. This was designed by an English sculptor to commemorate the animal soldiers that served and died under British Military command throughout history.

At the going down of the sun, we will remember them.

To count the dead
Bob Lock (SDWC)

Will no one count the dead?
In blood and bile scrawl numbers?
In shrieking wails anoint each bloodied head?
Chase broken limbs, to return them from whence they
fled?
And still no one counts the dead?

Day ends with gasp and unbelieving cry
For fields, where seeds and fruit grew, now yield a bloody
crop
And clouds shield a sorrowful moon in a bewildered sky
As only men find reason, cause, or flag, by which to die
Whilst the dead remain uncounted, where they lie.

Stars volunteer a bejewelled abacus
For those who wish to reckon the fallen host
In darkness the deed is done with little fuss
From scornful view the counting is hidden thus

But Nature watches Man with baleful eye and silent cuss
Wonders why in a human soul this practice is inbred?
What brings a mind to war or a heart to kill?
To cut the fragile strand of life like a piece of thread?
And from Earth's sweet bosom take all; leave nothing in
its stead?
Only those who have the nerve …

… to count the dead.

Twisted Thorn
Lynne Lomond (SDWC)

'There's a letter for you from Henry.'

Rose rushed downstairs and saw the longed for regulation envelope on the hall table. She took it to her room to read it in private, although she could sense her mother's anxious curiosity. It seemed so long since Henry had happily set off for what he saw as the adventure of a lifetime, terrified it would all be over before he could get out to the front. Less than a year ago, in March 1915, he had presented himself to the colonel of a newly forming regiment, armed with a letter from the sergeant major of the army cadet corps he had attended at school, it seemed so recently. In a few weeks he had been sent for training, told to get his hair cut, made lance corporal, and in the shortest time promoted to sergeant. After some months of training he was off to France.

It had been a joy to both families when the mutual attraction between Rose and Henry had begun to be obvious. Their parents had been friends since schooldays and their mothers had been delighted when their babies had been born within six months of each other. To the surprise and delight of all, the family joke that they would grow up and fall in love had turned to reality. Still too young for a formal engagement, they had nevertheless been allowed much of the freedom of a betrothed couple, both sets of parents trusting them not to abuse it.

They all felt a sense of pride when Henry announced his intention to join the army and fight for his country, the day he was legally old enough. Only in the privacy of their rooms did both Rose and Henry's mother shed tears at the

162

thought of his departure. On his final leave before sailing for France Rose and Henry had sworn their undying love, with many tears and passionate kisses.

Rose carefully slit open the envelope with her silver letter opener, shaped like a miniature sword, a parting gift from Henry.

He was full of cheer! *'We are kept very busy with wiring parties, patrols, and minor skirmishes. Last night we went on a raid up to the wire but something went wrong and it had not been cut. It was very exciting. We lost a couple of men but luckily most of us got back safely. You are not to worry about me, my dearest. I will soon be home with you, everyone says it will be over soon, and then we will be married. I think about you all the time.'*

When Rose went downstairs she could see her mother was longing to read the letter but realised it would be unlikely that Rose would suggest this.

'He's quite happy, Mother,' she said casually. 'He sends his love to everyone and expects to be home before too long. He says we will be married when he comes home!' She certainly wasn't going to let her mother see the passionate words with which he had ended his letter and had added the last bit to distract her. But her mother was far more excited by this news than she had bargained for.

'Oh, my dear!' her mother exclaimed, 'In peace time we would have expected you to wait a little longer to announce your engagement, but war changes protocol. I am so happy for you both, and your Father will be delighted.'

Although it had been taken for granted they would one day marry this was the first time anyone had put it into such explicit words. It seemed she wasn't even going to get the chance to say 'Yes!'

Later on she sat down at her little writing desk to

answer him. She imagined him, handsome in his uniform, bravely leading his soldiers into danger but careful to shield them from the worst of it. How she missed him and the happy times they had spent together. She told him how pleased her mother had been to hear of his proposal, about the new novel she had started reading, how proud she was of him fighting to protect all of them and ended with expressions of love only a little less passionate than his own.

Her mother told her the Red Cross were holding sessions in the village hall to knit socks and roll bandages. They went along, anxious to do their bit.

'Can you teach me to knit?' Rose asked the woman in uniform who took their names at the door.

'Can't you knit?' asked the woman in a mildly scornful tone. 'I haven't got time for that now. You can roll bandages.'

Rose joined a number of woman at a table heaped with a tangle of bandages of varying widths. She listened to the chatter and was soon being asked about herself. She felt proud to be able to tell them about her brave Henry.

The women came from different parts of the village and she had seen some of them at church but there was no one she knew well. They all had someone at the front, a brother, a father, a sweetheart, and she began to sense that her cheerful pride was not shared by them all. Some of them had received letters telling of life in the trenches, the mud, the water up to their waists at times, the long fearful hours of waiting, the shortage of food, the stench of rotting bodies. Her romantic view of her Knight in Shining Armour began to be a little shaken.

Nevertheless, the next letter from Henry shocked her to the bone. '*It's Hell out here, Rose, I am in Hell! Hell is not fire and flame, it is the ghastly smell of foul water up to your knees or worse, your body filthy for days on end, hunger, thirst, terror, perpetual terror. I don't know what to do, Rose. I can't bear it. A German soldier came across no man's land this morning and someone gave him a cigarette. He was just like me or the other men! How can I go and kill him tomorrow? This war, what is it for? I don't even understand. I can't bear it, Rose, I can't go on!'*

She was surprised the letter had got through, but the woman at the Red Cross had said censorship was not very thorough as yet. She wouldn't want anyone to read this! She felt sad for his suffering, but a little ashamed, too. They must all be going through the same conditions but she had never heard anyone else speak of this. Surely her Henry wasn't a coward! How could she tell her mother or father! Whatever would they think? She considered burning the letter, but in the end locked it in her treasure box. Not that anyone in her family would read a private letter without permission, she knew that. Perhaps she was hiding it from herself!

Next day, rolling the eternal bandages – she had found a woman in the village who was teaching her to knit but she was nowhere near good enough yet to join the knitters – she casually, she hoped, raised the subject of life in the trenches.

'Don't you think the men must sometimes wonder what it's all for?' she ventured, tentatively.

'They'd better believe in it, otherwise they'd go barmy!' a woman called Moll spat out.

'I think some of them do question it,' the vicar's wife said thoughtfully, 'but once they are out there, what choice do they have?'

'They'd be shot as cowards if they tried to run away,' said Marj.

'Quite right too, when men's dying to save us,' Moll returned.

'Would they really be shot? If they couldn't bear it?' Rose asked, shocked.

'Unfortunately, yes,' said the vicar's wife. 'Even if they

start to question the rights and wrongs of it, once they have enlisted they have to go through to the end, theirs or the war's. My husband was fortunate to be a man of the cloth, otherwise he would have been a conscientious objector and gone to prison.'

'And been despised for ever more!' returned Moll. 'Lucky he was a vicar then!'

'That's better than being shot, anyway,' said Marj.

Rose was now feeling deeply disturbed. Whatever was going to happen to Henry? She waited anxiously for his next letter, racing to the hall every time she heard the postman. Days went by with no news. The women reassured her that letters sometimes did not get through straight away. She began to feel sick with anxiety every time she left the house, as if being there would make the letter more likely to arrive. Her terror was that he had somehow disgraced himself, run away or refused to fight, and she was desperate to know if relatives would be informed of such a thing. Surely his parents would let her know if they heard anything! She went to see his mother, who greeted her with a hug.

'My dear, my future daughter-in-law! We are so pleased, though surprised Henry hadn't told us. Still, who knows what is going on for the poor boy. I hear things are terrible out there! But whatever happens, he now has the two of us to love and care for him.'

Whatever happens! Care for him! She imagined him with bits missing, covered in bandages, bravely grateful as she tended to his every need. The idea horrified her. This was worse than the disgrace. She wished she had kept quiet about the marriage proposal, if that's what it had been.

'Have you heard from him? I mean, when did you last hear?' she managed to stammer, hoping the shock in her voice would seem like the most natural concern.

'Not for a while, my dear, but please don't worry so. I

166

feel sure he will come home to us, and now he has so much to live for.' Her voice shook a little despite the supposedly reassuring words. Rose was far from reassured. How could she bear this waiting? She went home even more disturbed.

The waiting was broken by a telephone call from his mother.

'Now sit down, my dear, I have something to tell you,' came her gentle voice.

Panic rose in Rose's throat.

'You've heard something! Tell me! Tell me!' But she really wanted to put the phone down and run somewhere where none of this was happening.

'Yes, we had a telegram. Believed Missing In Action. But this could be that he is lying in some field hospital with no identity tag. So don't give up hope, my dear. We must pray and hope that he is still alive, that we will hear so before too long.'

Missing in action, wounded somewhere, or missing in hiding, having run away? Was that possible? Would they tell his family if it were? She didn't know how to find out without giving away what she knew, that he had said he couldn't bear it. But there was no doubt now, he was either a deserter or badly injured and she didn't know which would be worse.

She couldn't eat, she couldn't sleep, she couldn't tell anyone what she was really feeling. The weeks dragged on and she got through the days by being busy, practising knitting every hour until she was good enough to join the knitters, going to the new first aid classes so she could help in the hospital, pretending her concern was only for her beloved and hating herself for her true feelings. At last the inevitable call came from Henry's mother. Her mother answered the telephone and told Rose that she was to go over to Edward's house as soon as she could. It was the hardest walk she had ever taken. To her amazement she was greeted with joy.

'He's alive, he's alive, they're sending him home!' His mother hugged her painfully hard, all her pent up terror of the past few weeks which she believed Rose shared, released in the emotion of that hug.

'How badly is he hurt?' It was all Rose could think about.

'He was lying in a shell hole for two days before he was discovered,' his mother explained. 'All his identification had gone, and he was unconscious and delirious for all these weeks, but his injuries were not life threatening. He was very, very lucky. One of his legs was partially shattered but they managed to save it, although of course he will always have a severe limp. And he is blind in one eye, but that is all! And of course, he won't be fit to serve again, so he is safe!'

Her love for her son was so apparent. As long as she had him back, these injuries were nothing, and supposedly she was assuming Rose felt the same.

Rose was numb. The romantic, naive girl who had loved her handsome soldier had gone for ever and she no longer knew herself. Could she still love this shattered, disillusioned man who was coming home? Would they even know each other? Could she hide her lack of belief in him, her fear that he was a coward, her terror that she would be in honour bound to a deserter? Could she live with herself, knowing she had doubted him so?

It was still some weeks before he could be sent home but at last she received that long awaited letter. Her feelings as she opened it were so very, very different from those when opening that last shocking one. But his for her seemed unchanged.

'*My Rose, it seems as if you are the only thing that has kept me going. Your beauty of face and soul, your pure heart and my knowledge of your love have been like a bright flame amidst the horror I have been through. I pray*

168

your love will be my salvation, and help me to heal. I so long to see you and hold you. It won't be long, my darling, and I know you are longing for our reunion just as I am.'

She sat at her writing desk, pen in hand, staring at the sheet of thick, cream paper on the blotter in front of her. She wrote her address and the date in the top, right hand corner then paused again. She could so easily reply lovingly as he would expect from that girl to whom he had written, pretending she was still that girl. If she ever had been. Maybe they had each been in love with a romantic fantasy, and he was still seeing her that way.

But how cruel it would be to shatter his illusion now, when he needed something to live for, something to get him through the last few days or weeks. Eventually she dipped her pen in the ink and wrote quickly, almost unthinking.

'Dearest, I am so relieved to hear at last. I have been in a state of terror ever since your mother told me you were missing. She was overjoyed to hear you are safe. I can't stop thinking about the terrible time you have been through, and what it must have done to you. I only hope this ghastly war has not changed all of us beyond recognition, and that it ends before more and more young men are slaughtered. Thank God you were not one of them and are coming home to us to heal.'

At least that felt honest, and hopefully encouraging if not overly loving. Now she must wait.

It was a relief to go to the Red Cross group. She felt a degree of closeness with the women in the knitting circle she had not experienced before. Her old life felt so superficial now. Even before the war several of them had experienced hardships she had seen only at a distance and she understood their contempt for people like her, who had never known poverty. But now that was part of another life, and here they were equal in their anxiety and their comfort for one another. It was not only those who fought

169

who had changed. To her amazement, she found herself confiding in them.

'I'm frightened of seeing him, I'm afraid I won't feel the same,' she blurted out after telling them he was safe.

'That's only natural,' said Marj. 'You're young, you weren't even married. 'Course you feel anxious, like.'

'Don't know what his injuries might have done to him,' said Moll, and Marj nodded, clearly the same thoughts in mind. 'But you'll have to go through with it, whatever.'

'Well, of course! She wouldn't desert him after what he's been through!' Marj was clearly shocked at the implication that Rose might.

The vicar's wife spoke up. 'God will give her strength. He knows both their hearts!'

So that was it then. She had no choice. She would be despised as a deserter, just as she had in her heart despised him when she thought he might be one. She had never thought deeply about God, going to church because that's what you did on Sunday, so she could not count on Him being there for her. That would be hypocrisy too. Well, she and Henry would just have to find a way through it together.

A week later his mother phoned.

'He's on his way. Come over, my dear, so we can be here for him together, all of us!'

Rose realised his mother was anxious, too. She called her own mother and they walked across to Henry's home. It would be easier for that first meeting to be with his family.

After all, they would be her family from now on.

170

Battle of the birds
Shirley Anne Cook (external poetry competition highly commended)

They waited in line
chirping the old familiar songs,
a real feast of a dawn chorus.
Those with the brightest
plumage puffed out their chests,
and gave the orders to fire.
Soon feathers flew,
the chirping replaced
with squawking and screeching.
One by one the birds fell.
Even the old guard toppled
off their perches.

When the slaughter had ended
an eerie silence reigned.
Shell-blasted craters were littered
with bodies, bird on bird,
eyes sparked out
beaks still standing to attention.

Mother, please don't cry for me
Bob Lock (SDWC)

Mother please don't cry for me, for I have gone.
My pain's embrace has left, though you feel it still.
Turn your anguish to joy, for I am at peace.
In our trench's arms I lie; a sweet release.

And softly then the tender rain falls like blood
Upon our upturned faces that see no more.
Lovingly sweeps the red mud from sightless eye,
With purest tears wrought from God's own summer sky.

And our trench fills with a profuse torrent then,
Carries remains of its hopeless protection.
Earthen walls, sandbags and bodies, everyone
Seeks to escape the carnage we have become.

We're but empty vessels of our former selves,
The flow that seeks to wash away our remains
Blushes as it turns an even redder hue.
Shamed witness of those who know not what they do.

Mother, the foe were like us; all someone's child.
No malice in their hearts; there was none in ours.
Around their feet I beg you, let no blame pool.
Cheap were our brief lives; sent here by those who rule.

We were as but leaves on a great tree grown old.
But as the leaves fall, so shall the strong oak too,
Weakened, helpless to stand against folly wind,
Roots consumed from within by men who have sinned.

Leaders who knew the cost in our blood and lives,
At their spotless boots must all blame be now piled.
Vain, they called the piper, bade us pay the tune,
In granite should their shame be forever hewn.

So to grave we go; I hope for the best cause.
As symbols of the imprudence of conflict.
Peacefully safe with our friends, men: brave and true.
War that took so many …
… begun by so few

Man of the House
Fiona Riley (SDWC)

When Father left for war, Mother wept,
fussing with cap and collar
like she was afraid to let go.
Proud grey eyes twinkled
as he made me man of the house.

He fought at the front, so I carved myself a rifle
and lay safe in dry ditches, reading letters
giving lie to the horrors of the trench.
No hint of the stench of the dead and dying,
lying strewn over mud and barbed wire.
No sign of the fear and pain, it's now plain
were his constant companions.

We baked cakes and drew pictures to send
with socks and soap, in the hope
he drew comfort from the familiar.
We wrote that everything in the garden was rosy
because here, far from the madness, it was.

Father came home a broken man, and Mother fought tears
as I, stick-whittled rifle at my shoulder, gave a sharp
salute.
I'm going to be a soldier one day, Father, just like you.
His voice is a whisper squeezed through dry, cracked lips
Yes, my son, I rather fear you will.
Haunted grey eyes stare to the distance
and I know I am, forever, man of the house.

Paying the Price in the Great War
Marlene E. Harris (SDWC)

The Black Hand assassin his trigger did pull,
to kill a royal archduke and his wife.
His dark deed sparking a crimson flame,
fuelling anger to the Austro-Serbian strife.

And with so many European countries
living in a state of frail and fragile peace,
a mighty hell broke loose on its troubled lands,
unleashing an unstoppable brutal beast.

One great empire thus fought against another,
fighting frantically, forward to the fray,
whilst the Great War was surely coming closer,
with armies of millions heading far away.

For a first day's work in the British army,
a shiny shilling was paid out by the king
to khaki clad troopers so eager and willing,
to risk their young lives for country and kin.

And as the Germans rushed in so eagerly
on Belgian's neutral soil to seize and invade,
Britain stood proud for them to guard and protect,
now in the war for the brave actions made.

Our planes, submarines, and fleets of navy blue
faced fierce flack, fighting the enemy bravely back,
on war-torn ground in a relentless, endless fight,
with men blown to bits by the dreaded booby trap.

In bloodied, muddied trenches on foreign battlegrounds,
hungry eagles searched among the stench of death
in the muddy soil turned beetle black with blood,
from the shattered shrouds of the maimed corpses left.

Four years of dire destruction the war ensued
in, rivers, hot deserts, ice, snow, swamps and shores,
with the din of warfare and screams in dark nights,
against smoke screens, gas, shell-shock, and gore.

The fight at long last came to a victorious stop,
when on the west front German retreat was made,
with admission of defeat, and an Armistice signed,
our memories of the dead and decorated ne'er to fade.

Thus the crimson red poppies of Flanders fields,
remind us of the life and blood that was shed,
when our brave troopers fought so relentlessly
for a future generation to look ahead.

Tracks
Alan Bryant (SDWC)

The last mortar blast missed Ted by about ten yards, showering him with another coating of mud. Then silence came, as it always came. Sunday mornings at eleven o'clock in the Somme could seem, well, if not heavenly, at least somehow spiritual. If Ted had been a religious man he might have thought God was responsible. He supposed that, even though everyone blamed the Kaiser, in a way God was responsible. Being God, He could do anything. So why didn't He stop this bloody war? Everyone stopped for Him. Wherever they were, generals stopped for brandy, officers stopped for tea, the soldiers stopped and prayed. They all stopped, except for the snipers whose eyes peered through the drifting smoke, their expectant fingers caressing warm, polished triggers. But in the bunkers, in the trenches, and even beneath the ground in the tunnels they dug to plant explosives under the enemy, they stopped. And they prayed for mankind, all mankind. Then they lit the fuses and blew each other to pieces.

The Germans were in a trench fifty yards away. Between the two armies lay a torrent of rusted barbed wire. Any minute now the birds would come back to peck at the flesh that hung from the barbs that dripped and fell to feed the mud that was France. Private Ted Ellis took a long sniff through his blooded nose and noted the increased level of cordite in the air that day. There was another smell too. A few days earlier a horse had been shot nearby. It lay in a bomb hole about twenty yards away and was starting to decompose. The stench wafted over him on the wind. This war was not for cavalry, thought Ted. This land was not for horses any more. Also carried on the wind was a distant rattling sound that came and went with the weather. He wondered about that.

Looking around in the trench for something of interest to pass the time he noticed a finger sticking out of the mud. He bent to pick it up. It was not unusual to find bits of bodies about the ground. He wondered if it was British or German. He wondered what it had done with its life, what it had seen, where it lived. Did it once caress a lover? Ted's own sweetheart was waiting for him to return home.

He closed his eyes and breathed deep again, remembering how she felt in his arms that last time; Mair was soft and smelt of warm currant cake and Sunday teatimes, and sometimes all he wanted was to hold her and melt into her. Sometimes in the quiet times, like this, with time to think, he wanted to run and run till he ran back to her arms.

He looked at the finger again and thought about what would happen when the praying stopped, and the distance was measured to be right, and the fuse lit, and all those little pieces of flesh, bone, and soul would come raining down on them once more.

In the beginning he had been frightened. Now, life was no more than an acceptance of awaiting anonymity. Today he was here. One day he would not be here.

Ted relaxed against the wet clay of the trench wall and looked up at the sky that began to drench down on him again. And he wondered what was different about this Sunday.

There were no birds today.

But there was a noise, nearer now. A horrifying, metal-crunching evil, clattering noise, and then a roar roughly punctuated by a banging, spluttering cough that might have come from the depths of Hell. He recognised the sound, and it wasn't coming from Hell, nor from the German side so it must be from some sort of back up, he thought. If he was inquisitive enough or stupid enough he would have looked over the trench. But Ted was neither of those things, which was why he had stayed alive this long. The noise stopped. Ted waited a few minutes, then, only to amuse himself, he threw the new-found finger high in the air. Two quick shots from the snipers sent it spinning away. It would keep them satisfied for a while, and Ted settled himself into another state of boredom.

From his left now came a splashing sound, then his name sirened through the stillness.

'Private Elliiiiiiiiiis!' When the sergeant spoke to inferiors his voice could rise to a tonsil-splitting pitch at the end of each sentence.

'Yes, Sarge?' Ted looked over to the mud spattered sergeant. Amid the anarchic geography of foxholes the man was a rock. Sergeant Tudor bristled with bayonet and trouser-crease authority. Sergeant Tudor was a man who fought wars. He sought wars out. In his opinion there were not enough wars to keep a real man occupied. The day the Second Boer War ended the sergeant had cried inward tears. At home he was the husband of a shrew wife with two daughters, all of whom, it appeared to the sergeant, showed their sole and combined purpose in life to be grinding him into shivering surrender to female authority. Sergeant Tudor needed this war to re-establish not only his manhood but his reason for living. If no one had shot the Archduke Franz Ferdinand the sergeant would possibly have taken on the role of assassin himself. His finger beckoned Ted to the tarpaulin-covered office of the captain.

Rifle in one hand, and pressing his helmet tight on his head with the other, Ted ran crouching to the entrance of the hole in the ground that was the trench command hut. The sergeant barked again. 'Private Ellis, who is in charge of entertainment this Christmaaaas?'

To Ted, this seemed an odd question, it being only

September, but he answered. 'Private Mardew, Sarge,' he said. 'He's on tunnel duty today.'

'Bloody Mardew,' said the sergeant. Then he paused in thought a moment. 'Didn't you tell me once you could ride a bicycle, Elliiiiiis?'

'No, Sarge, I said Mardew could ride a bicycle. I pushed a wheelbarrow in the market.'

The sergeant was not one for mechanical details. 'One wheel, two wheels, all the bloody same, Elliiiiiis.' The voice rose and held the note with choral precision.

'Yes, Sarge.' Ted soaked up the remark with a trained and accepted yielding.

'Follow me,' said the sergeant.

Private Ellis followed him into the gloom. The rain battered against the canvas roof. Sergeant Tudor stood erect beside the captain who sat at a makeshift table. A hanging oil lamp reflected the pallor on the young officer's face as he struggled to fold up a huge grey blanket. Large applique shapes were stitched to it. On the table was a book titled, 'Great Tapestries of even Greater Wars'. Ted saluted, the captain shrugged.

A movement caught Ted's eye in the darkness of the small dug-away corner of the room. He could make out the shape of a man cloaked in a rain cape sitting on the floor.

Sergeant Tudor turned to the captain who was still folding the blanket. 'I think he could be our man, sir. Obviously has an engineering background.'

The captain looked at Ted. 'Haven't kept pigeons by any chance, have you?'

'No, sir, but my sister has a very popular pussy.'

'Less your insolence, Elliiiiiis,' barked the sergeant.

'Yes, Sarge,' said Ted.

The captain was young but already the enthusiasm of youth had been worn from him, and he was left with only an oblique concern for life's continuing madness. 'Would Private Ellis's sister apply in this case, sergeant?' he asked.

'I don't think so, sir,' said the sergeant. 'In my experience that whole area has a proven history to disappoint, sir.' The sergeant had been known to leap unarmed into trenches and frighten the enemy into surrender with a single, meaningful roar. However, when faced with any mention of the female form his uncontrollable instinct was for retreat into solitude. He took a small, involuntary step backward into the darkness. 'Anyway, sir,' he said, 'he's all we've got, what with everyone else praying and stuff.'

'Suppose so,' said the captain, and he rose from his chair. There was no attempt to camouflage the weariness in his voice. He walked to the side canopy of the office. 'This could be your chance for immortality in silk thread, Ellis,' he said. And with a small crochet hook, he folded back a portion of ripped canvas. 'Do you see that out there?'

Ted Ellis peeped through the ragged hole to the mud sea of the battlefield. 'Do you mean that leg, sir, the one still in the boot? Standing up in the muck?'

The captain eased the tarpaulin a little further to one side and looked through. 'No not the leg, man. That … over there, that … thing.'

'You mean the tank, sir?'

'Have you seen one of these machines before, Private?'

Ted nodded. 'We had them in Courcelette, sir. But they were males. Is this the female version, sir?'

'Male?' said the captain.

'Female?' said the sergeant, and took a further step back.

The corner shadow was lit up by a match setting light to a pipe. The scent of expensive tobacco came puffed, curling through the dampness. When the man spoke his voice aired the usual refinement heard only in officers' speech, but there was something else too, Ted thought, a

181

trace of an accent, possibly European. The man said, 'So, Private, you know what tanks can do.'

The captain took another look through the ripped hole. 'Do you mean to say they can actually, you know, actually … increase? Gosh, this war could really be over by Christmas, eh, sergeant?'

The sergeant's brow furrowed deep with the thought of approaching domesticity and all it implied. His imagination wandered onto the intricacies of mating machinery, and he tried to shake that too from his mind. With some reluctance he leant across to look through the hole in the canvas to see the machine. 'Where's the wheels?' he said.

'Great morale booster,' said the captain.

'I can't see any wheels on it,' said the sergeant.

'Male and female, amazing,' said the captain. 'Great Britain does it again, eh, sergeant?' His voice began to rise with the faintest surge of child-like excitement. He brushed his tunic with his hand as if to find some past vestige of vanity beneath the debris of war and weather and clinging apathy.

The pipe-man spoke again. 'They're machines, they don't mate,' he said.

There was silence as the words were digested by the men, the mood, and the mud.

'We call them male and female because one is smaller than the other, that's all,' he said. 'Each machine has a motor producing over one hundred horsepower.'

The sergeant cleared his throat. 'Talking of horsepower, sir, what about the cavalry, and the horses?'

'For the Christmas show?' said the captain.

'No sir, just thinking to myself, if we have these tank things, would we still need the horses, sir?'

'Probably not,' said the pipe-man.

'No cavalry?' said the captain. 'That won't be popular.'

'We could sell the horses to the French, I suppose,' said

the sergeant. 'They'll eat anything.'

'And the Norwegians,' said Ted.

'Are we at war with Norway now?' said the captain.

'Not that I've heard, sir,' said Ted, 'but Amundsen took dogs to the South Pole and then ate them.'

'Damned cannibal,' said the captain. 'Outrageous.'

'Whereas, sir,' said Ted, 'Although Scott did have some horses, they were foreign, so of course they weren't up to much.'

'Of course,' said the captain.

'All that garlic and stuff,' said the sergeant.

'So he mostly relied on machines with his lot,' said Ted, 'and they never got back. You can't eat a machine, can you, sir?'

The sergeant stiffened to what he considered to be true British rigidity. 'I hate to admit this, sir,' he said, 'but Private Ellis could be right about that.'

'Could be,' said the captain. 'I have to admit to not knowing much about these tank things.' He looked about the room as if to find direction from anyone available.

The pipe-man spoke again. 'Each tank has a full complement of eight men and two pigeons. I'm one pigeon short. Dashed thing died of fumes, or fright, so I'm looking for one more – or a runner.' The pipe pointed at Ted. 'Can you run, private?'

The sergeant splashed to attention. 'He can do better than that, sir. This man can ride a bicycle.'

Ted's mouth opened with the intention of correcting this last statement but he was deterred by the sergeant's tonsils again.

'Shardaaarrrrp!'

'Yes, Sarge!'

The pipe rose up. Its tobacco embers glowed, giving a red shine to the smooth though indistinct features behind it. It belonged to a man well over six feet tall. He wore a waterproof cape that reached the floor. It was obvious to

Ted that this was not standard army issue. The man walked slowly toward the captain, and from beneath his cape, brought out two envelopes. He handed them to the captain then his hands disappeared beneath the cape again. The captain took the envelopes and with some ceremony laid them side by side on the table. To Ted, the man with the pipe seemed to hover back to the corner with soundless ease.

The pipe-man turned to Ted mid-hover. 'In a short while, your captain will give you one of these envelopes,' he said. 'Take it back to the adjutant, and be as fast as you can.'

'Yes, sir,' Ted saluted.

The pipe-man made an odd hampered movement beneath the cape, then turned and levitated into darkness.

The three men stood looking at the envelopes in the grim light. After about a minute the machine roared and clanked again. The noise grew louder and when it seemed it would self-destruct, it rattled away. The ground shook and trembled with the spite of an earthquake seeking revenge for the sins of man that had turned nature's pure soil into a pock-marked, poisoned swill.

Ted stood listening, and guessed it was about fifty yards away towards the German line when the motor seemed to scream as if in fear of eternal damnation. The ground shook and jolted the three men to the floor. Next came the blast that mushroomed up and out and through the tunnel being dug by Mardew and his lads as the tank fell through into the dig, detonating the explosives. Ted, the sergeant, and the captain scraped, clawed, and fought their way out of the mud grave that wanted their ultimate sacrifice and found themselves back in the fume-swirling trench.

Kneeling in the water, the captain struggled for air. He held out an envelope to Ted. 'Take this to the adjutant,' he said, and pointed. 'Go that way.'

Ted took the envelope. There was no feeling in his hand, nor his legs, nor anywhere in his body. The sergeant took hold of Ted's shoulders and turned him to face in the right direction.

'Run,' he said. 'Ruuuun.'

Ted ran. The bullets zipped and spat and cursed around him but he ran and staggered and fell and ran again. The rain pelted down and hissed in steam as the rounds fired through, and all the time Ted kept on running.

'Run, Elliiiiis. Ruuuuun,' shouted the sergeant. 'And when you get there, come straight back. From now on you're in charge of Christmas entertainment. Bloody Mardew. And don't you come back without a bicycle. Now you run, hear me? Ruuuuun.'

But Ted could hear nothing. And he ran as though the very blast itself was carrying him along in its rage. All around him the earth exploded, erupted, and shamed the world with its lack of hope or love. He saw a hand landing in the mud in front of him. It might have been his hand. Ted never stopped to check.

The scent of warm currant cake and Sunday teatime swum through his head and filled his senses. Far off in front of him was Mair. Her arms were held open, spread wide in expectant embrace, waiting for him to come back, to melt into her.

Mercy Dog
Annabelle Franklin (SDWC)

He never knew exactly what injuries he'd received. The pain had been monstrous, immense, involving most of his body; now it had passed, leaving him in a state of dreamlike calm.

He could no longer hear guns or shells; an unearthly quiet had settled around him. He felt as if his churned-up flesh had become one with the churned-up muck on which it lay. The night sky seemed very close, and he could still see the stars when he closed his eyes.

'Am I dreaming?' he said, not sure if he'd spoken aloud.

'No,' said a soft, gravelly voice on his left.

Unable to move for the past few hours, he now found he could turn his head. Next to him crouched a dark shape. A ripple of anxiety invaded his calm.

'I thought I was alone,' he said.

'You're never alone,' the shape replied.

'Who are you?'

'Open your eyes.'

'They are open. I can see the stars and I can see you. I just can't see you properly.'

'Believe me, your eyes are closed.'

The voice carried a quiet conviction. An unbidden memory came to him of home, of his mother waking him up on a spring morning, urging him to walk the dog before he went to school. He could see the sun shining redly through his eyelids, feel the soft embrace of warm blankets seducing him back to sleep, sense the patient presence of Shep beside his bed, waiting to welcome him to wakefulness.

'Open your eyes,' the voice insisted.

He obeyed, half-expecting to see his sunlit boyhood bedroom, only to find himself still out here in the dark, miles from hope or help. But the darkness was no longer total. A gentle golden light shone from somewhere behind him, revealing the shape on his left to be a dog – a Border collie, with Red Cross saddlebags strapped to its back.

'Mercy dog,' he whispered.

'Yes.' The dog's mouth hadn't moved, but the voice had come from its direction.

'You can speak,' he said.

'Yes,' the dog replied.

'And I'm not dreaming.'

'No.'

He felt a stab of fear. 'Then I must be dead.'

'Not yet,' said the dog. 'Not quite.'

'But soon?'

'Yes.'

He kept his eyes fixed on the dog. The wisdom in its eyes allayed his panic.

'Did you take away the pain?' he asked.

'I did,' the dog replied. 'It's what we're for.'

He remembered it was the Germans who had first trained dogs to carry medical supplies on the battlefield.

'They're not all bad,' said the dog.

'What?'

'Germans. They're not all bad.'

'I know.'

The numbness was seeping away. He still felt no pain, just very cold. 'How is it,' he asked, voicing a thought that had troubled him since schooldays, 'that a handful of bullies can get so many other people to do their dirty work?'

'They have help,' said the dog.

'Help? Where from?'

187

'From behind the scenes of this world.'

'From the Devil, you mean? I'm not sure I believe in all that tosh.'

'Oh, it's real, all right. Maybe not in the way people think, but there are certainly spiritual forces behind the workings of this world. Whether they know it or not, bullies and warmongers align themselves with titanic forces of darkness that give them the power to achieve things they could never manage on their own.'

An icy chill crept through his shattered bones. Damp vapours drifted upwards, swirling lazily in the night air. 'I don't want to die,' he said, his eyes pleading with the dog's gentle gaze. 'Can't you save me?'

'There is no need for fear,' said the dog.

He felt his life shrinking around him, his memories fading, until it seemed he had never been anything but this patch of mud and mangled flesh. 'Is there an afterlife, then?' he asked.

'There is no before or after,' came the answer; 'Simply life. Consciousness never dies.'

His vision misted over and the dog's form became hazy; only its eyes remained clear. 'Are you here to take me to …?' He couldn't finish the sentence.

'No – I have other work to do. But there's no need for fear. Dying is as natural as waking up in the morning.'

Warmth entered his heart. He thought maybe the golden light was coming from a fire – he saw sparks rising into the sky and felt his lungs fill with smoke. Each breath was a conscious effort.

'Is it time?'

'It is time.'

With one last long outbreath he felt himself expand outwards and upwards, filling the night, effortlessly shedding his personality along with his ruined body. The vague sense of inferiority that had plagued him for most of his life, the attachment to home and family, the secret and forbidden love for his captain, the resentment at being sent into danger and death to fight a war he didn't understand for a country that abhorred and vilified people like him – all those things that had mattered so much were wiped out as if they had never been.

And yet he still existed. He was the earth and the trees, the stars and the sky – and himself. In that eternal moment of profound peace, he was more himself than he had ever been in his short, sad life.

Consciousness never dies.

Red Cross casualty dogs, also known as Mercy dogs, were first trained by Germans who equipped them with saddlebags of medical supplies. They sought out the wounded and gave comfort to the dying.

Source: http://www.examiner.com/article/dogs-of-modern-war-part-2-world-war-i

Verdun
Shirley Anne Cook (external poetry competition highly commended)

Walk as far as you're allowed.
'Interdit. Verboten. Forbidden.'
For the grey earth still yields
a deadly iron harvest.

Stop and gaze around.
You'll see green undulating hills,
but they were not always there.
A hundred years ago this place was blasted
with explosives and millions of shells.
In their wake a desert terrain
of pockmarks and craters,
brimmed with soldiers' shattered remains.

Go there today and remember,
those lush mounds shroud a living hell.

Silhouettes
Alan Murton (external short story competition highly commended)

James stood outside the recruiting office shifting from one foot to the other. The poster announcing 'Kitchener Needs You' was the reason he was there. At just sixteen he would not have received his call up papers for another year and even then, as a farmer's son working on the land, he might have been exempt from military service. The call to arms was an exciting challenge to him, he led a dull life on the family farm in the windswept hills of Lancashire, there was no prospect of his ever seeing anything of the world – he and his father scratched a bare living from their farm. He'd wanted to try for a job in the cotton mills in the nearest town but his father would not hear of it and his mother pleaded with him to stay at home.

He knew he was risking his father's wrath and his mother's tears but he'd made up his mind – it was the army for him and that was that. He went in to sign his papers. The recruiting officer ignored his patent lie about his age, sent him for a medical, and by the time he caught the bus home he'd already been enlisted in the county regiment, the Lancashire Fusiliers.

'Where were you this afternoon – I near enough broke my back hauling all those spuds in on my own – you're an idle sod sometimes lad, where did you get to?'

James took a deep breath and looked down the supper table at his father, 'I went to Preston to join the army.' He stopped waiting for the storm.

'You did what? You bloody fool … you would never

have had to go … any way you aren't old enough by nigh on a twelve month so they can't take you … we need you here I'm getting too old to manage this place on my own … I'll soon sort this out, I'll get down there myself and show them your birth certificate, that'll put an end to your little games … look at your mother there, crying streams – this could be the death of her …'

The would-be soldier found courage he didn't know he had, 'If you do owt to thwart me, Father, I'll leave home anyway and go off to work in the mills like I've always wanted and you'll never see me again …'

Tears still streaming his mother crossed to him, 'What have we ever done, Jim, to turn you against us so – why are you doing this to us? Why, oh why? Listen to your father; please don't do this to us …'

'I'm sorry, I knew that 'twould be hard to tell you, but I didn't want to leave home in the middle of the night and you not know where I'd gone … I didn't want to upset you but there's this terrible war against Germany and I want to do my bit … they say there'll be no peace in the world again until Kaiser Bill is beaten. Mum, Dad, please understand what I'm saying – nearly all my friends from the village school have been called up and I want to join them … I'd call myself a coward if I didn't do my share …'

'Yes son, and there's telegrams nearly every week saying that one or other of those friends is missing, dead, or hurt bad …'

There was a long silence, just the crackling of the fire in the kitchen range. James' father held his wife close before he said, 'You always were a headstrong young bugger, Jim, but I suppose we have to give way to you this time. It is a noble cause and God willing it'll be over long before you have to go to the trenches. I'll not stand in your way, truth be told I'd rather lose the war than lose my only son …'

All three were in tears as James' mother fetched the pie from the oven.

The following morning James helped his father with the milking before he changed into his Sunday suit and picked up the case he'd packed the night before. His parents came to the door to see him off and stared after him until he disappeared down the lane.

James walked the three miles to the station to catch the train to Lancaster. The booking clerk looked at his warrant, gave him his ticket, sighed, and said, 'I wish you the best of luck – you are no more than a boy but England needs brave boys like you ...'

Three months of military training and discipline later James was packed with thirty other young soldiers into a lorry which dropped them at the troop train on the start of their long journey across the Channel to France and the trenches. James had found life harder than he'd expected and the rigorous routine of those training months almost broke his spirit. He managed to say little about the hardships in his letters home. He showed aptitude as a marksman and was chosen to be a Lewis gunner, one of a two-man team who learned to fire the machine gun from its tripod on the ground or from the hip as they charged forward.

'You look after that weapon, Henderson,' the sergeant instructor told him, 'Your mates in France will be glad to see you come with it – they're new and the boys out there need all the firepower going to mow down the Huns ...'

The trenches sucked the strength and morale from many years older than him and there was no time for settling in; he had to learn to cope with the mud and the wet that was all pervasive in the rat-infested warren of burrows dug into French soil. The first battle of the Somme was getting towards its climax so there was a constant smell of cordite, the bombardment from the artillery of both sides was incessant, and it seemed that there were more and more names missing at roll call each night.

James woke from the sleep of utter fatigue and prepared to face the day. They were going over the top again; it was to be the last push to drive the enemy back from the river. He put on his steel helmet, checked the magazines of bullets for his Lewis gun, and cradled it in his arms. The silence in the narrow slit of their forward position was broken only by the noise of bayonets being fixed, rifle bolts ramming home a cartridge into the breach. Dawn was just breaking when the whistles blew and the soldiers, like robots followed their young officers out of the trenches and into the maelstrom of shells and bullets as they charged forward guns blazing ...

James stood at attention in the line-up for the medal presentation. The December breeze fanned his face and the sun reflected off the dark glasses which shielded his sightless eyes. He was dressed in his khaki uniform for the last time. Soon he'd be on his way to the care and training of a St Dunstan's home for the blind and a lifetime of finding his way around the world with a white stick.

He felt the grip of his guide tighten as the general officer commanding, Douglas Haig, stopped in front of him and the regimental sergeant major read the citation:

'To Private James Henderson of the 1st Battalion, Lancashire Fusiliers, the Military Medal for his bravery on 29th October 1916. Despite a continuous bombardment from the enemy artillery Henderson remained at his Lewis gun post and maintained covering fire for the attack which saw the retreat of the German Army from the Somme River to their trenches in the Hindenburg.'

He felt the general's hands on his battledress blouse as the medal was fastened into the serge.

'Well done Henderson, England is proud of you ...'

James felt the tug on his left cuff, the signal for him to

salute the officer.

The presentation party moved on; there were more medals to present, but the curtain had come down on the last act of James' military career.

He wished that he could leave the barrack square for the quiet of his billet but he knew that he was expected to stay at attention until the band played the national anthem, after which they would lead the parade to the barracks, playing the regimental march of the Lancashire Fusiliers.

He hated the loneliness of his blindness – he hated more the pictures that came flooding in when he was left alone. The images tormented him by day and by night and as yet he'd not found how to block out the sights and sounds of the years since he'd lied about his age to the recruitment officer.

As he stood waiting for the order to march off his mind wandered back to the day that condemned him to the black world he now lived in. He remembered looking from the foxhole he had scratched in the mud at the winter sun setting low over the battlefield and the last things he was ever to see, just a collection of silhouettes … of the barbed wire defences and the obscene attitudes of the bodies of soldiers caught in the web to die there, piles of abandoned equipment, the burnt-out shell of the tank, in action for the first time …

The mortar bomb which burst in front of him may have deprived him of his sight but it had burned those silhouettes into his brain to torment his every waking and sleeping hour …

Reconciliation
Sue Shannon-Jones (SDWC)

'Olive, where's my clean apron – I have to be opening the shop in five minutes.' David Jones – known in the village as Dai Butcher – called up the stairs to his wife.

'Where it usually is, Dai. Next to your lunchbox in the kitchen.' Olive sighed; this was a daily ritual, it was as if he needed the reassurance that she was still there looking after him. She heard the front door slam as Dai left the house in his usual haste. A hard working man and popular in the village, Dai always had a jolly smile for his customers, each of whom believed they alone were favoured and got the best cuts of meat. It's just as well they don't see the other side of him, she thought, what a temper he has, though it was rare he would lose his temper, to be fair. It was when he was arguing with Jack, their son, his usual ruddy complexion would take on a crimson hue and he would wave his large hands in the air as if they could somehow drive some common sense into Jack. Father and son had parted after the last row silently resentful and each one stubbornly refusing to acknowledge the other. As she thought of Jack a small tear threatened to escape. She missed Jack so and worried about him, longing for him to come home safe and sound. Olive finished making the beds and made her way down to the kitchen to start on the washing and cooking. The stove would take some time to warm and there was bread to bake. She thought herself lucky to have such a well-equipped kitchen that was large enough for the family to sit together to eat. It was the heart of the household, Olive's only regret was she did not have the large family she had hoped for. There was just Jack and his twin sister Nancy, who worked with her father in the butcher shop. When Olive and Dai had married she was just eighteen, they had planned a large family, but it was many years before Jack and Nancy made an appearance, and Olive was told then, there was no hope of any more children for them. It was a blow at the time, but over the years they had come to terms with the fact that their family was complete. Olive assumed Nancy would marry in the next few years and have a household of her own to run, then there may be grandchildren to look forward to. At seventeen, however, there was no sign of romance in the young girl's life. Nancy had declared that she had no interest in marrying just because it was expected, she wanted to have more freedom to choose her own life. She and Olive had clashed many a time over the issue, it was unheard of in their small village that a young woman would not want to marry and have a family of her own.

'Hello Mam.' Jack was standing in the middle of the kitchen smiling at her with his lopsided grin and crinkled nose.

Olive just stood there for a moment not believing what she was seeing, how could it be her Jack?

'Why are you here? We thought you would be gone longer, did they send you home? Are you in trouble?' She looked anxious for a moment wondering what Dai would say if Jack was in trouble.

He had said so in that awful row they had had before Jack went marching through the village with his friends on their way to the training camp. They had both been in some temper at that time and some dreadful words had been spoken. Dai could not believe Jack was old enough or responsible enough to go and fight for his country. He was convinced it was only because his friends were going, they had all egged each other on without knowing exactly what they were getting into. Not that Dai had any idea himself, no one did.

'No Mam, I'm not in any trouble.' Jack's voice was gentle and reassuring. 'Where's Nancy? Has she managed to take over the business yet?'

He laughed, knowing his sister was the ambitious one in the family. He, Jack, wanted to read books, study, and travel. It was a dream he had not thought would ever happen for him. For some reason, his father would fly into a temper every time he mentioned going travelling. Until war had broken out, Jack's life had been mapped out for him by his father. He was to learn the business of the village butcher and eventually take over, something that filled him with dread. His sister was far more suited for that, he knew, but his parents would not hear of it.

Olive suddenly leapt up from the chair she had gratefully sunk into.

'Goodness, there am I just sitting around and you just home, you must be hungry, I'll get you some food and a nice cup of tea.'

She started bustling around the kitchen.

'There's no need, Mam, I'm fine honestly,' then, 'when will Dad be home?' There was a tone of something Olive couldn't quite put her finger on in Jack's voice, it wasn't anxiety or resentment, but – something.

'It's half day today love, he'll be home soon.' Olive's tone was conciliatory, she didn't want the rowing to start up again; it had almost come to blows the last time.

She had never seen the men in her life so angry; it had taken all of her peace-making efforts to calm the situation.

'Don't worry, Mam,' Jack assured her, 'there won't be any problem from me I promise – now I think I will have that cup of tea after all.'

Jack sat quietly in the corner of the kitchen watching his mother work; he said little and answered her questions with little real information.

'How is Sidney?' she asked, 'Did he come home as well?'

'Sidney is fine Mam, just fine, but no, he won't be home just yet,' Jack told her.

Jack and Sidney had been inseparable since they were toddlers. They had been born within hours of each other, and Olive and Gwen, Sidney's mother, had become firm friends, helping each other with childminding and nursing the boys when they were sick. The boys had shared everything, even the measles. They would often be found in some mischief or other but no one ever knew which one was the ringleader. The boys would be close-mouthed about whose idea the prank was and take whatever punishment was meted out without protest.

When the posters went up in the village and the nearby town Jack and Sidney along with the other young men flocked to sign up. They were all convinced that as they were all going together, they would stick together and would all come home together as soon as the war was over.

'All pals together, anyway, if we go together, we'll come back together. Anyway, it'll be over by Christmas.' Jack had told his parents. 'You'll see, everyone is saying it.'

The people of the village were proud of the young men who marched off so bravely to war. Olive knew Dai was heartbroken, although he hid it under a veil of anger and disdain. He would scour the papers for news of the fighting, but there was little enough of that. A few weeks ago, there was a report Dai had become quite excited about. 'There's a big battle.' he said, 'Somewhere in France called the Somme, we are winning the day.' he enthused. 'It'll soon be over and we can have our boy back home where he belongs.' He gave a small cough, frowned and grunted, 'As he should be.'

The kitchen door flew open and Nancy entered in her

usual noisy, lively, way.

'The shop is quiet so Dad sent me home earl–' For once Nancy was shocked into silence, but not for long.

'Jack!'

She flew toward her brother, almost knocking him off his feet as she slammed into him.

'What are you doing here? How long are you staying? Why have they sent you home? Have you been hurt? Did anyone else come home with you? Are you on a special mission?'

The questions came pouring out without a break, Jack had no chance to answer so he just let her run out of steam.

Dai locked up the shop as the church clock was striking one. He was tired today, and would be glad of a rest this afternoon. In spite of the optimistic reports in the newspapers he couldn't help worrying about Jack and the other boys out there. At night, he lay awake thinking about his only son away in France. In his mind, the world was a dangerous enough place without a war to make it worse. Dai was no coward, he could hold his own in a fight and had proved it time and time again in the village – there was a small community centre where the men and boys would pit against each other in the boxing ring. He usually won, but would also take a rare defeat with a smile, shrugging off the bruises with a nonchalant air. Many a time he was asked to join the team in matches against other villages and towns, but he always refused. He had not left the village since he was a child unless it was unavoidable, the thought of going anywhere away from his comfortable safe life filled him with a dread he couldn't explain to anyone.

He had a vague memory of going on a Sunday school trip when he was very young and getting separated from the rest of his friends. He had no idea where he was or how to get home. Eventually someone – he didn't know who – saw he was very distressed and took him to the pavilion near the beach where lost children were cared for. He was assured by a kindly lady someone would be along soon to fetch him.

Dai had sat in the corner for what felt like many hours, he wondered what they would do with him when it was time to close up and go home. Would he have to try to find his way home? They had been on the bus for a very long time, it would take so much longer to walk, besides he didn't know which direction to take back to his village. Eventually his Sunday school teacher arrived in a fluster, she had been looking for him everywhere and had just heard over the loudspeaker that Dai was in the pavilion.

The memory of the event became faded and fragmented in Dai's mind, but the anxiety and fear of being away from home stayed with him and would become so overwhelming when he thought about going anywhere, he would cover it all up with temper.

That was the cause of the row with Jack the day he came home and said he had enlisted. Dai just flew into a rage, saying things to his son he regretted deeply. He knew in his heart Jack would eventually go from home; he had always been curious about the world and no matter what Dai said to him he would declare that one day he would go to this town, that city, or even another country.

What he hadn't bargained for was that his son would be marching into real danger. All Dai's hopes and prayers were that he would have the opportunity to be reconciled with Jack. As he reached home Gwen came rushing out from next door, she was waving a piece of paper excitedly as she approached Dai.

'It's Sidney,' she called. 'He's in a hospital, he's been wounded but not badly; he has been shot in the arm and shoulder. The nurse who wrote the letter says that he is recovering and will be home soon. Have you heard from Jack?'

Dai told her he had not heard since the last letter a few weeks ago.

'A lot of use that was,' he grumbled, 'most of it had been blacked out!'

'Well as long as we don't get those yellow telegram things, we know they are OK,' Gwen said. 'Someone was saying this morning in the Post Office that three of those had been delivered on the same day in Pentre.'

Dai's heart clenched at this, he didn't want to think about bullets or telegrams, he just wanted his boy home safe. He grunted and made his way to the kitchen door, he was puzzled as he neared the house, he could hear raised and excited voices. Nancy was excitable he knew, but Olive was usually quiet and Nancy would soon run out of chatter when faced with her mother's calm. He hoped they didn't have visitors, he just wanted a cup of tea and to put his feet up for the afternoon.

He was hoping for more news about the war, if the papers were right, the allied forces were winning. As he opened the door, he was greeted with a bombardment of excited chatter from both the women at once. He didn't hear a word, he just stood and looked at his son.

Jack. Home. Safe.

Dai felt weak at the knees for a moment and was on the point of rushing to hug Jack when he pulled himself up short and with great effort, stood his ground and said calmly, 'Hello, son, I see the army has had its fill of you then?'

They stared at each other for a long moment.

'Dad I –'

'Son –'

They both spoke at once, then fell into silence once more. Olive grasped Nancy by the elbow.

'Come on, there's something I want you to help me with upstairs.'

'But Mam I –'

'Don't argue, girl, come on. Leave your brother and father in peace for a while.'

Nancy rolled her eyes, but followed her mother up the stairs. The two men looked at each other. Jack shuffled his feet and spoke.

'Dad, I don't have much time, I really need to tell you how sorry I am for the way we parted. I can understand why you were so angry, but I felt it was my duty to go –'

'No need, son, it's me who should be sorry. I've regretted all those awful things I said. I'm so proud of you my boy, you are brave, braver than most people I know,' Dai said. 'I think we can put all the past behind us.'

They spoke at length, having a conversation such as they'd never had before. They both realised how much they had loved and respected each other over the years, but had been unable, perhaps unwilling to express that to one another until now.

'You know, Dad, I've always had a lot of respect for you, but I really had to go,' said Jack.

'Yes, son, I know. I was scared for you and it just came out in temper. I just didn't want to lose my only son. The heir to my little empire.' Dai smiled wryly knowing this was the last thing that Jack really wanted.

'About that, Dad, why don't you let Nancy learn more about the business, you know she would love to and would be much better at it than me.'

'You are probably right, son,' Dai grinned. 'She already bosses me around, telling me that I should be doing this or that to make the business better. But what will you do once this war is over?'

'Oh, you don't have to worry about that. Dad, I have to go soon, tell Mam and Nancy that I love them.' Jack suddenly stood up.

'They'll be back down in a bit, son, you can tell them yourself. Where are you going? Or aren't you allowed to tell us?'

Before Jack could answer, Olive shouted from upstairs,

'Dai – Dai! There's a boy coming up the path with one of those yellow telegrams in his hand. He's made a mistake, I don't know what poor soul it is meant for, but tell him he's at the wrong house.'

The telegram was addressed to Mr David Jones, it had his address on the front. Puzzled, Dai opened it to see who it may belong to, there were many David Joneses in the area, the War Office must have mixed up the address with another David Jones.

It is my painful duty to inform you that a report has been received from the war office notifying the death of

No: 41987 Rank Pte

Name: Jack Jones Regiment: 14th Welsh Battalion on the 14th July 1916 and I am to express to you the sympathy and regret of the Army office at your loss. The cause of death was Killed in Action.

I am sir, your obedient servant

*(*Here, an illegible signature)

Officer in charge of records.'

There was more, but Dai didn't read any further; this was ridiculous, he would have to inform the War Office they had got it wrong. He went back into the kitchen, perhaps Jack may have an idea who this may be.

Jack was still standing near the window, he smiled his special lopsided smile at his father, saluted smartly, and was gone.

Portrait of the Enemy
Maggie Cainen (SDWC)

Through my half-open eyes I see angels gliding to and fro, their long white wings floating out behind their backs. The light's so bright I can't focus so I sink back into the softness of my fluffy cloud and listen to the hymns sung by the heavenly choir. I know I'm in heaven because I can't feel pain any more and I can hear angels singing. The last thing I remember before I died was a voice whispering:

'You'll be all right, Tommy, keep your hand on this.'

Excruciating pain tore through me. I felt someone pressing my hand down hard on the dressing over the wound in my shoulder. That's all I remember about my death and now I've arrived in paradise I can't wait to meet up with my dead comrades, my old school friends, who all died long before me. They'll be waiting here for me.

As my mind clears details start coming back to me, how I'd sneaked off to the recruitment post before my sixteenth birthday, during the summer holiday in 1914. I did have a birth certificate but I didn't take it, obviously. Anyway I was tall and looked older than my years, working every holiday and weekend on Aunt Lucy's farm and eating all that good food had given me big muscles. The practice I got bringing down crows, magpies, and other vermin to stop them eating the corn had made me a crack shot too. You know I actually got as far as the first training camp but that's where Mum caught up with me. She marched in, breathing hellfire, brandishing my birth certificate. 'He's only fifteen,' she shouted much louder than the sergeant major! So that was the end of that. I

205

made it out here just over a year later though, when I was seventeen in 1915.

Hello, one of the angels is coming to talk to me. Better stop rambling on to myself.

'Well, young man, good to see you're back with us.'

It's a young woman, not an angel … No, it's not a young woman, it's a nun dressed in flowing white robes and some kind of head dress. She's got such a kind voice, with a slight foreign accent I can't place.

Am I a prisoner of war? Am I in enemy hands?

'Where am I?' I whisper.

'This is a Belgian field hospital near Ypres.'

'I'm not dead then?

'Certainly not, you just had a nice long sleep.'

Very gingerly I touch my left shoulder. It's covered in bandages, but I feel no pain.

'Why doesn't it hurt?'

'That'll be the morphine, wonderful stuff, sends you away with the fairies. Let me have a quick check and you can go back to sleep.'

It's dark when I wake again, desperate for a pee. I'm too embarrassed to get one of the nuns to help me with my bad arm, so up I get, blunder around on my cotton wool legs, feeling my way until I trip over something and land on my arse with a loud crash.

'Hell and damnation!'

'Now that was a silly thing to do, wasn't it? You need to urinate, don't you?'

One of the kind nuns gives me a bottle.

'Don't be a silly boy. Now, do you need a hand?'

I blush scarlet, as with a huge sigh of relief I fill the bottle.

'Am I going home, sister?'

'Now why would you need to do that? We'll have you fixed up in no time. Anyone would think you don't like it here!'

And bit by bit as I lie in my lovely clean bed under the care of the angelic nursing sisters I finally remember the nightmare of the trenches and I start to weep. All my school friends gone, most of the officers dead, and I'm wounded and I'm not even eighteen yet, not knowing whether I'll ever use my shoulder and left arm again. Will I lose it, am I to be a one-armed cripple for the rest of my life? How can I become a doctor now?

The only food they'd give me was sweet white bread and milk. I didn't mind at first but I was soon desperate for a bit of meat. I kept thinking about all the rats I used to kill in the trenches. I said I was a crack shot, didn't I? Rats weren't bad to eat, you know. You're probably thinking how could you, they'll eat anything, rats, well they do but if all you've been eating are tins of bully beef you really fancy proper meat, something to chew, it doesn't matter where it comes from. The secret was quickly to chop off their head, tail, and claws and then skin them at once. They taste quite like rabbit when you cook them, especially if you can get hold of some wild garlic and other herbs to flavour it. To be honest we only ate rats when we were literally starving and we'd finished all our rations on the march days before. We'd have eaten anything then; actually we did eat almost anything at times: dead mules, rats, and one day we found a freshly shot horse. It was appallingly hard work marching in all that mud and rain carrying our kit and when our ration and water supply failed men were falling down and dying by the roadside. Do you know we eventually got used to it, we couldn't see beyond the next few minutes.

I can still smell the mud. It's a smell you never forget. It coated everything: boots, battledress, rifles, food and everywhere that god-awful stink. The stench was worst coming out of some of the dugouts in the trench walls: the ones full of rotting bodies and dead mules with that whiff of gas lingering over everything. Our sergeant made us pee on our handkerchiefs and use them as masks when he thought gas was coming. At least we were lucky to miss that so far but we saw what it did to the blind soldiers who were crying and frothing at the mouth, wishing they were dead.

I remember the feeling of huge relief when we were told to go over the top that last time. The waiting had been grinding us all down, making us jumpy. We were running on pure adrenaline; my belly squirmed with nerves, spiders ran up and down my arms and legs, I was pumped up for a fight when we finally marched into no man's land.

Nothing prepares you for what hits you at that moment: ear-splitting noise, smoke, explosions, fire, gunshots and the awful cries of wounded soldiers. You can't see with smoke blinding you, you're deafened by the guns, cannon, and grenades. The gunfire was relentless and my buddies were falling to the left and right of me but I almost reached the enemy lines. I was pushing on looking for a target when something smacked into my left shoulder, a bullet, shrapnel, I don't know. It knocked me flat on my back straight into the mud of no man's land and I hadn't fired a shot.

Apparently I was lying out there in the stinking mud all day and all night long because it was coming up to dawn next day when the stretcher bearers found me right next to the British trenches with a German field dressing covering my shoulder wound. Someone had dragged me back there from the enemy lines. I might have bled to death without that dressing. Much later I found a creased envelope stuck to the blood on my battledress. Inside there was a photo of a pretty girl. There was writing on the back and an address written on the envelope too in continental fashion, from the sender somewhere in Frankfurt, in that spiky, difficult to read German script.

It was a mystery. Had a German soldier helped me? Wouldn't he have been court-martialled for helping the enemy? I tucked the envelope and photograph away in my kitbag and forgot all about them when I went back to England to convalesce.

I was sent to the big house, Thorpe Salvin, near my parents' home in the village of Harthill in the South Yorkshire coalfield. It was being used as a convalescent home. My grandmother had been employed as their cook housekeeper before the war and had stayed on. I'd always wanted to see inside the big house when I was younger, but of course everything must have changed now. All the big downstairs rooms were full of beds. My shoulder wound was healing well they told me, even my feet were growing new skin at last as the blisters fell off, but I kept having nightmares and shouting all night long. They moved me to a little room upstairs because I was disturbing the others. I thought I'd be sent straight back to the front from the field hospital, but perhaps because I was still only seventeen they'd sent me here to convalesce instead. I hated every minute. I was desperate to get back out there to fight and prove I wasn't a coward to my pals, but then I'd remember my old trench mates were all gone: Tim Evans, Jack Snow, Peter Lumsden, Ian Cole, all my old classmates. I really miss them you know. You can't live cheek by jowl with the same crowd without getting to know all their little foibles. You know who farts in his sleep, who snores, who talks in his dreams, who cries. The doctors gave me stuff to make me sleep but it made the dreams worse. I kept remembering the long marches, desperate for food and water and my feet bleeding so much I was too scared to remove my boots in case my feet fell off. Each time we stopped we'd fall asleep still standing upright. Every night in my dreams now I feel the mud creeping up over my face as I'm convinced it must have done in no man's land whilst I was unconscious. Every creak or noise sounds like gunfire to me. Once the doctor's car backfired and I jumped out of bed in my nightshirt and ran screaming downstairs to the coal cellar where I hid behind the coal.

Tomorrow is my eighteenth birthday and I think they're going to send me back to the front again. I know I should be dead. There's still a bullet out there waiting for me, but I have to go back.

September 1916: Conscription came in January this year for fit bachelors aged 18-41. I'm just eighteen now so they're bound to send me back to that hell hole. I'd be better off dead. I'd wanted to be a vet or a doctor when I was back at grammar school. I was a good student too but I couldn't wait to join up. None of us could. We saw all the posters, heard all the propaganda, listened to the old soldiers. All the boys in my class signed on, none of us were eighteen, and now they're all dead except me. We were desperate to do our bit and send the Huns packing all the way back to Berlin. No chance of me becoming a doctor or a vet now. I'll be lucky to survive another week out there.

'Can you drive, Ben?' It's the army doctor who's been looking after me, come to assess my fitness to fight. He's been testing my reflexes and moving my shoulder about.

'You've some splendid muscles on you, young man. Your shoulder has healed really well. I bet you've been driving farm vehicles for years, haven't you? All you farm boys start young.'

'I've been driving horse ploughs and farm machinery since I was ten.'

'Think you could drive a motor ambulance for us? We'll send you on a course, driving, engine maintenance, and some basic first aid. Those new motor ambulances are very heavy to manoeuvre but you should have the muscles for it.'

Is he worried I've lost my nerve? Or is my shoulder still a bit too unreliable to cope with the recoil from firing a rifle? No chance of me being picked as a sniper now.

December 1916 onwards: Driving an ambulance up to the casualty clearing stations proved very dodgy indeed. Those motor ambulances were big brutes to handle, and despite the Red Crosses on the sides and roof we were frequently under fire. You lived on your nerves all the time. Passchendaele in 1917 stands out as being sheer misery as we came under almost constant fire and the jinking about we did to avoid the shellfire hurt our wounded soldiers. I remember one who'd lost a leg and the rough movement set his stump haemorrhaging again. We had to stop to re-dress the leg before he bled to death and give him more morphine, but he still died. In a way it was a blessing, the poor sod had suffered a poison gas attack too and been blinded and couldn't stop coughing.

I still felt guilty about that German soldier risking his life for me by dragging me over to our own side. One of the ambulance drivers told me about a wounded German officer who was tortured for information before they'd treat his injuries. According to that ambulance driver he'd seen it happening before. It's sickening to think that ambulance drivers risked their lives several times a day just to see the men they'd rescued tortured for information.

We ambulance drivers had to drive through fields and acres of deep mud, trying all the time to keep the ambulances steady, not to jolt the suffering soldiers inside. It cut me up listening to their muffled groans, tears, and their involuntary shouts when we hit a rut. I understand now why the doctor had asked me about farm vehicles, that had been excellent preparation for handling those clumsy beasts but I can't help wondering if someone had talked about me in Thorpe Salvin as the sole survivor from my year in the local grammar school and they didn't want the whole class from the village to die.

Do you know that they actually let VAD women drive

some of the smaller ambulances right up to the front? That took guts. It was no picnic for any of us getting the wounded soldiers back from the casualty clearance stations, constantly under fire with virtually no visibility as we struggled along the quagmired tracks.

1920: It's a while since I've had time to write in this notebook just as I remember it. I think I should write about my experiences but still feel guilty that I survived and millions didn't. I've got to do something to prove myself. I suppose it was sheer luck that helped me survive driving ambulances for the last two years that's what made me so determined to train as a surgeon after seeing the dreadful injuries suffered by soldiers during the war. So I left the army as soon as I could after peace was declared. I'm studying hard now but it's tough going back to academic work after three years in action and being treated as an adult.

1930: The years rushed past and I did become a hospital doctor and found great satisfaction in healing rather than killing people. It gave me massive fulfilment swapping my rifle for a scalpel. In between my hectic hospital shifts I thought about the war a lot. Not so much about the wasted lives but more about the survivors' ruined lives, the broken families, the disabled one-armed, one-legged men barely scratching an existence. Ferreting about in the loft one day I came across my bloodstained battledress in a cobweb-covered bundle. As I unrolled it out fell that creased old envelope with the handwritten address on the back and the photo of the pretty girl inside. It made me think of my unpaid debt to the anonymous German soldier. What happened to him after he saved my life, I wondered? Did he suffer repercussions after dragging me back to our lines? Was he still alive today? Morbid curiosity made me start German evening classes when I could manage it with my hospital shifts. The mystery of the words on the back of that photo intrigued me. They're probably all dead now, I told myself, but perhaps I can help anyone still alive in his family. I'd read about the dreadful conditions in post war Germany, far worse than here in Britain.

Summer 1931: It's been a long difficult journey getting here to Frankfurt. I'm there now in my hotel room searching an old street map for Klagenfurt Strasse 9, hoping it's still there and someone knows something about Elise Noll who used to live there and sent her photo to a serving German soldier, who may have saved my life.

I knock at the door, practising my elementary German.

'Sprechen Sie Englisch?' It's my well-rehearsed opening line.

The door opens.

'Yes, I speak English,' replies an attractive, slim woman, followed by a skinny teenage boy. 'How can I help you?'

Mutely I hand over the much creased envelope and photo.

'I sent that to my fiancé Franz in 1916. I'm Elise. Come in.'

For a few moments I'm tongue-tied. The little house is spotlessly clean but sparsely furnished. Elise busies herself making coffee, watched by her silent son.

'He died at Passchendaele, you know,' said Elise.

'I didn't know. I think he saved my life when I was wounded in 1916 by putting a field dressing on my shoulder to stop me bleeding to death. He may have dragged me back to the British lines too. That envelope probably fell onto my battle dress when he was bending over me and it got stuck in the blood.'

'So, Englishman, you are alive and my Franz is dead, but what do you want with us? The war ended many years ago, why have you come now?' said Elise.

213

'I've been training as a doctor for a long time to become a surgeon but I wanted to return the photo in person and make sure you're OK, Fräulein Elise. And to offer you help if you need it.'

'No, I thank you, Englishman. We're fortunate, I've a good job as an interpreter. We have all we need. Go back to your own country and heal the sick. We must both pray we never have another dreadful war like that one.'

Her courage in adversity humbled me. I returned to my hospital and achieved my ambition to become a surgeon, specialising in the new discipline of plastic surgery helping rebuild faces and bodies wrecked by war. It was my way of repaying my near miss with eternity and the unexpected gift of my own life.

Into The Dawn
Coral Leend (SDWC)

April 1914

'Bertie. I say, Bertie!'

The stable lad driving the cart slackened the reins and turned around at the call. Waving his arm, he grinned as the horse and rider drew level with them.

'Master Theo. I thought you was gonna miss it this time fer sure.'

'Keep going,' Theo said. Loosening his feet from the stirrups, he grabbed the side of the cart and swung himself on board from his mount's back. 'Thank you, Bertie. I knew I could depend on you to bring my trunk,' he said, tying his horse's reins to the cart.

'Master Don must be already on the train.' Bertie glanced up at the sun and flicked the reins. 'Get a move on,' he urged the horse.

At the station Theo left Bertie unloading the trunk, as a porter ran up with a hand truck. Leaving them to it, he sprinted up the platform just as the guard, flag in hand, was already lifting a whistle to his lips.

'Hold on, please,' Theo called.

His father, General Sutton, was looking at his pocket watch, his face forbidding. He motioned to the guard to wait, as the porter hurried the hand truck along the platform to the guard's carriage.

'My apologies, sir,' Theo called, as an ear-splitting hiss of steam from the engine drowned his words.

'This indiscipline is noted,' the general rasped. 'You will also notice the discrepancy in your allowance.'

The whistle blew as Theo dropped into the corner seat, opposite his twin brother, Don.

'You actually made it.' Don shook his head. 'Why on earth do you rile the old man like that? I thought he was going to have a heart attack.' Don stood up to take off his jacket and folded it carefully before placing it on the overhead mesh. Theo tugged his off, and threw it to Don.

'Stick mine up there, too.'

'Our last term. I thought it would never come.' Don gave a satisfied nod.

'Well I'll wager you ten shillings that our blue team will beat your red one,' Theo said, referring to Lauton Public School's end of year equestrian competition. They captained rival teams in the Cavalry Corps and were fiercely competitive, especially with each other. But being such close friends, their rivalry was genial.

'Accepted.' Don reached over and shook Theo's hand.

'Although perhaps I ought to let you win. You'll need to get the Corps Sword of Honour to impress at Sandhurst.'

'Let me win?' Don howled with mock indignation. 'As if I needed ...' Theo saw his brother's dawning realisation. 'What do you mean?'

'That I don't intend going to Sandhurst.'

'You never told me,' Don accused. 'You're having me on.'

'I'm not.'

'Where will you go, instead? Oxford?' Then his voice rose in horror. 'You're never serious about being a vet?'

'I've written to a London veterinary college and they offered me a place. I think I'll accept it.'

'Merry hell! You *are* serious. You've always been a bit mawkish about animals, but the old man will never countenance it. Vets are just jumped up farriers.'

'Don't talk rot. You're beginning to sound like Pater now.'

Don threw Theo a disgusted look. 'Never in a million years could I be as blinkered ...' His voice trailed off uncertainly. 'Do I? Do I actually?

Theo grinned. 'No. But sometimes you quote him a little too seriously.'

'War is serious. And it seems there will be one very soon.'

Theo's grin faded. 'I am aware of that. A veterinary surgeon is a recognised profession; I could get an army commission. I would work with the animals, but I don't want to kill other men for something I'm not in agreement with.'

'What if it was our country?'

'If someone was actually here, attacking *us*, then yes, of course I would fight. But what has some foreign archduke's squabble to do with us? All those men dying, families bereaved – for what?'

'Theo. Don't let other people hear you talk like that. It sounds ...' Don frowned, looking away.

'Sounds what? What?' Theo demanded.

Don shrugged, avoiding his scrutiny.

Theo leaned forward, gripping his arm. 'What are you trying to tell me, Don?'

Don shook him off. 'I don't know,' he snapped. 'But I don't agree. Let's leave it drop.'

'Yes, let's,' Theo said, turning to look through the window, adding sotto voce: 'But I'd give my life for you without hesitation.'

July 1914

'Come on. Come on!' The school's Blue Corps sergeant screeched. 'Move yer arse ... sir, or Red's going to bloody beat us.'

Riding bare-backed, with the halter strap grasped in one hand, Theo raced his mount towards the white target

217

square marked on the ground, urging her on. Then, with his free hand he grasped the canvas belt cinched around the animal's girth. Nimbly, he vaulted off to one side of the racing horse, swinging both legs to thump down on the white area, before rebounding back over the horse, to pound down on the opposite marked area. With an agile leap he regained his seat, crouching over the animal's neck, aware of another rider almost alongside him, straining to get past. Theo's horse jumped the last hurdle and they crossed the line just in front of Don, with Theo throwing his brother a triumphant grin, and waving an arm to his own cheering team.

'Well done, sir.' The sergeant came to congratulate Theo and caught the horse's bridle, patting her affectionately. 'And you. Good girl,' he said, pulling an apple from his pocket as she nuzzled him for her treat. He then turned towards Don, feeding his horse a treat too. 'You nearly beat us, sir – but not quite. Better luck next time.'

'If there is a next time.' Don pulled a rueful face, reaching to shake Theo's hand, as Red sergeant came over, trying to hide his annoyance at the result. The rest of the losing team, aided by a horde of noisy junior boys, pulled Don from his mount and yanked a half-full nose-bag down over his head, showering him with oats, then dumped him in the lake. Laughing, Theo went to rescue his brother and surrounded by an admiring pack, they walked back to School House for a cold shower.

'You two are jolly well certain to be top cadets at Sandhurst,' Brodie minor shrieked, jumping up and down with excitement. 'No one else ever gets a chance. Do you take it in turns to win?'

'What? Let him win?' Don laughed. 'I would never hear the end of it.'

Everyone burst out laughing when Brodie exclaimed: 'But how can anyone tell for certain which of you has won?'

August 1914

'You what?' General Sutton roared at Theo, who stood at attention on the other side of his father's desk. 'You want to be a bloody vet? They're nothing but jumped up farriers. That what you want?' Red faced, he bawled a whole list of obscenities about vets and ungrateful sons, as Theo began to fear his father really was going to have a heart attack. 'What am I supposed to say when the commandant at Sandhurst writes to ask me why my son has turned down his place? After winning Lauton School's cavalry prize, for God's sake!'

'But …' Theo began.

'Shut up!' The general thumped the desk. 'Don't interrupt me. I've a good mind to take a riding crop to you,' he spluttered. Theo pursed his lips, hoping his father was not foolish enough to try to carry out his threat. 'You *will* go to Sandhurst and become a cavalry officer. I will *not* support you for any other course. Understood?'

'Yes, sir. Perfectly. May I go now?'

'No, wait. I also forbid you to accept any financial aid from your mother. Now keep out of my sight until you come to your senses.'

Concerned, Don was waiting outside the door. 'Are you all right? I thought he was going to attack you.'

Theo smiled ruefully. 'I thought he might try. I think he genuinely believes he still could.' Having both experienced the threatened punishment in the past, the young men smothered their laughter.

'So you'll come to Sandhurst?' Don asked.

'No.' Theo shook his head.

'But he'll stop your allowance.'

'I don't care, I am going to London. Hopefully I'll find work to earn my keep.'

219

'Doing what?' Don was unconvinced. 'Please reconsider. We've done everything together. It won't be the same without you.'

Agreeing, Theo sighed. 'I realise that. I've gone over it, so many times. But my mind's made up. I want to work with animals.'

September 1914

Men were volunteering in hordes to join the army, the war in full swing, when both boys began their courses. Theo, as a veterinary student in London, managed to support himself by working as a part-time tutor. A friend of his mother's, Mrs Toomey, had welcomed him, delighted someone could help her errant sons with Latin and Maths. Theo struggled to fund his college fees, but at least his room, and some of his meals, were free. He used any spare time assisting in a vet's practice, which was satisfying and incredibly helpful with his course. An ironic side effect was learning to shoe horses; Don would find that highly amusing.

December 1914

Eagerly, Theo hurried to meet Don for his promised visit during the Christmas break. At the station, hesitant, they stared at each other, each seeing his *alter ego* mirrored in his brother. Theo punched Don on the shoulder, who returned in kind, both trying to keep impassive expressions. Then, capitulating, they gripped one another in a brief hug, acknowledging their affection and isolation.

'Come on.' Theo took Don's bag. 'Let's walk. It's not far,' he added, not wanting Don to realise he couldn't afford a cab.

'So what sort of tutor are you?' his brother asked with interest. 'Any good?'

'Excellent of course. What did you expect?' He grinned. 'Let's say Mrs Toomey said her sons' marks have improved. And she's invited you to dinner this evening.'

'And Mother insists you come home for Christmas. She has Pater's approval.'

Theo raised sardonic brows.

'Well, perhaps grudging permission,' Don amended. 'Here is her invitation.'

Theo smelt their mother's distinctive perfume as he took the letter.

At home, the general paid Theo scant interest, treating him as a lowly private soldier, beneath his attention. Theo responded by ignoring him, seeking nothing from his father.

'They are calling for army volunteers,' the general pointedly remarked at dinner. 'Some boys even put up their ages.'

Silently, the family concentrated on their meal, unwilling to initiate an argument.

The following morning, they were seated at the breakfast table when a footman brought in the post, handing it around.

Not recognising the writing, Theo examined his envelope curiously before opening it, wondering if it was from his pupils. A white feather fluttered out. He gasped, a hand going up to his neck, feeling as if he had been punched in the throat. He coughed, his chest tight, heart thudding, and forced himself to raise his chin and look at the family and servants, all staring at him. His mother's eyes filled with tears; she threw down her napkin and rushed from the room. Don's face creased with dismay. The elderly footman scowled, grabbed the envelope and the feather, crushing them both in his hand.

'Whoever sent you that doesn't know you at all,' he spat, and stalked from the room, indignation in every step.

Theo scrutinised his father's aloof face, detecting a hint of triumph. He calmed his breath and swallowed hard.

'I will not remain for Christmas, after all,' he drawled, fighting to keep his voice even. 'That should please you, sir. There is a strange smell, as if something is rotten.' He got up and followed his mother from the room.

Western Front 1917

'All right, old girl.' Theo spoke softly to the trembling horse he was leading, as it floundered wearily. He stroked her muzzle as she flattened her ears when another blast of gunfire reverberated around them. Man and horse, exhausted after numerous trips, were both knee deep in glutinous mud, which clung tenaciously as they fought each step of the way with the cart. Inside were three injured soldiers, one of whom smothered a groan as the cart jolted into yet another trough.

Corporal Morris came over as they reached the field ambulance post. 'Who you got, Conchie?'

'Three men. One is hurt pretty badly …' Theo began.

'How'd you know?' Morris sneered.

Theo acted as if he never heard the intended insults, and silently leaned into the cart. Carefully avoiding the other men, he gently rolled the badly injured soldier on to his side and eased him onto a filthy stretcher as others appeared to help.

'Thanks, mate,' the soldier murmured to Theo. 'I owe you.'

'You don' owe 'im nuthin,' Morris bawled.

'Only my life,' the soldier whispered.

'Not a yeller-bellied Conchie,' Morris jeered.

'Shut it, or I'll do it for you.' Morris spun round to find one of the other injured soldiers had managed to slide off the cart unaided and towered above him. 'He got shot rescuing me and my mates. We'd all be bloody dead if not for him.'

When conscription was enforced in 1916, eighteen months as a veterinary student had been insufficient for Theo to become a Veterinary Corps officer. As a conscientious objector, he had arrived here over a year ago, to attend to the animals.

Theo helped carry the stretcher into the tented first aid post.

'You better get that seen to,' the stretcher bearer said, seeing the blood soaking Theo's damaged sleeve.

'I've got to see to the horse first. She's about to collapse.' He turned away before someone prevented him from leading the weary beast away for some attention, food, and rest. Once she was settled, Theo unwound his puttees and pulled off his muddy boots and socks, examining his feet for trench foot before putting on clean socks. Then he put his boots back on again, and rewound his filthy putties before returning for treatment to his arm.

'Your name's Sutton?' the first aider asked as he bandaged Theo's arm. 'Any relation to a Lieutenant Sutton?'

'Why? Is he here? Is he injured?'

'They said gassed, but I don't think ... '

'Gassed? Oh, Lord.' Theo snatched his arm away. 'Thank you.' He raced over to the officers' first aid tent, rapidly scanning the men on the camp beds, many minus limbs or sporting bloodied bandages, waiting for transfer to the field hospital. At first he couldn't find Don, then recognising his white blond head, saw he was curled in a foetal position his back to the ward. Theo pulled up abruptly.

'Oh no. Please don't let it be Don,' he whispered.

'Can I help you?' Dazed, Theo turned to find the medical officer behind him. 'Oh, Theo. I didn't realise it was you.' In spite of rank, Theo and the MO were quite friendly.

When the MO had first arrived, Theo's dedication and consideration towards animals and wounded men had caught his attention.

'Sutton? Do I know you? Your face seems familiar.'

Theo gave a half smile. 'I believe we both attended Lauton School, sir. You were head boy.'

'Really? Yes, I remember you now. Didn't you have a brother?' Theo nodded. 'The twins. We had a hell of a time telling you apart. You tricked us all constantly.'

Theo had laughed. 'We did.'

'But you were excellent scholars. So why are you here? Wearing this uniform?'

Theo had gone on to tell him the background and the MO had realised Theo's veterinary knowledge could prove useful with wounded soldiers, as well as animals. The field ambulance units were always understaffed, stretcher bearers were some of the highest war casualties, and he had trusted Theo enough to make use of his services when necessary.

Now, sensing Theo's anxiety about the patient in the bed, the MO asked: 'Who are you looking for? Do you know this officer?'

'I think it might be my brother, sir. But I haven't yet seen his face.' Theo clenched his hands, his glance straying to the trembling figure.

'For God's sake go and find out.'

Theo took two steps and his hope died. Don was shivering uncontrollably, an arm covering his face. This was not the Don he knew, crumpled and cowed, his eyes tortured pools in his face. Theo smoothed the limp hair back from his twin's forehead.

'Don, it's Theo. You're safe now.' He raised a questioning glance to his MO, knew his assumption was correct when he returned a brief nod. Shell shock. Neurasthenia. Whatever you name it! When a man's mind refuses to accept the callousness and cruelty of war. They called it cowardice. The MO, a discerning man, had never accepted this diagnosis.

'Is he is going to be sent home, sir?'

'I hope so.' The MO hesitated, knowing Theo understood. 'I am trying, but I can't promise. Get cleaned up and you have my permission to sit with him. Tell Corporal Lucas I said you can give him some phenobarbitone. To sedate him.' He started to walk away then paused. 'I can't promise he will be in the ward tomorrow.'

Slumped on a stool alongside Don later on, Theo recognised his brother's mental health was seriously impaired. But at least he was quiet since the sedation. Theo recollected what the MO had once told him about this condition.

'Their minds just shut down. All they need is rest and recuperation. But that fool, Field Marshal Haig, calls them cowards. Says the army must make examples of them.'

Theo knew what that implied. Was this to be Don's fate?

The MO's hand suddenly gripped Theo's shoulder. 'I have some hopeful news. A lorry is arriving tomorrow to take wounded to Blighty. I will personally try to ensure he is on it. Now get some rest. And that is an order!'

'Where's Lieutenant Sutton gone?' Theo panicked, on returning an hour later to find Don's bed empty and stripped.

'The MPs took him,' said an unrecognised orderly. 'We had a hell of a job to dress him in his uniform, poor sod. He's to face the firing squad at dawn.'

Theo felt physically sick. Forcing down the bile which rose in his throat, he dragged himself outside, scanned the sky, not yet light.

What can I do? Think!

Pulling himself together, he rushed across to the shelled

remnants of an old cottage serving as a prison; found the guard sprawled asleep outside, and slipped past the battered door. Squinting through the gloomy interior he spotted Don spread-eagled on a straw pallet, still comatose from the generous dose of phenobarbitone given to him earlier.

I know what to do.

At dawn two MPs entered to find their prisoner standing just inside the door, shoulders drooped, head hanging, but his uniform as neat as was possible in a war zone. They exchanged a brief glance of surprise.

'Lieutenant Donald Sutton, sir?'

'Yes.' His voice was subdued.

'You know why we're here, sir?'

Their prisoner, lifted his head and pulled himself erect.

'Of course! Get on with it!' His voice authoritative, clipped public school. 'When you return, be kind enough to give this note to the medical officer. It is *most important* that you give it to *him* and no one else. Many thanks.' He handed them a rather crumpled letter, clearly addressed to the medical officer, by name.

'I am ready now.' Raising his chin, shoulders back, he walked smartly out into the dawn.

Booze and Birthdays
Barbara Koethe (SDWC)

I am looking out at the white laced hems decorating the green waves. It is pleasantly hypnotizing to watch them push their way towards the beach. They jostle, fast, because there is a wind coming from the right.

My fringe flaps like a curtain over my eyes. The dry sand powders across my naked feet. It is cool and calm under my soles. Bracelet Bay - perfect spot for my alcohol-polluted veins and my throbbing head.

I feel good, content and enriched.

Now I know I cannot drink like Welsh fishermen. And I know that clichés and stereotypes are dangerous. I let myself fall back into the sand, I adjust my pencil and notebook in my back-pocket, fold my arms under my head, close my eyes and scroll through the memories of last night …

… I parked my VW bus beside a few mobile homes near Mumbles Pier. He immediately started talking to me, telling me there was no problem with overnight-parking, that he and his mates came here to fish at the weekends, that his name was Phil, that he knew my number-plate was German. I told him my name was Daniel and that I actually was German, that I had been an exchange student in Swansea ten years ago and was now on a long holiday, touring around Wales.

'A few of us are having a little something to drink tonight! You're more than welcome … come on over to my camper!"

At 9'o clock I clambered into the narrowness of Phil's

mobile home. Five people, most of them in their sixties, helloed me noisily. All just about fit onto the two earth-coloured settees opposite each other. Shots of spilling cider interspersed with bubbling laughter made me feel welcome.

It was like crawling into a trench of applely, malty alcoholic smells mixed with juicy fruit like eau de cologne and the Old Holborn tobacco I used to roll as a student.

'Hi! Great you made it!'

Phil passed a can of Strongbow cider to me, looked at the others, and said, 'This is Daniel. He's German. His English is perfect … so, you better watch your gobs.'

I took a big slug from my can and laughed with them.

'Squeeze in here!'

As they untangled their legs and shifted up I tried to be polite. 'Don't worry! I'm alright standing up,' and a small voice in my head said, 'Don't be such a stiff German!'

I was grabbed and pulled down into the friendly chaos and found myself surrounded by shiny faces. Craving for the alcohol to kick in, I gulped down my Strongbow and tried to ignore my stupid-looking posture with my knees right up my chin.

'I'm George, alias Tom, Tom Jones. This is Paula!'

'I'm Dave, this is Marianne – Marianne, this is Daniel!'

I hardly got their names in the middle of the cheery clanking of brandy glasses, cider and beer cans – at the same time trying to get used to the English with the Welsh accent again.

George, aka Tom Jones, was sitting across from me, our shoe-tips touching. Fascinating fellow: he didn't call himself Tom Jones for nothing: He *was him* – with his elegant, body-hugging light-blue shirt and the matching dark-blue tie, the perfect tight Tom-Jones-locks, dyed black. And wow! The proud expression on this huge face with the tanned wrinkles when he struck up in the perfect voice of 'The Tiger':

228

'Sex bomb, sex bomb, you're my sex bomb!' Fantastic! We roared with laughter. Now the alcohol had kicked in, I clapped and cheered.

The fun was real and the stale air no problem.

With a boasting grin Phil explained, 'Tom makes money as an entertainer, he is the one with the *arian*!'

Paula must have seen the questioning look on my face.

'Welsh for money,' she whispered.

I noticed she was a beautiful young blonde with an angelic smile. She was the only one about my age: late twenties or early thirties. It took a couple of seconds before I noticed Tom Jones' hand on her thigh. Embarrassed I quickly looked away – only to then see that her pear-shape was responsible for the limited seating-space.

Another 'can of something' was pushed into my hand.

Marianne nudged Phil with her elbow, 'Go on, show Daniel your camera!'

As if Phil had waited to be asked he immediately dragged an impressive apparatus out from under the settee.

'Wow, this is not a toy! Are you a photographer, Phil?'

'Go on, you hold it!'

'Oh! It weighs a ton! The lens looks·like the arm of a sumo-guy!'

My staccato pronunciation created a picture of me as the 'Jawohl! German' in my head.

'Yup, this is the real McCoy! I take the shooting-stills for *Doc Martin*, the series, you know!?'

No, I didn't and Phil looked disappointed.

Another can helped here. We all became louder. I loosened up. We all did and Marianne's dress did, too. Her *décolleté* was inviting and feminine, even with her breasts having entered the sagging phase. I tried not to stare.

Dave, who seemed to be the quiet one, distracted me by stretching across and producing a guitar from above my head. I'd avoided looking at him because his face was distorted and made me feel uncomfortable. He had no lower jaw ... Maybe severe orthodontic problems, maybe a traffic accident, or even a war injury?

For lack of space he placed the guitar somewhere between his left armpit and his right ear. He started singing softly.

'Marianne's a jolly good fellow, she's a jolly good reason ... she's the jolly good re-eason ... to celebrate today ...'

He had me spellbound with the beauty of his voice. We all put our festive faces on and sang with sincere gusto like a Welsh choir.

'Happy birthday to you! Happy birthday to you! Happy birthday dear Marianne... happy birthday to youuuu!'

Congratulations, cheers, drinks spilled, drinks topped up – a wet and loud rumpus!

'I bet you wouldn't think she was fifty today, would you?'

I shook my head, signifying disbelief. I rose from my squatting position and kissed her cheeks, feeling their limp softness on my lips. For a second the uneven surface of her nose made me think of a rose-coloured cannon-ball; too many cans of something? She gave me a crooked smile. I had to divert my glance from her watery eyes under her fluorescent light-blue eyelids. I winked at her and escaped by asking Tom Jones:

'There is another big round birthday this year, a one hundredth anniversary, isn't there?'

Tom's eyes lit up, 'Oh, yes! There are great programs on telly all the time. I loves them!'

'Yeah, I watched *A Poet in New York*. Saw that?'

'N-no...?'

I didn't get the confusion: 'It's a beautiful film! Brand new, BBC ...'

'No, what film is that? About Wilson? Was he a poet?'

Which way was this going? I blamed the alcohol.

'Don't know, Wilson who?'

'Woodrow Wilson … wasn't he president then?'

'I am getting pretty confused here! I am talking about the one hundredth birthday of Dylan Thomas.'

'Oh … Dylan! Yes, right! It's his birthday, too, this year. But I was on about the war.'

Jawohl! My trench-association came back. 'The war? Which war?'

'Hey! The First World War! It's the one hundredth anniversary of the Great War!'

'Oh, right … Sorry, I wasn't thinking …'

We looked at each other as if we were from different sides of an invisible border. Tom couldn't hide his disbelief and said scoffingly, 'Don't you have lots of documentaries on German telly?'

The temperature dropped and the sound thinned around me.

'Well, we probably do … but me personally, I haven't followed any, really… yet …'

'But you do know that World War I was the war where more soldiers died than in any other war before?'

A nervous tickle was growing in my guts.

'I'm not sure. You people seem to know a lot more about the great war than we do… or maybe it's just me… not being interested enough.' Feeling like having trapped myself in the moron-corner, I tried to wiggle myself out of it. 'Well, how do I put it? I think the impact of the Second has covered over the importance of the First World War. We younger people know and speak about World War II. It's still part of our lives because we get the vibes of the collective guilt from our parents and grandparents. When my mother was young she never spoke in public, when she was on holidays, so that the Spaniards or Italians wouldn't know she was a German!'

This was getting very awkward. Maybe I should leave. But then Tom slammed his flat hand on Phil's leg.

231

'We never shut up, do we? No matter where we are!'

We all cheered and lifted our cans and glasses and I could relax again. Booze can make or break an evening, I thought.

Phil put on a serious face. 'Anyway, it's the anniversary of the Great War we're on about now. They killed like fuck because they *could* with all the new lethal weapons they had: Flame throwers, machine-guns, all the chemical shit, torpedoes on compressed air, the bloody Fokker, you know?'

'Mmh ...'

I felt Phil's impatience: 'Hey, come on, Daniel, you must know something here!'

'Well, this is not so much my thing ... weapons and stuff ...'

Phil was right in my face: 'What the fuck – pardon my French – do you know?'

What I did know was that I'd never get myself into this kind of situation again. Uptight I was, not comfortable. I felt my head jerk and saw my fringe fall back in front my eyes. What do I say? Will I play the smart-ass German? The honest toe-dipper or the diplomatic empty-phraser? I took a deep breath.

'Well, wasn't World War I just a silly game of dominoes?'

Was it the cracking of the thin ice of my semi-knowledge or the quiver of my voice echoing in my boozy head as I went on. 'Because of stupid extreme nationalism? There was the – do you say crown-prince? – Franz Ferdinand. He was killed in Serbia. That triggered it. Austria-Hungary struck back – they declared war on Serbia – Russia became allies with Serbia – Germany then declared war on Russia and the French and British on Germany, then Austria-Hungary on Russia. Just click – click – click like a chain reaction without brains.'

I took another deep breath and peeped through my

fringe. Dave looked amused:

'Not bad, boy! Yes, dominoes … never looked at it that way … Did you, guys?'

Phil was not convinced. 'Yeah, so what? Fact is, Germany was the producer of all that shit that killed so many and kept the war going for ages. You can't deny that, my German friend!'

Fight, flight, or freeze? I looked at the others. Their eyes looked glassy. Good Paula smiled at me. Marianne's eyes were on me too. I returned her look, not knowing if I myself had just triggered a click-click-reaction without using my brain.

Marianne smirked and raised her eyebrows, 'Here we go …' Philboy had a drink too many and is showing off!'

Did she sense that I wasn't good at this kind of thing? I felt so much safer smiling with the girls. I wasn't sure if I had to decide which team to join: the peace-girls or the war-boys. For lack of saying something, I winked at Marianne, just for good measure.

Tom nudged Phil and pointed at Marianne with his chin, 'Saw that? Looks as if a Welsh-German alliance is forged there! Is our birthday girl getting bored with us?'

Marianne took a slug of her brandy, played with it looking at Phil, swallowed, and coaxed in a rough sexy voice, 'Darling, actually I am. Why get carried away over war when party and love are in the air? I want my special guest here to feel comfy with us Welsh. And aren't we a peace-loving folk? Famous for our hospitality, remember?'

Her eyes became piercing, her voice snappy. 'We all bloody well know who lost the damn war and stuff but there is no point in dragging it out now! We're here to have a bit of fun, aren't we?'

Phil grabbed Marianne's hand with his hairy paw and kissed it. 'Isn't she the smartest woman in the world? I loves you!'

Roars and clapping! … And I sighed with relief. What

an easygoing way Marianne and Phil had! It made me feel grey, dense, and anxious, my head full with all the big serious war words like 'national identity', 'cultural differences', 'dreadful historical occurrences'.

Then Phil took hold of my wrist. With a serious and honest look in his eyes he guided my eyes to a faded beige photograph in a black frame above the driver's cabin. It felt like a short-cut out of my muddled theoretical war-approach straight into his very personal life. The picture sat between dried flowers hanging with their heads down, stickers from different fishing associations, leather bands with a blue eyestone, a yin-yang-pendant, and some torn children's drawings. I was strangely touched. The photograph showed a smiling woman with a baby on her lap.

'See that? This is my grandmother, Elisabeth. Wanna hear her story?' It was as if he was opening a window.

'Yes.'

'She married my grandfather, Bruce, on June, 15th 1916. I have their marriage certificate, I can show you! He played football for Carmarthen. He was a soldier in the 12th battalion, which was a training reserve battalion. The two, Elisabeth and Bruce, went on honeymoon – just for a couple of days. A few weeks later the 12th battalion was sent to France to support the 2nd Worcestershire battalion. Because down there in the Delville Wood the 2nd Worcestershire battalion had just lost three hundred men. They were heavily shelled on the 21st August. You have heard of the Somme trenches, haven't you?

'At the beginning of September my grandmother got a letter from a nun from the General Hospital in Rouen. She wrote about how sorry she was to tell her that her husband was shot in the head on August, 26th and that he was taken to the closest hospital 80 miles away. He was not dead but had a very bad head wound and wouldn't last long. After another few days my grandmother got another letter from the same nun saying that her husband had woken up from his coma, recovered a bit, but sadly died on the 31st August. He was buried in Rouen cemetery. Now, listen to this: On the 14th April 1917, my mother was born. My grandmother never married again, she was a widow her whole life and my mother never had a father.'

I felt a strange prickly mixture of embarrassment, sorrow, and warmth taking hold of my heart. This evening's 'discussion' was not about figures, measuring knowledge, or about pitting national identities against one another, not about winning or losing. This was about real people.

There was nothing to add apart from kissing Marianne, thanking Phil and her for the lovely evening, and wishing each other a warm 'Good night!'. We all left Phil's. Far too drunk, but all friends again, we went off to sleep in our own mobile homes ...

... The wind has dropped. The sky is very blue. The white clouds are very far away. The waves lick across the sand. The throbbing in my head is very faint now.

I feel something in my heart that hasn't been there before: the warmth of gratitude. Gratitude for the very personal story Phil shared with me. It is as if I was given a present.

A mild buzzing is interrupting my solitude. It comes closer. I open my eyes and see a brown creature hovering clumsily above me. I am strangely intrigued. I whisper: 'Maikaefer' – a maybug – what a rare sight! Another present!

As I follow it with my eyes, the words of the children song come back to me:

'Maikäfer flieg, dein Vater ist im Krieg, deine Mutter ist in Pommerland, Pommerland ist abgebrannt, Maikäfer flieg'

Every German child knows this song about the war.

I have an idea! My heart and mind jump with excitement: This song will be my personal gift for Phil! Slowly, not to frighten the beetle, I sit up, fiddle pencil and notebook out of my back pocket and start to translate terms, to render rhyme and rhythm.

Dear maybug fly
Your father fights to die
Mother's in the land at the sea
Which burnt down entirely
Dear maybug fly ...

I feel inspired by the little verse. Yes, I am doing something meaningful ... and I keep creating more verses ...

Dear maybug fly
Every child asked why
In Germany's long history
And the answer they can't see
Dear maybug fly ...

Dear maybug fly
This song made children cry
One hundred years it has been sung
In their German mother tongue
Dear maybug fly ...

Dear maybug fly...
Our children do not lie
It's our children's biggest fear
To lose the ones that are so dear.
 Dear maybug fly ...

Just a Postman
Ann Potter (SDWC)

'Age?'

I looked into the distance above the sergeant's left ear – and lied.

'Nineteen sir.'

I needn't have worried. He didn't seem to care.

'Schooling?'

'Les Frères School in Bruges, sir.'

'So I suppose you can speak French?'

'Yes sir. We had to – all the time.'

'How long were you there?'

Careful! This could be a trick. 'Er … I started in 1912. There was an intake of European students that year. So … three years sir.'

'Interesting! Come on, lad, I want you to come and meet my colonel.'

Oh bloody hell! Now I was for it. He must have realised I was only seventeen and would probably put me in prison for falsifying my age, or worse still, contact the monks or my father.

Well! I was here now and up to my neck. Should I salute when we got to this colonel's office or just shake hands? I thought I'd better shake hands. After all, I wasn't a proper soldier yet.

The sergeant was muttering into the colonel's ear and then he saluted smartly and left.

The colonel stroked his moustache thoughtfully, leaned forward, and shook my hand.

'Now then, Thomas Taylor, isn't it? I am interested in the fact that you can speak French. Quite fluently, I understand. I think it may be very useful in the army.

'You will have to do the same training as all the others

237

who have enlisted, but after that you will be deployed to serve with the Royal Engineers and receive special instruction in postal delivery. If you're willing to do that Sergeant Harris has left me your enrolment papers. Understand all that? Well then – sign here.'

With a hand that shook … I signed.

'Now then – Private Johnson will take you through to pick up your uniform and have your medical. Good luck!'

I was in! I was going to serve my country and be … a bloody post man!

Still, they did really need me. He'd said so – in a manner of speaking!

Well, I couldn't have gone back to school. It was, after all, in occupied Belgium. But then I'd seen the poster pasted up everywhere, with that man with a big moustache pointing at you and asking for people to enlist. I just knew it was the right thing to do. Nobody saw me leave so I read the poster carefully and followed the directions to the recruitment centre. I didn't like the school anyway. The monks were just a bunch of frustrated old men.

Johnson jostled me along to join the other lads to get my kit. The uniformed men in the rooms shouted and swore and pushed us about. The monks had been cruel and quick to use the cane and punish us whenever they could, but they hadn't sworn all the time. These soldiers used wonderful words I'd never even heard of.

The medical was worse. They treated us like pieces of meat. There were so many of us and we all needed to be vaccinated. That needle went in one arm after another. My name being Taylor put me at the end of the line, and it was really blunt when it got to me. Hurt like hell! Then there was the 'bend over' and the vice-like grip on our privates. I was amazed how the medics seemed to take a real delight in reducing us to shivering wrecks.

Over at last, we went to the barracks, made up our beds, stored our stuff, and had 'Inspection'.

After being called every name under the sun for a crinkle in a blanket, we went to the mess for some food. It was six o'clock by now and I hadn't eaten since breakfast, so I ate the sloshy stew and grey potatoes swimming in water quite happily. It was just the same as school food after all. Then after a rice pudding you needed a knife and fork for, I finally went with the others back to the barracks for the night.

Once there I could at last speak to some of them. The lad in the next bed was called Tom like me. He had ginger hair and freckles (which, of course, in a very short time became his nick name) In another bed further down a poor chap was snivelling away under his covers, having probably come from a home where his Mum wiped his bum for him. Poor lad he became the butt of many a joke. Unlike some of them I was quite used to the company of others the whole time and I fell asleep the minute I got into bed.

Christ! We didn't know we born before we came here. We used to hate some of the rules and practices at the monastery – but here it seemed the sergeants who trained us were actually out to break us. We carried haversacks loaded with stones for miles and miles, marched round the parade ground until we were literally falling over, we had rifle practice, and gym, and wrestling, and scrubbed the floor of the barracks till it shone. One smear of polish or a blade of grass that had come off a boot, and it was: 'Pick that up you 'orrible little turd. Who do you think you are coming here with your filthy ways, you stinking bastard.'

Once a week we had time to write a letter home. I didn't have to do that. I hadn't got a home. Well, not a proper one. I was adopted when I was five by a man who also adopted thirteen other boys at the same time. Although I was now Thomas Taylor, I'd been Tomos Jenkins before that and come from Wales. 'Father', as we were taught to call him, was a very perverted sort of man and subjected us l to many unpleasant times. He was strict disciplinarian too so none of us could ever change our lives. What could we do? He'd have tanned the hide off me now if he knew I'd escaped. I expect he was wondering where I was but I didn't want to 'better my education' any more.

The third week we were at the camp I was having a wander while all the others were doing their letters and I saw two older men from another barracks leaning on a wall smoking and talking to each other in very low voices. This was wartime now. I must be aware!

I used the cover of a bend in the wall to creep closer and listen. I couldn't hear what they were saying clearly, but it was something to do with a raid. They were both privates and I thought it odd that they knew anything about a raid. Suddenly I saw Major Crawford striding down the roadway – so did the two men. I dropped behind the wall and doubled up to run back to my own barracks. The two men must have been doing something untoward because they too stood up quickly and, acting casually, saluted the major, and walked off down the road.

That night I was telling Freckles about them – how I wondered what they were doing, muttering to each other about a raid like that. Well Freckles is a miner's son and much more solid and down to earth than me, and he didn't half pull my leg about imagining things.

'Did you think they were Germans who were infiltrating our camp, then, Tom? Come to plant a home-made bomb? You're an idiot. You let your imagination run away with you, you do.'

The incident stayed on my mind though and I thought it was really my duty to speak to that colonel I'd seen when I first enlisted, so asked if I could see him. He'd call me all sorts probably – still!

'Well, Private Taylor, what did you want to see me about?'

I told him what I'd seen and described the two older men and their talk of a raid. Of course by this time I was truly sorry for my request to see him and quite sure I would be on 'jankers' and painting coal or cleaning the latrines for punishment, but –

'Ha, Private! I see we have someone who keeps his eyes open. Those two men are in the ranks to listen out for any untoward goings on. Tomorrow there will be a search of all barracks. We hear there are those among us who are not what they seem. Well done! Keep this to yourself though.'

'Oh he gave me a ticking-off and told me not to be such an arse,' I told Freckles, later on. I am ashamed to say I found lying quite easy.

Next day we saw three soldiers being marched off after having all the barracks thoroughly searched while we stood to attention by our beds. I wondered if I'd find out one day what had happened to them. I never did though.

In time, of course, we finished our training and came out of it ready to jump off a cliff if we were ordered to do so.

Next day I was loaded, together with my kit bag, into the lorry that was to take me and a gang of others to join the Royal Engineers – Postal Section. Of course I had to say good-bye to Freckles and all my other mates. Amazing how quickly all the lads had become 'mates' in such a short time. I wondered if I'd ever see Freckles again.

If I'd thought the job of 'post man' would be easy, I was completely wrong. One of the things my training involved was learning how to drive lorries. The route was split into various sections and I would be driving on the last leg of the journey through the heavy shell fire to the serving soldiers on the front line. French would come in handy as we'd be going through French towns and villages.

I must say I enjoyed learning to drive and met some

great chaps in the Postal Section. Rusty was my special pal and we knocked around together. He was the same age as me and confessed to also being under-age. Most of them, though, were older than we were but, luckily, quite willing to help us along. I liked them all – except Sergeant Rawlins.

'Keep out of 'is way son! He's a bastard of the first water – he is!' If you lost your bayonet before inspection, as I did once, he was likely to make you march on the spot until you dropped. That time someone kindly passed me his before Rawlins got to me.

We heard about the fighting – and the dreadful casualties – the conditions – the mud and the rats. I wondered if I deserved what seemed like was going to be an easy life. Little did I know then, what was in front of me.

Getting the letters to the troops was a complicated business that I'd never even thought of before. Now it was wartime every letter had to be censored before they left home, in case someone had either accidently or even on purpose given some information useful to the enemy. After that they were taken to Dover, ferried across to France, and then dropped at various stages to men across the country. The final drop was to men right in the thick of it at the front. It was a very satisfying job to do as everyone was pleased to see you. It was hairy too.

Together with my unit I moved up the various stages – first delivering to men just on their way through France and then on to the more dangerous regions. I worked with Rusty most of the time. There was a lot of bravado and we couldn't wait to get to deliver to the front.

As we drove deeper into France we saw dead bodies littering the roads and at first it made you retch, but in time you became sort of numb – oblivious to the gruesome sights. Sometimes we had to get out and move a body to the side of the road before we could proceed. There was blood and ambulances and body parts and mud everywhere. Our lorry constantly skidded in the muddy conditions and we had to use old blankets to put under the wheels to give them a purchase. When we finally arrived at our destination, bullets sizzled though the air all around us. Somehow you didn't believe there was one for you. Poor Rusty took a bullet in his face and had to go to hospital. We were billeted close to this hospital and slept in tents but the lorries were able to be parked up safely under cover in the hospital grounds.

Every day we left to liaise with the other post lorries who had come to meet us from the earlier run. While I crossed the driveway to go in and visit Rusty I often saw the patients arrive in field ambulances with labels attached to them – a red label for the seriously injured, a blue label – serious but not life threatening, or a white label – a minor injury.

Fortunately Rusty's wound soon healed and he was discharged but I still went to talk to some of the white labels. I felt they would probably enjoy a chat, unlike the more seriously injured patients who would prefer to be left to recover quietly.

One night I was sitting with a man called John Calloway. He'd caught a bit of shrapnel in his arm and didn't expect to stay there long. He was telling me about this really callous Doctor Heller who ruled over everything on this ward. He called them all 'yellow bellies'. In telling me about it John was getting quite worked up so I changed the subject and asked him about home. He told me he was from Bristol and showed me a picture of his two kids and his wife and asked me if I had a family photo too but I told him about the adoption and my aloof, cruel, and severe father.

'That's a real shame. After the war you really must search for your real mother and father.'

'Oh! They obviously didn't want me – they gave me

away to someone else. I'll never understand how anyone could do that.'

'You don't really know what happened, Tom. Perhaps circumstanced forced them to do what they did.'

When John was due for discharge he shook my hand. 'Do as I say, mate! It's the only way to chase all those demons away.'

It was only a short time after that when I walked over to find the place in turmoil.

A short stocky man in his late forties, with a bandage covering his right eye, had been admitted and had had the usual treatment from Doctor Heller.

'Nobody calls me a "yellow belly",' he yelled. 'You may be a bloody doctor but we're all doing our bit. Think you're way above all of us with the letters after your name, don't you? Just because you've been assigned to poke shrapnel and bullets out of wounds and not do the big life-saving operations. You are a *mochyn du*.' And he lay down with the sheet over his head until the doctor stalked out, unable to think of a reply.

I went over to the bed and gently pulled at the sheet.

'What do you …? Oh! Hello, lad.'

I sat down.

'He was out of order and none of these little shy mice would tell him. Well let's hope he behaves a bit better now. Doesn't matter what walk of life we're from.'

We chatted on till his red face cooled down and he was able to talk normally.

'Anyway, what does "*mochyn du*" mean and what the hell language is that?' I asked. He laughed. 'That's Welsh, boy! It means 'black pig' which that doctor is. Amazing how Welsh comes in handy sometimes, even over here.'

I got to know Dai, as he called himself, quite well after that. He had to stay for two weeks because his wound became infected before he could go back to the fighting.

I asked him if he had photos of his family. He pulled out a very creased and lined sepia photo of a pretty girl, much younger than Dai, and a little boy of about five. I saw there were tears in his eyes, which soon spilled down his cheeks. Must have been killed in a raid, I supposed.

'She died of T.B,' he said. 'After that I couldn't cope. I couldn't go to work as well as look after my boy. I was mad – with grief – I suppose and I let that chap have him. He promised a good home and a good education. He was looking to adopt and help a group of boys. My Tomos cried and cried – but I hardened my heart and made him go. But after ... well I never could forget what I'd done. How could I have given away my only son? I searched and searched but I couldn't find him – with his new smart life and different name.' He hung his head.

I spoke slowly. 'Actually I think you have now ... Dad!' I said. I swear his hug nearly broke my ribs.

'I'll see you again after the bloody war – God willing!'

Of course I've written to that man who adopted me to thank him for the life he'd given me. He wrote back a short letter to say it had been a pleasure and that he wished me well in my adult life.

We're home now in Bristol. Dad lives just down the road from me and Ivy, and we have given him three grandkids who visit him every day. I think that, at least for me, some good came out of that terrible, wicked, bloody war.

Badger and the Zeppelin Conspiracy
Steve Jones (SDWC)

Captain James "Badger" Badgerworth turned west over the river. After climbing for five minutes he held the Airco DH 2 fighter in a shuddering turn against the torque of the engine. Completing a hundred and eighty degrees he straightened out, careful not to overcorrect. Four thousand feet below the city was a map in the moonlight. Directly beneath him the silver ribbon of the Thames bisected by Battersea Bridge. To the north he could see the lights of the Embankment. Further north again, the glow of fires burning on the King's Road. Of the air-ship that had caused them there was no sign.

After a moment listening to the reassuringly even thunder of the Gnome, nine-cylinder engine he decided to risk a little more time searching for it. He turned towards the black emptiness of Hyde Park intending to fly east towards Euston Station then pick up the A3 and follow it south-west. The aircraft sank slightly in the downdraft over the park as he used the ailerons to make a shallow right turn over Marylebone, careful not to lose his bearings. There were no conveniently large fields between here and Croydon. He thought what an irony it would be if he were killed crash-landing in South London after surviving April in France.

Keeping the fighter level he undid his harness one handed and reached for the flashlight stowed under the seat. With his shoulders free he ducked below the air stream and used it to check his instruments. Nearly five thousand feet at fifty knots, even in a climb he still had a good ten miles an hour advantage over his quarry. In another four minutes, well before he hit his landmark, he should have the height advantage. After that, even if the zeppelin crew saw the fighter they wouldn't have the speed to get away. Gripping the control yoke between his knees he reached forward to check the mounting lock on the Lewis Gun. He thought about firing a quick burst as insurance against a jam, but decided against it. The tracer might be spotted.

In the city below, and about a mile directly ahead, two white lights flashed in rapid succession. A second later he heard the boom of the explosions and felt the shock waves strike the airframe.

In the place where the bombs had struck an orange glare appeared and brightened. Badger eased the nose of the aircraft in the direction of the fire, scanning intersecting strings of street lamps, looking for a moving patch of deeper darkness. He saw the zeppelin two hundred feet beneath him, and half a mile ahead. It was beam on as it headed south towards the estuary at a steady forty-five knots. Badger levelled off, using the blip switch and fuel lever to reduce speed, creeping up on the dirigible. As long as he stayed head on and kept his air-speed down the pusher design would hide the tell-tale exhaust flames. The zeppelin maintained course and speed as the DH 2 stealthily made up the distance. When he was close enough to feel the turbulence in the leviathan's wake he opened the fuel valve to full power.

He began a shallow dive, intending to overfly the hull, putting a full magazine of mixed hard-point and tracer into it, when he noticed something twinkling just forward of the giant rudder. Muzzle flashes, thought Badger, astonished, as bullets from a dorsal turret he didn't know existed slammed into the side of the cockpit, smashing his spare ammo drums and ripping away the elevator controls.

Without elevators the tail dropped. To counter the stall he gave full right rudder, desperately slamming the control stick forward. It didn't help. Torque from the powerful rotary engine flipped the DH 2 on its back, collapsing the rigging under the starboard wing and tearing away the fragile tail-booms. In a second the Airco was a broken kite. As he fell from the cockpit a thought occurred to Badger. In the heat of the moment he'd forgotten to re-fix his seat harness.

He landed heavily on top of the zeppelin, bounced once, and stopped face down. Winded, his relief at being alive and unwounded was tempered by certainty that the DH 2 would land on top of him or at least crash elsewhere on the dirigible, sending them blazing to earth. Nothing happened. The wreck of his aircraft had by a miracle, missed.

Badger raised his head and looked around. He was lying crosswise on the three hundred yard long hull. The airstream was from the right, therefore, he reasoned, the stern of the zeppelin and the turret that had shot him down must be to his left. He cautiously turned his head in that direction. A hundred yards away was a fabric horizon with half the rudder showing above it. They couldn't see him. He tried looking to his right. Next to him a dome-like structure, a foot tall and three feet wide emerged from the hull. There was a handle labelled 'Für den Notfall'. Not falling was exactly what Badger had in mind. He reached it and tried turning it: it didn't budge. He tried harder. This time it gave way, releasing the hatch cover to spring up a couple of inches, fluttering in the airflow. Cautiously he pulled himself against the cowling and shoved the hatch open far enough to get his head underneath. There was an aluminium ladder and far below a pale circle of light. Keeping hold of the rim of the hatch he squirmed inside, closing it above before climbing downward.

Badger emerged onto a dimly lit metal walkway. He judged he must be in the centre of ship: this would be the axial corridor running the entire length of the vessel. He could hear the deep growl of the zeppelin's mighty thirty-litre Maybach engines and on either side were the huge netting-encased gas bags.

He considered his tactical position. In one pocket of his leather coat was a penknife and his pistol with five rounds of ammunition. In the other, his wallet containing a two pound notes, a ten shilling note, two sixpences, and a couple of farthings. Bribing the crew with two pounds eleven shillings and a ha'penny to drop him off at Croydon seemed an unlikely option, as did forcing the ship to descend by puncturing the gas bags with his knife. The amount of puncturing would necessarily be limited by its two-inch blade and the resilience of the wire netting surrounding the bags. He guessed that even if he slashed away for hours they would be over Belgium before he had any effect on the buoyancy of the airship. That left the pistol. Discharging it inside a vessel which used hydrogen as a lifting gas was beyond risky, but he might be able to use it to hijack the zeppelin by taking the crew hostage.

The more Badger thought of it, the more plausible the idea seemed. The whole crew was probably fifteen or perhaps sixteen men but the bridge crew only five. There would be the captain, the navigator, the flight-engineer, helmsman, and rudderman. Five Germans could be influenced by a single determined Englishman armed with a Webley, he was sure. He just needed to take them by surprise.

For the ambush to work he'd need direct entry to the bridge, which was located at the front of the control car, under the nose. He picked a direction hoping it was the right one. As he walked the sound of the engines reassuringly diminished, confirming his choice.

After he'd taken control of the bridge there were the gun positions in the forward engine pods to consider of course. They could fire on the control car, but he was sure the 'maschinists' wouldn't take the risk. They'd know that as well as killing their own comrades a spark would put an end to all their lives.

An electric bell suddenly rang in short bursts followed by shouts and footsteps. Badger stopped in his tracks then dived off the walkway and clambered into the service tray underneath it. Seconds later he heard two of the crew call out to one another before stopping above him. After speaking quietly for a few moments they strolled off in different directions. He waited, puzzled by their lack of urgency. He checked the luminous dial of his wrist watch. It showed five minutes past twelve. Midnight to most people, but in the navy he remembered, 'eight bells.' Despite being thousands of feet in the air, this was a ship. The bell hadn't been an alarm. It signalled a watch change. Even so, Badger decided, his new hiding place offered a significant advantage over the open walkway. Although crawling along beneath the footplates would be a good deal slower than strolling the corridor above, he was almost immune from discovery. He continued onward, careful not to snag any of the control cables or electrical junction boxes.

Progress was slower and more difficult than he'd anticipated and after ten minutes Badger was soaked in sweat. Despite the protection it gave his elbows he decided to leave his heavy coat behind, reluctantly squeezing out of it. He kept his gloves, telling himself if ambush proved impossible he could always stuff them into a pulley junction and jam the zeppelin's rudder and aileron controls. That would at least inconvenience them for a while. It was not a particularly good plan as they would soon find both the problem and him and it risked being shot as a saboteur, but it was the best he could come up with.

After what felt like hours of painful progress, stopping every time a crewman walked overhead, he encountered the first downward shaft. It was helpfully labelled

'Wasserballast', which even Badger's limited German told him must lead to the ballast room. It was not what he needed but at least proved he was moving in the right direction. Another spell of wriggling over pulleys and control wires brought him to the 'Bombenschacht'. This was further confirmation he was moving in the right direction. The bomb-bay was in the rear part of the gondola. He thought there was likely to be a connecting corridor from here into the wireless room and control car. This would be easier and quicker than his agonizing progress under the walkway. All the 'bomben' had already been dumped over London so there was unlikely to be anyone down there. But Badger hesitated. He couldn't be sure, and the idea of discovery after coming so far was unbearable. He decided to continue a little further, hoping for a more direct route to the bridge.

After another twenty minutes of grazing his elbows and knees on the plating he allowed himself a short rest. He told himself it didn't really matter when he took control of the ship. In some ways the longer he left it before making his move the better. The crew was more likely to be off-guard.

Cushioning his head on his gloves, the exhausted Badger found himself dozing. Frightened he might sleep he forced himself awake and continued doggedly on. After another half hour of crawling he decided to reward himself by stopping for another rest. He awoke with a start to the sound of voices somewhere in front of him. A few yards further and he was looking through a grating into the bridge.

This far forward the deck plating was no more than ten feet below him. He silently lifted the hatch and was about to jump brandishing his pistol when he noticed his ears popping. The engine note had changed too, becoming quieter and less insistent. Irregular bursts of power were being selectively applied. Horrified he realised the airship was landing. In the same moment he knew it was impossible. The zeppelin base in Brussels was two hundred miles from London. Even in ideal conditions it would take four or five hours. He was sure no more than an hour could have passed.

The engines stopped and there was a slight jerk as they docked. From below came a round of polite applause. The voices ascending the shaft took on a different tone. Conversation broke out, jovial and confident. From outside there were shouts as the mooring was made secure at the front. He heard a ladder dropped and the bridge crew talking and laughing as they began to disembark.

Badger waited until all was quiet before cautiously climbing down the access shaft to stand on the deserted bridge. Through the windows he could see the rooftops and part of the facade of an English country house. The airship was attached by its nose to a short flagpole fixed to the battlements of a tower built into the front of the property. A set of folding steps led from the bridge to its paved roof. From there a lighted stone staircase curved down into the rooms below.

He walked over to one of the side windows for a view of the floodlit lawn thirty feet below. A banner had been spread out decorated with two Maltese crosses. Printed on it in gothic script were the words, 'Welcome L33 and our Friends from Germany.' Even more strangely, Badger could faintly hear dance music.

There was the sound of feet on the steps and a young man in evening dress entered. He turned and helped in an elegantly dressed young woman.

'What about this then, Darcy?' he said, with a grand but unsteady gesture taking in the bridge of the zeppelin.

'What's he doing here?' she asked, pointing at Badger.

'Oh, Lord. I thought they were all downstairs,' said the young man in an aggrieved tone, 'Sprecken sie English, Old Chap?'

'Perfectly,' Badger replied, 'I went to school in England.'

'Golly, yes,' he said apologetically, 'a lot of you people did, didn't you? I keep forgetting that. Which school was that?'

'Walton Hall,' said Badger

'Ah, don't know it, sorry. I went to Eton myself of course. Father insisted. The Bressinghams have always gone to Eton. It's tradition, you see. Next year I shall go up to Oxford.'

He joined Badger at the window looking out at the house and lawn. 'Impressive, isn't it? Not quite as spectacular as some of your castles on the Rhine, but not bad for Surrey. Father says that's why we need to be together on this, to keep the right people in charge, people with breeding and values. If that damned Welshman had his way all this would be turned into an orphanage tomorrow.'

Badger nodded. 'Did you know this airship raided London a couple of hours ago?' he asked.

'Good, Lord, yes. It'd look damned queer if one of these things popped over the Channel and didn't drop a few bombs. That's why Mother insisted on the party, to make sure nobody got hurt.'

'Very thoughtful of her,' said Badger.

'Rather,' said the young man, 'That's Mother all over, always putting other people before herself.'

'I'm bored,' said a female voice behind them, 'I'm going back to the party.'

They both turned in time to see Darcy lifting her satin dress preparatory to re-negotiating the steps. The young man hurried to her side. 'I'm with you, sis,' he said. 'I could do with a top up anyway.'

Before leaving he turned to Badger, 'Can I send you anything?' he asked, 'The other guard chappie at the back has had some sandwiches and a beer pulled up.'

253

'Oh, don't trouble, sir. I expect I'll have some of his,' said Badger.

'Fair enough, Pater will have finished with your Kommandant Von Altmann by now anyway, and you'll want to be going soon.' He gave a small wave before trotting down the steps in pursuit of the bored Darcy.

Badger pulled up the folding steps before taking out his pistol and opening the bulk-head door at the rear of the gondola. It led to an empty radio room where a powerful set left turned on fizzed and squawked. All the mod cons, thought Badger. He wondered when radios would be light enough to be fitted to aircraft. Beyond the radio room was the companionway leading to the bomb bay, ballast room, and crew quarters. His young lordship had mentioned only one man who'd had food pulled up. Therefore, reasoned Badger, there was only one German on the airship and that German didn't know he was there, or they would certainly have met by now.

In the bomb bay both bomb racks were as he'd suspected empty, signifying a successful raid for L33 and the murder of dozens of innocent civilians.

The water tanks in the ballast room next door were half-full, giving L33 the reserve buoyancy she would need for the return trip. Beyond the ballast room were the crew quarters and ready room. Badger knew this was where the sentry would be. From there the whole of the underside of the ship would be visible, as well as the house and the grounds thirty feet below. He had surprise on his side, but the sentry would be armed with a rifle compared to his pistol. On the other hand in the confined interior of the airship that might work to his advantage. Badger cocked the Webley and taking a deep breath kicked open the light wooden door.

The electric landing lights on the lawn filled the room with light and shadows. It was empty, as were the bunks beyond. To the rear of the sleeping quarters he found an open escape hatch where a rope ladder had been fixed. Resisting the temptation to stick his head out he detached it and dropped it to the lawn below. He made his way back to bridge just as the lights on the lawn were turned off. A metallic click followed by an amplified voice came from the radio room.

'Captain Badgerworth?'

Badger made his way back through the companionway and cautiously picked up the microphone. Pressing the speak button he said, 'This is Badger.'

'Lord Bressingham here, Captain,' said a voice from the radio speaker, 'I believe we need to talk.'

'Can I ask how your Lordship knew I was aboard?'

Bressingham gave a sardonic laugh. 'Oh, I didn't. Fortunately my son and daughter recognised the famous Captain James "Badger" Badgerworth of the RFC immediately. "Daddy, we have a gate-crasher", they said. How did you manage it anyway?'

'Manage what?'

'To get aboard my zeppelin,'

'I dropped in,' Badger replied.

'I see. In that case I think you should consider dropping out. No harm will come to you if you surrender to us now.'

'And if I refuse?' asked Badger.

'Then I'm afraid things could get very hot for you.'

Badger dropped the microphone and went through to the bridge and looked out. The top of the tower was covered with tarpaulins extending protectively down the front of the house. There were several large drums of water and a coiled fire-hose. Men in fatigues manned a sledge-mounted machine gun aimed at the bridge while two others dressed as game-keepers and armed with rifles guarded the gun crew. Movement in the darkened grounds directly below caught his eye. Another disciplined group of his Lordship's military style gamekeepers were fanning out in front of the house. He walked back into the radio

255

room and picked up the microphone.

'Did you have a look at our preparations?' enquired Lord Bressingham conversationally.

'Yes.'

'Excellent. And what did you see?'

'An MG08 heavy machine gun, the kind your house guests use to kill British soldiers on the Western Front.'

'Oh please, Captain, no speeches. The real point as I'm sure you know is a five-second burst from that gun will make that zeppelin your funeral pyre.'

'What about your house?'

'It's kind of you to ask, but as you can see we've taken precautions. Anyway, the house is in no danger. The reason you have such a good view of its elegant frontage is because the wind is from the north. When the mooring is released the burning hydrogen will lift the zeppelin out over the downs. It will be quite spectacular. I'm almost looking forward to it.'

Badger asked, 'Am I supposed to believe you would sacrifice a zeppelin just to kill me?'

'Yes, my dear boy, you are. I hope it won't come to it, but compared with what's at stake here tonight one zeppelin is neither here nor there. The crew is safe, and we would dock another as soon as there was favourable weather. In fact, thanks to you we may have to destroy it anyway. It will be light soon and it's a landmark I could do without. As I said, one five-second burst from that gun and in less than ten minutes all that's left will be a handful of ash and a few girders.'

Badger knew his Lordship was absolutely correct in his summation. He also realised he wasn't bluffing.

'Do I have your Lordship's word I will not be harmed if I surrender?'

'My dear boy, you will merely be locked up until the cessation of hostilities between our two great countries, no more than three weeks at the most, and as you can see in very agreeable surroundings.'

'I need time to think,' said Badger slowly, hoping Bressingham wouldn't think he was playing for time and respond early with the promised five-second burst from the heavy machine gun.

After a tense moment the peer ungraciously acceded. 'All right, Badgerworth,' he said, harshly, 'I'll give you three minutes to decide whether or not you want to die gloriously.'

Yes, or just die, Badger thought. He couldn't imagine any circumstances in which Bressingham would really let him live. As he'd said himself, the stakes were too high. Five minutes after surrendering he was sure he'd be put up against the nearest wall and shot. There was a click as Bressingham closed the transmission.

Badger wondered whether the noble lord had discussed his plans with the zeppelin's crew. If he had they'd forgotten to remind him of some small but very important details of their craft's construction.

He went quickly through to the crew quarters and opened the access hatch to the port engine pod. It took him a few seconds to scramble up the ladder in the dark and into the maschinist's seat. There, as he'd hoped, he found the Parabellum MG14 machine gun fixed in the stored position. The roof of the tower was about fifty yards away and fifteen feet below him. The lights they'd set up there illuminated the nose and bridge of the zeppelin as well as the preparations around the MG08, but most of the air-ship including the engine pod where he was sitting was in shadow.

Another of his Lordship's game-keepers arrived on the roof, carrying a long acoustic megaphone. He raised it to his mouth and experimentally pointed it at the bridge. Badger swung the gun up into the ready position, locked it in, clipped on the twin drum belt magazine, and cocked the weapon. He lined up on the MG08. The man with the megaphone checked his wristwatch before raising it to his lips again.

'Your three minutes is up, Captain Badgerworth,' he called out. 'His Lordship requires your answer.'

And he shall have it, thought Badger grimly, squeezing the trigger. The roar of the anti-aircraft machine gun echoed back from the front of the house, the hail of bullets shredding the tarpaulin into floating filaments. High velocity rounds found the MG08 gun crew, spinning them lifeless over their shattered weapon. A gamekeeper managed to raise his rifle, only to stagger backwards as the 7.9 mm bullets stitched a pattern across his chest. More nickel-jacketed lead raised a cloud of stone dust and tore into the steel drums, spraying fountains of water over the flagstone roof. Megaphone man and the remaining game-keeper dived for cover behind the parapet.

Badger swung the gun towards the flagpole and fired another sustained burst, hoping it wouldn't overheat. Splinters and sawdust flew as the pole sagged then separated. Released, L33 began to float slowly backwards over the garden and away from the house.

Out of ammunition now, he ducked out of the pod and clambered back down to the crew quarters. Exposed on the ladder he heard the reports of rifles from the ground and the fizz and thwack of bullets hitting the framework around him. Racing back up the companionway he made it to the better-protected ballast room. He sat on the reinforced plating with his back against a water tank while the dirigible floated out of range. He knew the black hull would show up badly against the dark pre-dawn sky. Provided His Lordship hadn't been given a German searchlight to go with his German machine-gun, and L33 didn't snag any tall trees he thought he'd get away with it.

Later, out of range of Bressingham's gamekeepers, Badger was on the bridge discovering he'd made a miscalculation over the ballast. The airship was at five hundred feet and still slowly ascending while drifting over sleeping Sussex villages towards the English Channel. With only one crew member it was slightly, but definitely, positively buoyant. To complicate matters the sun would soon be up. When the heat penetrated the black hull its buoyancy would increase still further. Another small problem was his chums in the RFC and RNAS. They would soon be running dawn patrols and would eat the crippled zeppelin for breakfast. He had to find some way to make L33 descend, and quickly.

The ballast room had seemed the obvious place to start but offered nothing other than the opportunity to dump water, which would have the opposite effect to the one he wanted. Giving up for the moment he went back to the bridge and sat in the captain's chair, watching the sun rise above the horizon. At a thousand feet dawn had broken. Down below in the shadowed English countryside it was still night. Although he knew the sunlight spilling through the windows of the bridge would add to his difficulties he found the sight cheering after his long and testing night. One way or another, it would soon be over.

Exhausted, he pondered the nature of gas. There was a gas stove in the kitchen in the basement of the officer's mess at Croydon. It ran on coal gas of course. If it had used hydrogen they'd have had to turn the taps upside down and put it in the loft. Problematical, he decided, for washing up as the sink would have to stay in the basement. Water was heavy and liked to flow down. Hydrogen, on the other hand was light, lighter than air, and liked to go up. There'd be hell to pay from the batmen and maids if they had to run up and down stairs all day between the cooking and washing-up. That was why in L33 the ballast room was at the lowest point of the lower deck, and the gas vents in the top of the hull.

A light went on in Badger's head. 'Of course,' he said aloud, 'it's up, not down. The water goes down, the dashed hydrogen goes up.'

He climbed back onto the axial walkway and ran along it to the point where he'd emerged the previous night. Finding the ventilation shaft he began to climb the ladder. It was already warm in there and his perspiring palms threatened to slip on the thin triangular rungs. After a minute of climbing he began to think he must have been mistaken. Then he saw the valves. There was one on either side of the shaft mounted on back-plates, unhelpfully labelled, 'Abschnitt 3' and 'Abschnitt 4'. Badger surmised where there was a '3' and a '4', there was probably a '1' and a '2' and almost certainly a '5' and a '6'. He thought there was probably, zeppelin owners' manual somewhere, warning it was 'verboten' to open 'Abschnitt 3' or 'Abschnitt 4' before opening 'Abschnitt 1' and 'Abschnitt 2' or some such slavish Germanic nonsense. Not a man to be concerned with piffling detail he opened both valves as far as they would go, the hiss of escaping hydrogen increasing to a roar.

'That should jolly well do it,' he said to himself, sliding down the ladder onto the walkway then jogging down to the bridge to check the altimeter. Through the windows he could see that the morning sun had reached the fields below, but L33 was already descending. He watched the dial drop below nine hundred feet and continue falling. Then the rate of descent slowed. The attitude of the zeppelin became progressively more nose down, the horizon gradually slipping up out of view as the pitch increased until objects began to slide off the navigator's table.

Badger re-entered the now steeply sloping axial corridor and climbed up the walkway until he was above the valves he'd already opened. He was pretty sure the attitude could be corrected by venting gas nearer the stern. This would reduce buoyancy aft, compensating for the reduced buoyancy of the forward section of the hull.

Picking the access shaft leading to the rudder gun position he found 'Abschnitt 9' and '10'. This time wary of overcorrecting Badger decided to try opening just one of the paired valves. After the roar of escaping gas stopped his pilot's instinct told him the zeppelin had levelled out and the renewed popping in his ears that it was descending once more.

He was about to step back down onto the walkway and return to the bridge when he felt a shudder. At first he thought he'd been bounced by a flight of RNAS Avro 504s. Typically late to the party, they'd finally noticed the unpowered zeppelin and decided to shoot it down and him with it. After a moment of silence the shuddering returned and developed into grinding and crunching. Badger knew this was no attack by navy aircraft: they'd hit the ground. He braced himself inside the access shaft for a final impact that never came. Suddenly the movement stopped and all was quiet except for occasional popping and snapping sounds. He dropped down into the twisted axial walkway and made his way to the bridge to find it wrecked. Through remnants of shattered Perspex he could see the treetops of a forest. Beyond that was a coastal town and in the distance the sun sparkled on the green waters of the Channel. Standing on the warped plating with a hand resting on the bough of an English oak he reflected the zeppelin was not the first aircraft he'd crash landed, and probably wouldn't be the last, but it was certainly the biggest.

Badger was at the 255 Squadron mess in Croydon helping himself to another thickly buttered muffin while his batman poured his second cup of tea. Sitting across from him was his cousin, Lieutenant Charlton Inglby Caruthers, known as 'Sissy'. He was reading the morning edition of *The Times*.

'I say, Badger,' he said, 'there's something about your

zeppelin in here. I thought you'd been sworn to secrecy and all that?'

'I have, Sis, old boy,' said Badger between mouthfuls, 'why, what does it say?'

'Claims it crash landed on the South Downs, all by itself.'

'That's fair enough. The average Jerry couldn't fly a balloon on a string. It's a miracle they got across the Channel in the first place.'

'Apparently the crew were rounded-up by Lord Bressingham and some of his estate workers. One or two of them were killed in the process and the old stately home took a bit of a pasting by the look of it.'

'You don't say?'

'I do say. Old Bressingham seems to have made a good show of it. It says he's up for the Empire Gallantry Medal. It must have been shaken him up though. He's left the War Office for a diplomatic posting in the Honduras, it says here. They've let him take his family and his staff with him, including the right honourable Herbert and sister Darcy, so I suppose it must be for the duration.'

'I'd say it probably is.'

Badger dropped a spoonful of jam on his muffin, took a bite, and chewed reflectively. 'I say, Sis,' he said after a moment of consideration, 'Where are the Honduras anyway?'

'No idea, old man.'

'Nor me. A long way from here though, I'd guess.'

'Oh, I should say,' Sissy replied, 'I'm pretty sure they are. In fact I'm almost certain they are.'

Those Who Come Home
Julie Hayman (external short story competition highly commended)

June, and there's talk of a permanent memorial going up on the green, made out of stone, would you believe it? It's a new idea, a way of showing respect and whatnot and getting to grips with things. The next village along, Monkton Chaney, has just had one put up, with an angel on top and a soldier's tin hat in her hands. They're a thankful village because everyone came home, just about, most of them in one piece and with their wits still attached.

Mrs Jenkins says, 'That memorial will cost a pretty penny.' and Mrs Howe says, 'It's all right for you, yours came home.' 'Not all of them.' says Mrs Jenkins, 'You're forgetting my Stephen.' spitting the name so as you'd think she was a cat. '*You're* forgetting your Stephen.' says Mrs Howe, and turns on her heels and walks right out of the fishmonger's without her order, her face stone. Mrs Jenkins eyes glow wet as a freshly dead fish's.

I'm stood at the back of the queue watching them. I never had a Stephen Jenkins to lose, nor a Billy Howe, Robbie Howe, Percy, Harold or Dickie Howe, and it's all too late for that now, just about, because I'm thirty-six come August. Me father says I'll die an old maid now for sure. 'Don't matter none to me,' I say, and Dad, he laughs his sour laugh and says, 'You'll turn out like your mother, if you're not careful.' He doesn't mean no harm: he just jokes a bit rough. He's fifty-five and has had a hard life and gets about on two sticks and is no good to anyone and wasn't sent anywhere by His Majesty, so he's all right, and he's the only man in our little family. Mother's away with the fairies since her funny turn a few years back and I've got my work cut out looking after her at home. She'll live as long as anyone, though she won't get no better, my dad says, and he's surprised, what with all that's gone on in the world, that there aren't more like her to keep her company. Well, he always was a misery.

'What'll you have, my love?' asks Mr Peck, hands red as salmon, moustache silver as a stickleback.

'Trout, please, Mr Peck,' I say.

'And what do you make of the memorial?' he asks, passing over the dull-eyed ones to get me a nice bright-scaled fish.

'Oh, I don't know,' I say, breezily, and I don't. Wouldn't bring them back, would it?

'It'll have to be a bloody big memorial to fit all the names on,' cut in Mrs Sumsion, arms folded over her chest, empty shopping basket on the floor at her feet. Mr Peck laughs gently to ease the tension but Mrs Sumsion isn't tickled.

On the way home, I get to thinking that the village is a good deal quieter now than it was before. No idea why I hadn't thought that earlier: the war's been over for a couple of years, after all. People don't pass the time of day in the street much now, and no one stands on the doorstep chatting to neighbours, and if you go round the back of the houses on the avenue by way of a shortcut, some of them never open their curtains fully no more, and you'll see weeds growing high over vegetable patches that always used to be well tended, and one white face and then another staring out of back parlour windows at nothing, and no one waving or nodding or showing that they'd seen you.

It's sunny and warm for once after all the rain we've had, and so I stop at the bench looking out over the park for a minute. Old Mr Smith is doing his daily perambulation round the circuit, and there's armless Ernest

Wells taking in the sun who judders and jolts when he walks so that the children giggle and copy him till they get a swift clip round the ear from whoever's nearest, and there's Mrs Jeffries pushing the pram with Mavis in. Mavis gets a lot of attention round the village, being one of the few babies we've got.

The apple tree on the north side of the park has late blossoms on it, hanging their heads down in blushing little posies. Mrs Harris's Elsie had a bouquet of apple blossoms at her wedding to Charlie Betts the summer he went off to fight. After the ceremony, she gave it to Minnie Bell rather than to me, but that don't matter none: Minnie's not going to get married any sooner than I am. It didn't do Elsie much good, either: Charlie's name'll be on the memorial.

I close my eyes for a minute or two as I sit on the bench. The sun makes me see red everywhere under my eyelids and I think it's too hot in the sunshine because my eyes water and I have to wipe the wetness away quickly, before anyone sees. I'd heard about girls going away to Maudsley or Netley to nurse those soldiers who were taking a long time to get better, and some of them married them, and that seemed like the best thing to do to me, though I didn't know if I'd be able to tend all the masculine bits and pieces that needed tending, though I'd have a go. Miss Dugden the schoolmistress always said I was a quick learner so I expect she'd have given me a testimonial if I'd asked. Anyway, it's all just a dream because I have to stay here and look after my mother and me old dad because there's no one else to do it. I get up from the bench. Best get the dinner home before Dad starts sounding off.

Stepping down the drung (that's what we call an alleyway round these parts) a big fluffy ginger tom comes trotting towards me. 'Hallo, my love,' I say, and it wraps itself round and round my skirts and I bend and stroke its head and run its feather-duster tail through my fingers and think how its colouring is just like Fred Macey's what used to come running after me in the road as a boy for a boiled sweet from the packet in my pocket. He'd carry my bag home for me if it was heavy and none of his mates were about to see. His body's mashed somewhere in a field in Belgium now.

I go on, not thinking much of it, but then I see a black-and-white cat and a grey one sitting together, companionable, on a wall, just like Eric Grant and Dickie Howe used to do, and the grey cat's eyes are pale like Dickie's. They both get up and yowl at me as I go past, flicking their tails. And further on, another cat, a tabby, in the same tree that Joe Appleby fell out of and broke his thumb on his twelfth birthday, jumps down out of it at me. And a white kitten runs into my path and cries in its tiny wheezy voice and I pick it up and kiss its head and set it down again and say, 'Hallo, little fella, and who are you?'

Now, what am I to think?

Just as I'm almost home, there's Mrs Howe, her face dark as the sea, talking to Mrs Williams. 'It's too soon for many,' says Mrs Williams, wiping her eyes on her sleeve. 'My Eddie would've been thirty-eight come Saturday.' I know they're talking about the memorial and what had happened in the fishmonger's.

'Don't worry,' I say as I go by, 'The men will find their way home.' I nod and smile a big smile at Mrs Howe on account of my seeing her Dickie, who always was the best-looking one of the bunch. I smile too at Mrs Williams because, although her Henry is in hospital in Scotland with shrapnel holes where his eyes should be, her Eddie is dead and so ready to come back. Eddie will be padding around again soon, I'm sure.

'Silly cow,' says Mrs Howe as I pass, talking about Mrs Jenkins again.

My old dad likes the trout well enough. I don't give him the lot but flake off a bit and put it outside the backdoor later on a saucer so the men can help themselves. And I think: there's a tortoiseshell over by the lane that's got a missing ear and half a lip: that must be Stanley Hiscock, blown-up at Wipers; and there's one with a white marking like a slash under his throat: that must be Georgie Kellaway who couldn't stand it out there no more.

A great big scarred tom watches me from the back fence.

They can build that stone memorial if they like and stand around it, for all the good it'll do them. I'll feed the men and laugh to myself because now I've got my pick and can have the whole lot of them, if I want, and they'll all be calling on me: Fred and Eric and Dickie and Joe and Stanley and that big tom in the garden, while I look after my old dad and my mother and keep my own counsel. You won't catch me looking out of the back parlour window feeling sorry for myself.

And now, with the window open at bedtime to let the air in, I won't know for sure whether what I hear is crazy Mrs Chivers having one of her bad nights, keening and rocking and sobbing for John and Harry and little Pete who, when he grew up, was going to be a stonemason like his dad, or whether it's the homeless toms crying and calling and yowling to me in their foreign tongues.

Doing my Lines
Polly Jenkins (SDWC)

I watch the News and all I can see is dead people:
   Victims of terrorism, children molested, honour killings.
   I finish my porridge, read the celebrity gossip and get to work,
   Brushing away the sense of unease.

Later that day I'm driving, listening to the radio about fighting in Gaza
   And a Malaysian airplane shot down over the Ukraine.
   At lunch my best friend hints at domestic abuse.
   I count my calories and change the subject by making her laugh and forget.

After I'm tired of fighting over a stapler and second-guessing the next office politics move,
   I go home and watch a film on World War I. I now know the reason.
   I feel ashamed that over sixteen million people (who knows how many exactly)
   Died for all this. A hundred years has taught us nothing.

Then my three-year-old runs over and plants a wet kiss on my cheek.
   I feel responsible for the entire planet, in the eyes of the fallen,
   That we have squandered any wisdom and succumbed once again to hurting each other.

But I'm also so grateful that you gave me and my son a chance to breathe.

One of us may put things right some day, in your honour.

Answered Prayers
Marlene E. Harris (SDWC)

It was a warm summer's evening in 1914, and John and Alice sat at their dining table. The brown chenille tablecloth shimmered in the warm glow of the oil lamp as they waited for the kettle to boil. They had recently moved into their cosy terraced house in Carmarthen Road, Fforestfach, Swansea after their wedding at the nearby Bethlehem chapel in Cadle. John was a collier at the nearby Mynydd Newydd Colliery, and Alice an excellent seamstress who worked from home. However, less than a month after being married, news broke out on 28th July that the Great War had started. Little did they know how much their lives would be changed. They usually reminisced about their happiness together in the evenings, but it was now August 4th and their conversation was about Britain declaring war on Germany that morning.

'My cariad, there's a public meeting at the Albert Hall on 16th of September, to recruit a Welsh battalion to fight in the war,' he told her nervously.

'Oh, John, I hope you are not going to have to go to war,' Alice bit her lip anxiously.

'Let's hope not, my cariad. There is not much likelihood of that anyway, as you have to be five foot, six inches to join the army and at five foot, four inches, I am not quite tall enough,' he said, assuring her.

Alice hugged him, not ever wanting to let him go, saying softly, 'Oh John, I hope so. I couldn't bear for us to be parted.'

One day in October Alice sensed something different about John when he came home from the colliery, black

270

from head to toe in coal dust as usual. There was a worrying silence as he sat in the tin bath by the warmth of the black-leaded fireplace. He wasn't his usual happy self. No singing or even whistling. He just sat there deep in thought.

Alice waited patiently until he had his tea, then asked, 'John, what is wrong? You are very quiet tonight,' she added.

'My cariad, please sit down, I have something important to tell you,' he said in a sombre tone.

Alice sat down and started to sense that John was going to be the bearer of bad news.

'At the colliery today we were told that they have decreased the height of recruits for the army to five foot three, and this means that I am eligible. I have also been doing a lot of thinking, my cariad, and feel it is my duty in volunteering to serve our king and country.'

Alice went white with shock.

'Please Alice, please understand. This is something I have to do,' he pleaded.

'I don't want to lose you now, John. I can't bear the thought of being without you,' she cried out as tears rolled uncontrollably down her face.

He put his arm around her to comfort her, saying, 'But I have to, my love.'

Alice remained silent for a few moments. 'Well if that is what you really want to do then I cannot stop you, my love,' she said as she clasped his hand.

John felt her pain. But he felt he needed to be on his own for a while, and to drown his sorrows.

'I'm going down the road to The Mile End for a pint, my cariad. I won't be long,' he said as he kissed her cheek.

Alice sat alone with her thoughts and fears, thinking about what her life would be like without him. She went to the cupboard under the stairs and pulled out a bottle of sweet sherry and poured herself a glass. They usually had one small sherry together in the evenings whilst they chatted happily together, but now, even this was going to change. She poured herself another.

Meanwhile, John quickly downed a few pints of ale, and staggered up the road back home.

Alice was feeling slightly inebriated from the sherry, and was so glad when John finally returned. They just hugged and kissed and helped each other up the stairs to bed.

The next day John walked down to the Guildhall to enlist. He also passed his medical with flying colours.

He started preliminary training at St Helens rugby ground, which had a rifle range built under the grandstand. In December he marched with the 14th battalion through Swansea to Victoria station, for his journey to Rhyl to continue his army training.

Clouds of white steam rose from the train's engine as John and Alice stood on the crowded platform kissing, hugging, and saying their goodbyes. She noticed with heartache how handsome he looked in his khaki army uniform. His shiny black hair was slicked back and his neat moustache framed his generous lips. His clear blue eyes radiated his honesty and intelligence. She loved every single thing about him.

He touched her soft, braided, golden hair and looked into her large, sad, green eyes. He thought how lucky he was to have such a beautiful wife.

A band was playing and the song 'Tipperary' was being sung with fervour.

When the guard blew his whistle John jumped on board. All the doors were slammed shut one by one. As the train noisily chugged away, Alice waved her wet handkerchief until he was out of sight. She felt that her heart had been torn from her chest. She felt bereft.

John felt emptiness and fear overtake him. He was so much in love with Alice and wondered how he would ever get used to not seeing her beautiful face next to him on the pillow every morning. But he had to be strong. He had to find the strength to go forward, not knowing what horrors lay ahead.

As the long lonely months rolled by Alice missed him so much. She felt the house was just an empty shell without him. The lonely evenings by the warm embers of the fire gave her much heartache. She went to chapel as often as she could to pray for him. The last time they were to be together was when he had leave a year later, before the Welsh regiment embarked for France in December 1915.

This day was the saddest day of all for Alice as the realisation hit her of the possibility she would not see her love again.

She tried hard to busy herself, but a couple of weeks later she learned that women were being taken on at the munitions factories. She had heard about explosions and poisoning in munitions factories and knew it could be dangerous. The days would also be hard and long, but she needed to get out of the house as the loneliness was starting to drive her mad. She needed to be with other people.

The following morning Alice took time with her appearance to make an impression, in her hand-made cream blouse, long black skirt, and warm coat. She then made the journey to Pembrey.

As she got nearer to the factory she felt nervous, and wondered if she had made the right decision.

Finally, at Reception she found her courage. 'Have you any vacancies?' she enquired.

The manager carefully looked her up and down, asked a few questions and took her on a tour of the factory. The factory was extremely noisy. The smell of sulphur was strong and hundreds of women in overalls and headscarves were filling shells with explosives.

'I can take you on to work full time, but I must ask if you are pregnant?'

'No, certainly not,' she replied, but wondered to herself why he should ask such a personal question.

'OK, you have a job. Can you start Monday?' he asked.

'Yes, certainly,' she said excitedly. She felt she was playing her part in the war now. When she got home she wrote a letter to John telling him her news about the job.

A few weeks later she received a letter from him about his traumatic experiences fighting knee deep in mud in the trenches. He always ended his letters with how much he missed and loved her. These romantic words meant everything to her, but she had bitten her nails to the quick worrying about him, and now she had also started to feel sick in the mornings.

After a couple of months she began to realise that she must be pregnant, but she didn't say anything to anyone about it and carried on in denial as if everything was normal, until her workmate Jane started to notice.

'You're not pregnant are you?' Jane asked.

'Well yes I am – that's not a problem is it?' Alice asked.

'Oh dear, you don't know do you?' Jane replied.

'Know what?' she asked.

Jane studied Alice's face and could see a yellow hue in her skin and noticed that even her blonde hair now had a yellow tinge.

'You may be at risk of having a canary baby,' she replied.

'A what?' Alice asked, with a surprised look on her face.

'It's the TNT that we are working with, it can affect the baby, it can be born yellow – and you don't look too clever either.'

Alice had to sit down to take it all in. She was roughly seven months pregnant. She looked at herself in the mirror when she got home and realised that her skin was indeed tinged yellow and so was her hair. She hadn't felt very well for a while but had put it down to being tired from the long hard days of work. Now she started to realise why the manager had asked her if she was pregnant.

She panicked and went to the doctor the following day. He told her she was jaundiced and ordered her to stop work immediately and rest until her baby arrived.

Meanwhile, in July 1916, after surviving months in the muddy trenches in France, John fought in one of the deadliest battles in Mametz Wood which was part of the Somme. The constant fighting turned the wood into chaotic disarray, with dismembered bodies everywhere. Casualties were high and John had to endure the constant sound of bombardments, explosions, shrieking shells, and the whistling of rifle bullets. Even worse, was hearing the endless screams of dying soldiers. He was in a living hell.

Meanwhile, Alice felt sadder and lonelier than ever now, and finally wrote to John about her pregnancy.

A month later she found herself in labour, and the midwife was called to her home where her canary baby arrived a month early, and was a distinct yellow. She named her Primrose.

When Alice regained her healthy glow and Primrose's skin turned a healthy pink she had her baptised at the chapel. She looked more like John than herself. She had bright blue eyes and dark hair. She was a very contented baby and Alice was grateful for that.

When John received Alice's letter he was overjoyed and filled with pride, and it was the news that gave him some renewed strength for a while, but gradually he started to have nightmares, heart palpitations, diarrhoea, and terrible anxiety. He dipped into a dark depression and became disorientated to the point that he could no longer pull a trigger. He was now barely functioning as a human being and was no longer any use to his battalion. He was subsequently put on the casualty list as 'Wounded-Shock, Shell.' All he could think of now, was to be home with his family.

One cold bitter November morning as Alice was on her knees scrubbing her front step, she heard the squeaky, iron gate open behind her. When she turned around, the much feared telegram boy was standing behind her. She stood to her feet and clutched the telegram with soapy hands. She went inside and felt sick as she opened it.

It read, 'We are sorry to inform you that your husband has become ill in the line of duty. He has been taken from a casualty clearing station in France and is waiting to be transported back to Britain to be admitted to St. Teilo's Hospital in Cardiff. We will inform you further of his arrival.'

She had been expecting it to read 'killed in action' and gave a heavy sight of relief. She felt her legs go weak from under her and quickly sat down, reading the telegram over and over again.

She waited anxiously for the letter from the hospital. Two more weeks went by until one day a manila envelope arrived.

She opened it nervously and the typewritten letter informed her of John's arrival at the hospital. All she could think about now was her journey to her dear husband.

A couple of days later she arrived at the hospital with Primrose, who was warmly wrapped up in a thick woollen shawl. The matron led her to John. She explained that his particular type of shell shock was psychological rather than him having nerve damage, which was good news.

When she clapped eyes on John she hardly recognised him. He looked thin and frail and his hair had started to grey prematurely at the sides. He was shaking and talking to himself. She held his hand and said, 'John, my darling, it's me, Alice.'

John raised his head and although his tormented mind

was in a blur, he recognised her immediately. 'Oh, my cariad, you're here at last. I've missed you so much,' he said, as tears ran down his face.

'My darling I've brought your baby daughter. Would you like to hold her?' she asked.

John reached out his shaky hands and held his beautiful three-and-a-half-month old daughter for the very first time.

'She's the image of me, isn't she, my cariad?' he said with such pride that Alice noticed a glimpse of John as he was before the war.

'I want to be home with you and Primrose,' he said.

'You will do, love, but you have to get better first,' she replied.

This was the first of many weekly visits that Alice and Primrose would make to see John. Gradually, after several months, he began to improve. The doctors had feared that his symptoms would be long lasting but John seemed to improve beyond expectations and six months later he came home with strict orders to rest. However, he would jump out of his skin at the least unexpected sound, but the shaking had stopped and he had put weight back on. He was still severely depressed and having nightmares, but the doctors hoped that being back with his family would help alleviate it.

Primrose was crawling everywhere and John was in awe of her. He was the perfect father.

Alice felt complete again and tended to John like a nurse.

The war finally ended when an Armistice was signed on 11th November 1918, between the Allies and Germany.

John and Alice could hear the faint sounds of hooters and sirens blasting at the docks. The news quickly spread through the town and thy danced with joy when a neighbour knocked their door with the news.

At 11 a.m. they heard the gun discharged on the beach by the military authorities to mark the formal cessation of hostilities.

Almost all work ceased for the celebrations to begin. And as evening approached, fireworks boomed and flashed all over the town which affected John really badly, but somehow he got through the night knowing that at last the war was over.

He continued to improve and was awarded a gold stripe for his part in the war. It was also a sad time for him, as so many of his fellow soldiers had been killed in Mametz Wood. He knew he would never be able to erase the terrible memories of the war.

'I'm so glad I got you back,' Alice said to John as they settled back to their happy evenings by the fire.

'My cariad, I'm so grateful to be alive. I will treasure each moment of you and Primrose for the rest of my life.'

Alice smiled contentedly. And felt that all her prayers had indeed been answered.

Step Dance
John MacBean (external poetry competition highly commended)

Take your partner by the hand,
Promenade, strike up the band.
Fix positions, ready to go,
Circle round and do-si-do.
This dance begins with cannonade,
Forward march, you're on parade.
Ancient wrongs are seldom righted,
'Injustice fester', fresh dawns blighted.
The beat is catchy, make your stand.
Altogether, it's hand to hand.
Left foot, right foot, jump and prance,
At the retribution, step dance.

Rhythmic mortars, blues wailing shell,
Strike up the music, this way to hell.
Wrong tribe, wrong caste, different creed,
Power seduction, corporate greed,
Bayonet, bomb, musket and ball,
'Friendly Fire.' the innocents fall.
The seeds of anger in the past were sown,
'If only we hadn't, if only we'd known.'
General Bungle's buglers blow,
'Over the top lads, fast not slow.'
Young lives unlived, secure 'Advance!'
At the payback, step dance.

Forward together my brave hearts all,
With right on your side, head high, walk tall.

279

Step to the rhythm, take up the slack,
This dance is timeless, there's no going back.
So forward, but backwards the dancers move,
'Freedom.' they cry as together they groove.
This dance will end in grief and pain,
And why when ended, must it start again?
Come gallant lads and lasses all,
Who'll join with me? Who'll heed my call?
Let peace be the victor. Give it a chance.
Step back. Step down. Stop dance.

SDWC Members

Alan Bryant: Swansea and District Writers Circle welcomed Alan as a member in 1987 and has been an ongoing influence in his life since. Most of Alan's writing consists of plays that will never leave the page, some awful poetry, and short stories that might never be read. Even so, it is a pleasure to be amongst people who share the love of writing. One of the joys of being a part of the Circle is seeing new members achieve results in our competitions. Circle members have continued to enrich Alan's life with kindness, advice, and inspiration and he feels privileged to count them as friends.

Maggie Cainen: A retired everything: former French teacher, lecturer, examiner, and water sports instructor. She's always written: editing magazines, newsletters, academic articles, official reports, and teaching materials. For several years a staff writer for *Diver* magazine, she also wrote Tesco book reviews online. She's had articles, short stories, reviews, and letters published in books, magazines, newspapers, and online and won prizes for her writing. She gained a Master of Arts degree in Creative Writing and Media Studies eight years ago. She joined Swansea Writers Circle eighteen months ago and has welcomed their support and inspiration ever since.

Catrin Collier: When I found the courage to walk into the reference library in Swansea in 1977 and join Swansea and District Writers' Circle, my life changed. I found myself surrounded by kindred spirits who also sat up half the night writing books in the hope that one day they might see a printing press. I also discovered kind supportive people among the members who became lifelong friends. They taught me many things, but perhaps the most important was also, (with hindsight) the most obvious. If you seek publication, write for markets. Within a month my articles and short stories were being published in magazines; novels took a little longer – thirteen years longer to be precise, but throughout all the ups and downs (and there were more of the latter) the members of the circle were behind me, cheering me on.

Decades have come and gone, the world has changed, but the one constant has always been the support and friendship of other writers in the circle which has enabled to continue writing. I can't thank all members, past and present, enough.

Annabelle Franklin spent most of her time in school writing stories, whether she was meant to be doing it or not. Since then she worked in an artificial limb and appliance centre, studied radiography and music (not at the same time), played in two bands, and taught children to play the piano. She lives on the South Gower coast, in an area of outstanding natural beauty that gives her plenty of inspiration. Annabelle has written and performed in plays and made a short film. Her children's novel, *Gateway to Magic*, is available on Kindle and she is currently working on another. Annabelle shares her home with Millie and Pearl, two beautiful rescue dogs who allow her to see the world through their eyes.

Marlene Harris is a retired self-employed homeopath, reflexologist, and crystal healer. Whilst living in Spain she enjoyed doing healing weeks abroad. Has also lived and worked in Guernsey in the Channel Islands. She is a member of the Swansea and District Writers circle and is busy editing two books and various short stories for children. Writing poetry is also a favourite pastime.

Polly Jenkins is originally from Russia and moved to

South Wales in 2005. She runs a financial paraplanning business and devotes her spare time to books: reading them and writing her own stories. She is in love with words and the English language.

Steve Jones is a retired nursing lecturer who has been writing short fiction for around two years. He is married with two grown up children and lives in Morriston, near Swansea in South Wales.

Barbara Koethe: A period to play and ponder; 2014 is a sabbatical year for Barbara. Born in Cologne in 1958, working in Brussels; with a son in Switzerland and a daughter in Scotland she is doing what she always wanted to do: travelling in a VW-van, (Wales, Scotland, England, Germany, France), going with the flow (joining the SDWC ☺ ☺ ☺) and picking up her love of writing (short stories and poems).

Cheryl Leend, one of the authors of the best-selling, *Bangkok Blondes* book has now returned to Swansea after working overseas for twenty-five years. Cheryl taught in Kenya and Saudi Arabia before becoming a Head of Primary in two separate International Schools in Thailand. An avid traveller, she has visited over fifty countries, and looks forward to writing about her exploits with the support of the SDWC.

Coral Leend, a Welsh International Gymnast in her youth, then passionate racing yachtswoman, began a new hobby of writing whilst employed as a hospital pharmacy technician. Encouraged by SDWC, she has had over eighty short stories and articles published, before becoming a RNA New Writers' Finalist with her first published novel. *Shadowed Waters* was quickly followed by her second book, *Free Spirit*.

Bob Lock was born on the Gower Peninsular, Wales, back in the Dark Ages when there were no computers, televisions, or FTL spaceships. (OK, there still aren't any FTLs whilst writing this, but who knows how long this bio might be around?)

First published in *Cold Cuts* 1&2 (Horror anthologies) 1993/94

Debut Dark Fantasy novel *Flames of Herakleitos* published in March 2007

His Urban Fantasy novel *The Empathy Effect* (set in Swansea) published in September 2010

http://bob-lock.blogspot.co.uk/

http://www.scifi-tales.com/

Lynne Lomond has been writing since she was six, and still has her earliest stories and poems, saved, to Lynne's surprise, by her mother and rediscovered on her death. Lynne had made a few half-hearted attempts to get things published over the years, but it wasn't really until she joined the Writer's Circle that she began to take her writing more seriously, and has greatly benefitted from the support and friendliness she has found. So maybe this is the start of a new career!

Will Macmillan Jones lives in Wales, a lovely green verdant land with a rich cultural heritage. He does his best to support this heritage by yelling loud encouragement at the TV when Wales are playing international rugby and drinking local beers. Having been an accountant for much of his working life, he writes fantasy and horror books in a desperate attempt to avoid terminal brain atrophy. A fifty-something lover of blues, rock, and jazz he has now achieved a lifetime ambition by extending his bookcases to fill an entire wall of his home office.

www.willmacmillanjones.com

Jill Moffat lives on the beautiful Gower Peninsula. Born to eccentric parents and raised to be a free spirit, Jill has travelled the world over and lived a thousand lives but now is committed to a life of writing. Besides inventing stories and characters for children and young adults, Jill works part-time as a nurse and runs a home for waifs and strays (animals of the two- and four-legged type) with her kind and unassuming husband. Jill's trails and tales are also recorded in a daily blog about nature and their lives.

Jean Moir lives with her husband in Oxfordshire. She likes languages and music and has always loved reading: studying English in Edinburgh. Jean worked in management and administration in mental health and care of the elderly, and upon retirement took some courses in creative writing. In 2013 Jean won a year's membership of SDWC with her poem 'Tearing Back Centuries'.

Ann Potter trained as a nursery nurse and had four daughters so it was inevitable that she started her career writing children's stories. She joined Swansea and District Writers Circle in 1985 and thereafter received terrific help and support. Over many years she has written magazine articles, newspaper articles, four unpublished books, a local guide book, and most recently an autobiography.

Fiona Riley writes short stories and poetry and thinks about writing every waking hour. She enjoys the feeling of accomplishment upon completion of a piece. After practising procrastination for many years, Fiona joined SDWC and is now in the early stages of writing two very different novels.

Sue Shannon-Jones has recently retired from a forty-year career in nursing, the majority of the time in mental health. This, along with bringing up a family and her liking for academic study, left little time for writing fiction. This short story is Sue's first attempt at submission for publication.
http://sueshannonjones.wordpress.com

Dawn Smith writes fiction and poetry for pleasure in her spare time. Most of the time she runs a translation and copy-writing business in West Wales. She has had two poems published in the past, as runners-up in competitions. She is currently studying part-time for an MA in creative writing at the University of Trinity St David, in Lampeter. She lives in Pontyberem with her partner and stepson.

Anthea Symonds was born, went to school, and worked in West London for first twenty-five years of her life. She travelled widely in Europe on the hippie trail after 1963 and lived on a kibbutz in Israel, coming back in Six-Day War in 1967. Anthea went to university as a mature student, first to Bath and then Sussex, graduating with an MSc. in Social History in 1977. She achieved her PhD in Birmingham and taught in FE and the Open University in South of England until coming to Swansea in 1985. She was lecturer in Swansea University until retirement (semi!) in 2006. Anthea has just taken up creative writing which is massive change from academic writing, was married to a local GP for twenty-four years, and now lives with her dog. Anthea is busy with U3A and her new-found interest – writing, along with walking the dog, and supporting Chelsea.

Ann Marie Thomas: Writing poetry and making up stories since she was a child, Ann only began to write for publication when her children left home. Her ambition is to write science fiction (with three novels at various stages in a series called *Flight of the Kestrel*). She was distracted by a major stroke and began to research local history, an interest that culminated in the publication of her first book, *Alina, The White Lady of Oystermouth*. Early retirement has given her more time to concentrate on her writing. The success of *Alina* led to the penning of a second local history book *Broken Reed: The Lords of Gower and King John*.

Joy Tucker is a Scottish writer who has lived and worked in Scotland, England, and Wales. A former columnist and feature writer with *The (Glasgow) Herald*, she has had several short stories and poems published in anthologies, newspapers, and magazines throughout Britain, as well as having her work broadcast on BBC Radio 4. Her radio credits include children's stories and poems. Recently Joy has turned to play-writing, with one-act dramas produced in Sussex, Devon, and South Wales. She now lives on the Gower Peninsula. Her 'day-jobs' have been as a Treasury civil servant, an advertising copy-writer, a Citizens' Advice Bureau manager, and a voluntary worker for the former Independent Television Commission.

Wendy White lives in Kidwelly, West Wales. She studied Religion and Ethics at Lampeter University and worked as a library assistant before training to become a primary school teacher. She has taught in schools in Carmarthenshire and Berkshire. Wendy joined SDWC after her poem 'Our Town' won their inaugural national poetry competition. Her children's book, *Welsh Cakes and Custard*, published by Pont Books, was awarded the 2014 Tir na n-Og prize, a video for which can be found at wendywhite.org.uk.

Gail Williams is an asset management specialist, a freelance editor, and keen crime writer, who really needs to learn to sleep. Has self-published a thriller, *Foreshadows*, on Amazon and continues to seek a publisher for a full-length crime novel series based in Merthyr Tydfil, while also submitting short stories for various competitions. In 2014 was shortlisted for the Crime Writers' Association Margery Allingham Short Story Competition.

Short Story competition entrants

Winner: Di Coffey, ex-designer/maker, ex-freelance journalist, and current leader of Falmouth U3A Creative Writing Group, is evangelistic about encouraging people to write. Some of her poems have been awarded prizes and all have been published widely. She is currently working on a collection of short stories.

Joint second: John Keenan is a retired probation officer who hopes one day to utilise the hours he spent with criminals in some form of crime writing. Meanwhile he is on the third book of a trilogy action adventure set in the early 1900s. He also writes short stories which occasionally win prizes including, rather embarrassingly, a short piece on horror and another one on erotic writing. He wishes he had stuck to writing when he was only twenty and the market was so much simpler and publishers did all the work. He lives in his head a lot but fortunately he has an understanding wife.

Joint second and highly commended: Julie Hayman teaches Creative Writing at university. Her work has been included in anthologies and she has received awards in a number of writing competitions. She lives in Bath and is working on a novel.

Highly commended: Carl Morris is from Swansea, South Wales and has been working his way around different parts of the world for most of his adult life; though Swansea is always considered to be home. Currently a teacher of English and Psychology in the Middle East, Carl enjoys writing poetry and prose and is fascinated by the challenges and changes of the human condition; convinced that wherever there appears to be a way, there is usually a dark and troublesome path leading through it. Carl has found that writing is a productive outlet for the many observations and thoughts of life that remain a constant source of wonder and despair.

Highly commended: Steve Brodie lives on the Lancashire Coast. Steve spent ten years writing his first novel, a comedy in which the central character is a fine, upstanding, and athletic Richard III. Shortly after its completion, the actual body of Richard III was discovered under a car park in Leicester where it had lain hidden for over 500 years and it turned out he wasn't as athletic as Steve had portrayed in his novel. Steve will be spending the next ten years on a rewrite.

Steve is a member of a local writing circle, the Fylde Brighter Writers, has failed to play guitar despite many years of strumming in hope and agony (for those listening) and is hopelessly addicted to watching the lows and deeper lows experienced by his local football team, The Seasiders.

Highly commended: Alison Leighton moved to South Wales in 2012 having been the head of the Education Advisory Team in Rutland, England. She immediately joined a local writing support group and also became very involved in helping to run her local theatre. Alison enjoys including a history dimension in her short story writing as she previously taught history for twenty years and she has also written a play to tie in with the First World War centenary commemorations.

Highly commended: Peter Martin grew up in Gloucestershire and runs a veterinary practice in Sidmouth, Devon. He has enjoyed writing short stories and poetry from a young age. His other interests include military history, travel, hard science fiction, watersports, and the outdoors – themes which frequently find their way back in to his stories. An advocate of animal rights and vegetarianism, he draws inspiration from authors including Robert Westall, Arthur C. Clarke and Wilbur Smith.

Highly commended: Alan Murton returned to his native Cornwall in 1994 after early retirement from his job as head of Personnel. He combined creative writing with travel, golf, and bridge and is a regular contributor to DIAL 174, a subscription magazine. He chairs Truro Creative Writers and has had many prize winning entries locally and nationally

Poetry competition entrants

Winner: Janet Killeen: Born in Yorkshire in 1947, Janet taught English in London for more than thirty-five years. After retirement, she began to realise the dream of writing and has self-published, including a collection of short stories, *There is a Season*, some of which seek to explore the ways in which both world wars continue to haunt us. She also enjoys cooking, loves wild flowers, travel, and above all, celebrates friendships.

Joint second: Stuart Randall is a retired teacher who enjoys writing poetry and performing with Moorside

Writers, a small but supportive group in Chesterfield, Derbyshire. He has published two collections, *From Where I'm Standing* and *Growing Up in Wartime*, which reflect his interests in family, jazz, cricket, peace work, and walking in the Derbyshire countryside.

Joint second: Robert Kennedy: brought up in Renfrewshire, Robert is a retired college lecturer in English, a graduate in English Lit., and a graduate of the Open University. Robert has been writing for a number of years, and now has the luxury of deliberation and refinement. Published in a number of anthologies (Anchor Books, Forward Press, United Press) and literary magazines (*Orbis*, *Poetry Nottingham*, *Envoi*, *Lamport Court*, *Poetry Now*, *Other Poetry*, and *Cafe Review* in Portland, Maine). Robert took diploma awards on two occasions in the Scottish International Open Poetry competition and was editor's choice in *Poetry Now*. He also writes short stories and literary reviews.
Robert writes in response to a world constantly closing its doors on common understanding; about things beyond what he thinks he is writing about.

Highly commended: John D Mac Bean worked in the health service and was based in Swansea for twenty years. On retiring he resurrected his interest in the written word and completed an MA in Creative Writing at Trinity College, Carmarthen. Since then he has published a fantasy story for children and a collection of short stories. He is currently working on a novel which is set in the valleys during 1939-1977: a period of great change. The novel follows the fortunes of a group of people as life's events gradually shape their lives. A further collection of short stories is also nearing completion.

Highly commended: Rosemary Cortes was a teacher and

293

careers advisor until retirement, after which she worked for a year with an Anglican mission in Peru. She lived in Spain as a young woman and on return acted as interpreter for the local police and social services. Her personal hobby is literary translation, and she is currently translating a trilogy by a contemporary Spanish author.

Highly commended: Shirley Anne Cook is a poet and author of children's books. Her poems have been published in a wide range of magazines and anthologies, and have won or been placed in an assortment of competitions. She also recently she won first prize in the Swanwick Writers' School poetry competition. She is a former teacher and lives in Buckinghamshire. Shirley can be found online here: http://shirleyannecook.wordpress.com/

Other titles you may enjoy

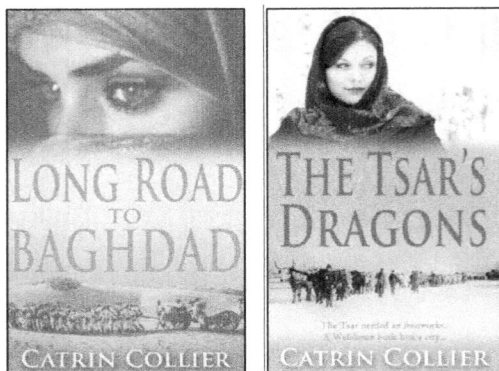

For more information about

other **Accent Press** titles

please visit

www.accentpress.co.uk

For news on Accent Press authors and upcoming titles
please visit

http://accenthub.com/

Lightning Source UK Ltd.
Milton Keynes UK
UKOW06n0704280116

267237UK00001B/7/P